# BLOOD
## ON THE
# MOUNTAIN

## David Burton

By Light Unseen Media
Winchendon, Massachusetts

# Blood on the Mountain



Original cover art, cover design and interior design by Vyrdolak, By Light Unseen Media.

This is a work of fiction. Names, characters, places and incidents are either the products of the author's imagination or are used fictitiously, and any resemblence to actual persons, living or dead, business establishments, events or locales is entirely coincidental.

Perfect Paperback Edition

ISBN-10: 1-935303-69-4
ISBN-13: 978-1-935303-69-5
LCCN: 2023934444

Published by
By Light Unseen Media
325 Lakeview Dr.
Winchendon, MA 01475

Our Mission:
By Light Unseen Media presents the best of quality fiction and non-fiction on the theme of vampires and vampirism. We offer fictional works with original imagination and style, as well as non-fiction of academic calibre.

For additional information, visit:
http://bylightunseenmedia.com/

Printed in the United States of America

0 9 8 7 6 5 4 3 2 1

# The Blood Justice Series

*Dedicated to all those who go to the mountains not to save the mortal world, but to appreciate their beauty. And, of course, to Dee.*

# Chapter 1

Around ten o'clock at night a few days after Justine returned, someone knocked on Harry Frazier's apartment door. Harry grinned. Justine must have forgotten her keys again. She'd only been gone two hours, shopping and just looking around. He knew she was trying to reconnect with her home after the last few months away. His grin faded. Why bother to reconnect when she'd be leaving again to go after Teresa?

He muted the TV and pushed up off his comfy couch. Aware of the pitfalls of mortal-vampire romance, he still loved her. He'd take any time with her he could.

Expecting her, he opened the door.

But it wasn't Justine with her cute pouty chagrined expression.

Two men stood there, caps pulled low over pale faces, one man slightly behind and to the side of the other.

Vampires. Harry sucked in a steadying breath. Not all vamps were bad. They might be from Darwin. Maybe they knew Justine.

"You Harry Frazier?" the front one, who had wide-set eyes and wide shoulders, asked.

By the tone of the guy's voice and the tension in his shoulders Harry knew they weren't good vamps. "Who wants to know?"

The second man, burly with a wide frog mouth, handed Shoulders a photo.

"You're him," Shoulders said.

Harry slammed the door, then reached for a gun stashed under a small table next to it.

The door crashed open, splinters flying from the shattered jamb.

Harry grabbed his gun as Shoulders seized his arm and flung him onto the floor.

Shoulders dropped to his knees and opened his jaw inhumanly wide while twisting Harry's head to expose his neck. Intent on blood, the vamp forgot about the gun.

Harry couldn't get a shot at his head. But two bullets into his body got Shoulder's attention.

At the door Frog had opened his mouth and extended his canines in anticipation of his share of Harry's blood. Before he stepped into the room, the staccato of rapid footsteps mounting the stairs outside distracted him.

Justine smashed into Frog. They tumbled onto the open landing, coming to a stop in front of Bailey's door. Frog was a tough one. He threw Justine off him. She smacked hard into the door. But Justine was tough, too. In full vampire and Kung Fu mode she kicked his leg. He returned with a punch to her ribs, the crack loud in the quiet night. She straightened up with a punch to his body, a punch to his jaw, and a sweep that knocked his legs out from under him.

He fell right on his ass.

With Frog stunned for a moment, Justine yanked a slim, modified machete from its sheath strapped to her thigh under her khaki trousers. It took her three strikes to cut through his thick neck. The head rolled between his legs and stopped a few inches away from Bailey's bare feet.

Still with full vamp face, Justine looked up at Bailey staring down at the head. Bailey's face couldn't decide what emotion to show. Justine didn't know either.

Two gunshots came from Harry's apartment. Justine ran to Harry so fast she appeared to vanish from Bailey's sight.

Shoulders gripped Harry's gun hand by the wrist. His other hand forced Harry's neck toward his wide open jaws.

Justine rammed her blade through the back of the vampire's neck, separating his spinal cord. She wrenched her blade right to sever half his neck. With one long stroke she cut through the other half, catching the head before it hit the floor.

"Hooo…ly shit," Bailey said from the door. Behind her, her partner Susan took in the scene with wide eyes and hands over her open mouth.

Justine froze with full vamp face, bloody blade in one hand, severed head in the other. The only movement was Shoulder's body slumping to the floor.

Still facing the women, Justine slowly set down the head, and brought her face back to normal. To Harry she said, "I guess it's time to have the talk."

Two hours later Bailey and Susan left. Bailey said, "Thanks for finally telling us, ah…everything. It definitely wasn't what I thought it would be. I'd give you guys a hug, but I'm still a little weirded out by it all."

Susan, who'd said little, seemed to accept the situation more easily than her partner. "Doesn't mean we won't let you borrow a cup of sugar if you need it."

Snuggling on the couch a few minutes later, Harry said, "That went better than I thought it might."

"I just hope I never have to do it again." A few minutes later, Justine asked, "Do you think that was the last of the Sinakov followers who'll come after us?"

"No." Harry took a deep breath. "You're going after Teresa soon, aren't you?"

"I talked to Simone earlier. The Families have a good lead on where she is."

"When are you leaving?"

"Day after tomorrow."

"Where to?"

She sat up and faced him. She took his hand in hers and flashed him a sly smile. "You ever been to Columbia, Harry?"

Harry had never been to Columbia, but as he gazed at her crooked little smile and her dark vampire eyes that nevertheless had a slight twinkle in them, he knew he'd go wherever she asked.

He'd been in love with her since they first met, when he was investigating the auto accident that killed her husband and the woman he was running away with. He didn't see her again for some years, until the brutal murder of her daughter. Vampires were a myth to him until Justine persuaded the three-hundred and seventy-something year old vampire Simone Gireaux to make her a vampire, as well. It was the only way to get justice for her daughter.

Since then he'd had more than his share of dealings with vampires—good and bad.

# Chapter 2

Ever alert, Justine Kroft and Simone Gireaux followed two other vampires, guides from the Guerro Vampire Family, through the streets of Cartagena, Columbia. They each had a 9mm pistol under their long coats and a machete held along their forearms.

"Stay alert," one of the vamps warned. "Rubicon's people could be anywhere."

It was ten at night, in an area tourists were advised to avoid. Justine and Simone were not worried about pickpockets or purse snatchers or any other interference, even without their local guides. They'd dealt with much more dangerous creatures than some small-time criminals.

They walked down a narrow dirt street past small pastel colored houses, most fronted with low concrete walls topped by security bars, the flicker of televisions their only illumination. Occasionally eyes peeked from behind curtains. The streets were deserted but for the four of them.

At an intersection with a slightly wider street, this one showing the remnants of an asphalt surface, their guides stopped. They inspected the cross street, then pointed to a larger two story, pastel blue house on the corner.

"*Entramos allí.*"

Justine studied the thicker, taller wall and bars that surrounded the house. "Looks like a safe house to me. I hope we can get out."

Simone squeezed her arm in agreement.

A patio on the right side of the house had a tile roof that continued around the house. A wide gate to the left allowed access to a three-car garage with an apartment above it, separated from the house by a breezeway wide enough to drive through.

A male vampire opened the heavy front gate from the inside. The last one to enter, Justine hesitated. She felt something—other vampires. They were in the Guerro Family territory so of course she'd sense them in the area. Vampires can sense other vampires, but she sensed many at a distance who—possibly just her paranoia—seemed to be concentrating on her. Gripping the hilt of the machete pressed back against her forearm, she stepped warily through the gate. She started as the gate clanged shut with solid finality.

Another vamp opened the front door. Inside Justine took in the wonderful smells of spicy Columbian cooking and, to her, time-wise still a young Blood, the not so appealing aroma of old blood and old death. Maybe in a few decades or centuries she'd appreciate it.

Their guides led them upstairs and down a long hall. Justine figured they were about to enter a room above the patio.

"*¿Hablas español?*" the woman guide asked. "He English not so good."

"*Sí. Los dos hablamos español,*" Simone said.

The woman shrugged and nodded to her partner who unlocked the door. "Please not to kill him."

"We'll try," Justine said and entered the room.

Jorge Cortez hunched over as he wrapped thin arms around his emaciated body. The skin on his long face hung slack as if he'd lost a lot of weight quickly. The last few weeks had been hard on him: kidnapped by the Guerro Family and held hostage for Justine and Simone. He stared at the two women with eyes sunken by worry and fear.

"*Señor Cortez,*" Justine said. "We have only a few questions. Answer them and you will be free to go."

With a voice as defeated as he looked, Cortez said, "Go where? Everybody want to kill me. That is why you here?"

"*Non, Señor,* we wish you a long life," Simone reassured him.

"Huh." Looking at the floor in resignation, he said, "*¿Qué deseas?*"

"We want—"

A loud cry and several gunshots interrupted her. The clang of machetes, a few more shots, and cries cut short were followed by footsteps running up stairs and down the hall.

The male guard shouted into the room, "Rubicon's people found us. Guard him."

"They'll never stop them," Justine said. "The window."

Justine slammed and locked the door. Simone raised the window and kicked out the bars that blocked it on the outside. At full speed she slipped through the window onto the short patio roof. Justine dragged Cortez to the window and pushed him through while Simone pulled.

The attackers hammered on the door, shaking the house. A kick splintered the jamb.

Justine said, "Take him. I'll slow them down." She readied her machete and stood against the outside wall next to the window. Simone lifted Cortez and jumped off the roof.

The first vamp, a male, stuck his bald head out the window. "¡Ahí!" he said, pointing at Simone and Cortez.

Justine cut his head off with one swipe of her razor-sharp blade. She grabbed his arm and yanked the rest of him through the window. The second vamp, a young guy with a white sidewall haircut, stuck his head out. He saw Justine, too late. His head rolled down the roof and landed with a thump on the grass. She grabbed his jacket, hauled his body halfway through the window, then took his long blade and jammed it through him into the wooden sill. She pulled the window closed on him then jumped off the roof and joined Simone.

In seconds they were over the high back wall and hustling Cortez down an alley. They turned right onto a wide deserted street lined mostly with small businesses, none of which were open.

"So where to?" Justine asked. "I don't think the Guerros are going to be much help at the moment."

"I do not know," Simone said. "I do not know this city. We must find shelter. Perhaps a hotel?"

"Are you going to kill me?" Cortez asked.

Justine said, "I hope not."

"I have small *hacienda* outside the city. You *Americanos* may call it a ranch."

"Would not everybody know where you live?"

"It is my getaway place. Nobody knows it. Nobody lives there. It is under a different name."

"How far?"

"Perhaps thirty kilometers."

"We'll need a car." Justine scanned the street for vehicles. There were not many. With her enhanced night vision she spied a forty year old Chevrolet sedan that looked like it hadn't been washed since it drove off the lot. "Next block. An old Chevy. If we can make it without getting killed."

"They are searching. We must go now, *vite,*" Simone whispered. "We carry him."

"No, I walk," Cortez insisted.

"No, we carry you."

Ignoring his protests, the two vamps grabbed his upper arms and ran to the car, reaching it in about five seconds. A quick search of the unlocked car produced no keys. No problem. Justine had had the foresight to learn some things from Harry, her mortal detective lover, when they had some time together. Without need of a flashlight and with her superior strength she had the old Chevy running in a minute.

Justine slipped behind the wheel and asked Cortez, "Where to, *Señor*? And while we're going there, tell us all about Switzerland."

Cortez guided them out of town and onto 90B, a good four lane highway which at that late hour was mostly populated by trucks, big and small. Small trees lined the highway that went through an otherwise arid landscape.

"Anybody following us?" Simon asked.

"Not that I can see. A couple pickups followed for a while then turned off."

Simone, sitting in the passenger seat, turned around and caught Cortez's gaze. With her no-nonsense glamour voice she asked, "Señor Cortez, anybody else know about this house?"

"*Mi amante.*"

"Your mistress? *Mon Dieu.*"

Justine said over her shoulder, "Does she love you?"

Pure misery. "No."

"So she would, will, tell. Probably won't even need a vamp to ask."

"Do the Guerros know about her?"

"*Si.*" More misery.

Justine said, "Okay, I think the Guerros have a traitor. Those attackers didn't just happen to be there. We have to assume that Rubicon's minions know about her and have already found out about your little love nest."

Simone, looking out the back window, said, "A vehicle, approaching fast."

All three tensed, watched the approaching headlights. The vehicle, an old pickup, came up on their bumper then swerved into the left lane and passed them. It continued at speed and was quickly lost to sight.

"*Mon Dieu*, I thought maybe we have to fight. But, Justine, did you sense a vamp?"

"Maybe. They went by pretty fast. How much farther, Señor Cortez?"

"Two or three kilometers."

"Where is Rubicon's laboratory and how do we get in?"

"You will kill me if I tell you?

Simone turned and said, "Señor, we will kill you if you do not. Speak."

With no choice, he told them.

Afterwards, Justine said to Simone, "You're the language maven here. Did you understand what he said?"

*"Oui…and non."*

"Great. Señor, can you explain—"

*"Aquí,"* Cortez said. *"Por mi casa, a la izquierda aquí."*

Justine stomped the brakes and turned left onto a dirt road barely wide enough for two vehicles to pass. On the right side of the road, a few clumps of trees rose from the dry landscape. On the left, a steep bank about a meter high opened onto a sloping field.

*"Dos kilometres mas,"* he said. *"¡Atención!"*

A pickup truck raced out of a dirt track on the left and slammed into the old Chevy broadside, driving it off the road into a tree. The right side door gave way, crushing Simone against Justine. It happened so fast neither of the vamps even had time to swear before they briefly lost consciousness.

# Chapter 3

"**S**hit!"

"*Merde!*"

Justine hurt. Her left side hurt from the pickup and her right from smashing into Simone. A glance to her right revealed a rough tree trunk much closer than it should be.

"*Ca va*, Justine?"

"Yeah, I'm great. Just great."

"That is good to hear," a German tinged male voice said from outside. "She will be so pleased."

Justine looked left. Through the window a pale square face grinned with cheerful vampire malevolence. He somehow looked familiar.

"If you are feeling so great, you may come out." He reached in and grabbed her head. Still groggy, Justine didn't put up much of a fight. A second man, with dark hair and dark eyes in a pale square face, aiming a shotgun at her may have been a factor.

Once free of the wrecked car, she hit the back of the first vamp's knees and tried to twist away. All she got for her effort was a smack on the head with the shotgun barrel and her arms held behind her back with heavy made-for-vamps handcuffs.

While Familiar-German guy knelt on Justine's back, Dark Hair reached in and grabbed Simone's arm to pull her out. Once she was outside of the car, Simone drew a small knife strapped to her leg and jammed it into his arm.

"*Hündin!*" Dark Hair let go. Simone pushed hard against the smashed door, propelling her clear of the wreck and into Dark Hair. They tumbled onto the dry ground, Simone on top. She stabbed his body a couple of times. Those wounds would have incapacitated or killed a human. She tried for his neck, but that just pissed him off.

He blocked her strike, gripped her arm and twisted her off him. As he rolled over her she managed to jam her knee into his crotch. Human or Vampire, a knee to the balls has a similar effect. That small distraction was all she needed. With full force, she swung her small blade into his neck and sliced halfway through. Springing to her feet, she drew out a well-used, thin bladed machete and with a backhanded stroke jammed the blade through his skull.

Without a thought to the fully dead vampire—in her three hundred and seventy some years she'd taken her fair share of heads—Simone turned to Justine and Familiar German guy.

Still kneeling on Justine, he held the shotgun to her head. "She will not be happy if I have to shoot off her head."

Simone and Justine locked eyes.

"She?"

They knew it couldn't be anyone else. "The Girl," they said in unison.

"I believe you are acquainted with her, *ja?*"

"*Oui.*" Simone flipped her machete, caught it by the blade.

"Do not do it," he warned. "Even without my head, I will shoot your friend."

Simone flung the machete sideways at the German—not at his head, but the arm holding the gun. The razor-sharp blade sliced through his wrist before his finger could pull the trigger. The gun and hand dropped away. She ran up and kicked him in the chest, sending him sprawling in the dust. Leaping to his side, she raised her blade to take off his head.

Behind Simone another vamp, a young Hispanic with neck tattoos, rushed out of the dark toward her. Justine, on her back, kicked him as he rushed by, making him sprawl into a tough desiccated bush.

"Simone!"

Simone spun, took a step and struck, removing the top half of the Hispanic vamp's skull. In one fluid motion born of centuries of fending for herself, she whirled back, looping her blade down on German's neck.

On her feet, Justine said, "Nice move."

"*Merci.* One or two hundred years from now you will do the same."

"Something to look forward to. Can we get me out of these things?"

Key in hand, Simone moved toward Justine. A shotgun blast grazed her leg, knocking her to one knee. Four vamps appeared, well armed and all with no-bullshit attitudes. "*Guten nacht,* Simone," a square-faced vamp with long black hair said pleasantly. "She will not be pleased. Hans was a favorite."

"You take orders from The Girl, now?" Justine asked, not trying to disguise the implied, "You pussy."

He shrugged, "What Rubicon wants, The Girl wants. You will come with us and tomorrow night she will speak with you. With some pain, I expect. Come."

"Cortez?" Justine asked.

"Dead. Did he tell you his secret?"

"That he had a private *casa* around here? Yes."

In an instant Square-face pressed his blade to her neck. "That is not the secret I mean. As you well know."

Justine looked over at the wrecked car. Cortez slumped in the back, his bloody head at a very wrong angle. With a shrug she said, "No. Nothing. *Nada.* He was waiting until he was safe in his *casa.*"

Square-face stepped back. "You should have told him he was not safe until he told you."

She pointed with her chin. "I don't think he would have been safe, either way."

He chuffed. "Perhaps. Come. Or do you want to walk back in the sun?"

If the four had been mortal, Justine and Simone would have had no trouble escaping. With those four vamps, they had no chance, so they went.

In two SUVs, one the requisite black, one dark green, they transported Justine and Simone, in separate vehicles, back into Cartagena. Once through a private gate into a compound attached to a large two story pink colonial mansion, more vamps escorted them into a four-vehicle garage and down stairs where they were shoved into a solid looking room with a thick wooden door.

Once the door thumped shut and the bolts shot, Justine said, "Once again, alone at last."

"So it seems. Perhaps a white knight will rescue us."

"He'd better. But I'd prefer to do it myself."

"I am waiting."

# Chapter 4

Harry Frazier wasn't happy. He didn't like the hotel room because the AC didn't work most of the time. It wasn't that he didn't like the local food, it was more that it didn't like him. He was used to simple, plain, non-spicy fare. Most of all he didn't like being left behind, and he didn't like that the trackers that Justine and Simone wore had disappeared out of range.

He didn't like to worry, either. But he did. Those two women could take care of themselves, but they did have a penchant for getting into trouble. They were headed south into open land. Where the hell were they going?

The door opened behind him. It was supposed to be locked. Hand on the gun in his lap, he turned to look. He saw a woman, her long dark hair in a ponytail, with a full mouth and intense dark eyes, probably thirty-five years old when she died. "Jade, you could have knocked."

"Señor Harry," she replied with a fetching, if fake, smile. "It is more interesting to enter a man's room unannounced."

Harry shrugged agreement. "Is Jade your real name, or do you just use it to project hardassery?"

"It is my real name, *gracias madre y padre*. I do not need a special name for my badassery."

Harry turned back to the computer. "I'm sure you don't. They've gone out of range. Where is that?"

Jade leaned over Harry, her cheek next to his. He knew she did it to unsettle him, but for reasons of self-preservation he made himself ignore it.

"Ah, *si*. Cortez has a secret *casa* in that area."

"Do you know exactly where it is?"

"No." She plopped onto a well-stuffed floral print armchair. She crossed her arms and allowed a who-gives-a-shit smile to curve her full lips.

"Who does?"

"Tito maybe." Tito, the head of the Family who actually made sure stuff got done.

"How long to get there?"

"Driving, a half hour. If I turn into a bat, ten minutes."

"Funny. I don't like that she didn't call to tell me where they were going."

"I think they were in a hurry."

He swiveled in his chair and gave her his best non-glamour mortal stare. "You think?"

"They were attacked at our safe house. They had to run with Cortez. He is taking them to his *romántico escondite secreto.*"

"Who attacked? Never mind, it had to be Rubicon's minions. Why are you here?" He waved his hands in the air. "Why aren't you out… doing… something?"

Jade sat forward in her seat. "Harry, my job is to protect you. You and Justine are *amantes.* Yes?" Harry jerked a nod. "If Rubicon's people had you, what would Justine do?"

To calm himself, he sucked in deep breaths. He knew what she'd do. She'd come after him, exposing herself to a trap—to The Girl.

"You think you can protect me against Rubicon's unlimited minions?"

Jade grinned. "I am a badass, remember?" She looked past him and pointed at the computer.

Harry saw two dots traveling up the same road they'd traveled down. "Looks like they're coming back. And they're in a hurry. Why don't they call?"

Two minutes later he called Justine. Voice mail. He tried Simone's number. Voice mail.

"Something's wrong." Three minutes later he asked Jade. "Where are they going? They just turned away from here."

In a second she was there, studying the map of Cartagena on the screen. "*Mierda.* I think your friends have been *secuestrado.* Kidnapped."

"Kidnapped? How the hell could they get kidnapped? You said that was open country. And how would Rubicon's minions know where they were going? Justine and Simone didn't know anything about Cortez's *casa.*"

Thinking hard, Jade said, "*Yo no sais.*"

"Who else knew about Cortez's *secret* hideaway?"

Together they said, "*La novia.*" "The girlfriend."

"Follow them. Find the address where they stop." Jade snatched up her cell and had several conversations in rapid Spanish.

Harry, barely able to keep himself from running out the door after the moving dot, stared at it, willing it to turn toward the house they had rented on their own. Jade was the only Guerro vampire who knew its location.

"The girlfriend is dead," Jade said.

Harry blew out a deep breath. "Vampire?"

"*Si*. And several of the Family."

Eyes on the dot, Harry slumped back in his seat. "So when Rubicon's people missed Cortez at your safe house…. How did they find that house so quickly? Someone tipped them off as soon as they arrived. You have a traitor."

Standing beside him, Jade stared at the dot slowly moving through Cartagena's Old Town. "Ricardo," she said through clenched teeth. "He is not happy here. He wants to live the big life, move up to big cities: Paris, London, Hong Kong; Palaces, Society, Money. A promise from Rubicon and he would turn on his Family."

"If you can't trust your Vampire Family, who can you trust? They've stopped. Do you know where that is?"

"*Si. Yo sais.*"

Harry jumped up. "Let's go get them. Can you get some backup?"

"I am your backup."

"What? What about others in your Family? We need help."

Harry felt a pressure on his chest that slammed him back against the wall. Jade held him there with his feet a foot off the floor. Eyes wide with surprise, he stared down at her, watched her two vampire teeth emerge from her snarl.

"You want the 'others' in my Family to help. Many of them are dead, mortal. Many are injured. Many are on the run from Rubicon's little army. The army that is here because we… helped… you. You want to find your witch friend. But we are paying the price. The only reason I don't rip your throat out is because Simone did our Family a great service in the past. We owe her a debt. *I* owe her a debt. I will help you find your *Bruja*, but do not push it, *¿entiendes, sangre?*"

Harry did. "I'm sorry. This was supposed to be a quick, quiet in and out operation. I'm sorry the Guerro Family got caught up in this. Maybe it doesn't matter now, but we very much appreciate your help. I believe that rescuing Teresa is important to everybody, vampire and mortal."

He felt her eyes penetrate deep into his, searching for truth. Then Jade dropped him and went to stare at the two dots on the computer.

Unnerved, Harry dropped to a crouch against the wall. He was a vampire's lover, had fought with them and against them, had faced one of the most dangerous vampires around, yet this brief encounter with Jade had unsettled him more than any other, enhanced as it was by guilt. As a cop for 18 years he had rarely felt guilt for what happened to the peripheral persons—families, kids, employees—when he arrested someone. The guilt for ruined lives was on the criminal, not him.

But there were only sixteen members of the Guerro Vampire Family in Cartagena. How many were left? Twelve? Ten? And it was Justine's and Simone's and his fault. He chuffed and stood up. They were vampires, already dead, and he felt guilty. Showed how hanging around vamps could skew one's priorities.

*"Vamos, mortal…* Harry. We go and save your friends. Then you go and save the world, yes?"

*"Si."*

Harry grabbed his .38, jammed it into his belt holster, checked that his machete was loose in its hidden scabbard along his right thigh and followed Jade out the door and down the stairs. They banged through the heavy metal gate and headed for Jade's car.

Jade stopped, head raised as if searching for a scent. As she reached for her blade two vamps rushed from the bushes, slamming her against the car.

Holding her by the neck against her car, a young pie-faced Black vamp said, *"Non, chienne Guerrero,* we will take over the world."

"Maybe, but not you." With a free arm Jade reached into her pocket, pulled out a switchblade with a four inch blade, stabbed him in the belly and slit him open to his chest. Not a killing blow, but it got his attention.

He backed off, gaping at his guts spilling out. Jade stepped forward ready to swing her blade at his neck. But the other vamp, also young with a pockmarked face, punched her chest, knocking her down. He raised his machete to take her head.

Harry didn't hesitate. He shot the pockmarked vamp in the head. The vamp was down and out, but Harry wasn't taking any chances. He knew by experience that until the head was off and destroyed a vampire was still dangerous. He stepped up and with one practiced swipe decapitated the vamp.

The gutted vamp grabbed Harry's arm with the hand that wasn't holding in his intestines. He head-butted Harry and reached for his blade. That's as far as he got before Jade split his head, topknot to neck.

While Harry caught his breath, they both scanned for more attacks. Except for several dogs barking, all was quiet.

*"¿Estás bien?"* Jade asked.

Harry shook himself. "A bit of a headache." He studied the black blood handprint on his sleeve. "A sore arm and a ruined shirt. But okay. Thanks."

"We are even, I think."

Harry nodded. "*Vamos.*"

# Chapter 5

While they waited, Justine inspected the room. There was no way to get out without explosives, except the door. Sure, they could beat a hole with their fists through the concrete walls, in about a year or two. They were not in a comic book and their superpowers were limited.

"I don't think this room was made to be a cell," Justine said as she roamed the fifteen by ten foot chamber.

"A storeroom, *probablement*," Simone said as she circled the room in the opposite direction.

They came together by the wooden door, which had thick rusty iron straps and a five inch square peep hole covered by a steel plate on the outside. Justine touched the door. "Wood, old, two inches thick. What do you think?"

Standing off to the side, Simone said, "Maybe try the peephole first?"

"Sure, why not?" Justine flexed a fist.

Too late—Simone punched through the hole. The steel plate slammed back on its hinges. She stepped back, then graciously said, "You can look."

"Show off."

Justine put her eye to the peephole, then jumped back as the muzzle of a shotgun poked through.

A deep German accented voice said, "You are to be kept in one piece, but if you come through I will shoot you. *Sie verstehen?*" He didn't give them a chance to respond, just withdrew the gun and slammed shut the plate.

"Oookay," Justine said to the room. They looked at each other with raised eyebrows, then sat down against the concrete wall covered with crumbling stucco, out of sight of the peephole.

Simone broke a few minutes of silence. "Do you think Harry will remain *un policier* when you return home?"

"I think he wants a regular life."

"With you."

"Fool that he is."

"Did you think your life would be like this when you asked me to change you?"

"I wasn't thinking of anything but finding Sinakov and killing him."

"Which you did."

"Sort of. I had to do it twice."

"And you, a regular life?"

Justine laid her head back against the wall. After a humorless chuckle, she said, "I don't know what a regular life is anymore. Maybe when Teresa is safe we can all go back to Oceanside and be one big happy family. That includes you."

"Maybe, but *chère*, even for vampires we have to live one day at a time."

"Yeah, guess so."

After a few minutes of reflection Justine said, "You know, he only said he'd shoot if we came through. Did he mean just the peephole?"

"*C'est vrai*, I think. He said nothing about through the door."

"No, he didn't."

Simone stayed relaxed. "Do you think Harry will come to rescue us? I do not know if I trust the new trackers in us to work."

"I'm sure they do and he will, but it might be easier for him if the door is open."

"*C'est vrai, ma amie. C'est vrai..*"

✴ ✴ ✴

At three-thirty in the morning Jade drove slowly past the gates. "This is one of the oldest houses in Cartagena, maybe two hundred years old. You can rent it for ten thousand dollars a week."

"Have you been in it?"

"Once, years ago. A party. It is very lavish, though I did not see much, the first floor and one of the bedrooms." She flashed a grin. "Mostly the bedroom."

"I don't think that will help much. There's probably a dungeon. You know any back doors?" He checked his laptop. As far as he could tell Justine and Simone were within three hundred feet of them.

She parked the car half a block down. "I wasn't staring at the ceiling all the time in that bedroom." She gave him an eyebrows up leer and punched him lightly on the arm. "*¡Vamonos!*"

At that time of the morning only the occasional rumble of a truck on the main street broke the silence.

Jade led Harry down the cross street, then left to a three story business building in back of the mansion. A heavy gate blocked the main entrance, but Jade stopped at a small gate that led to the side of the neighboring single-story building.

A chain and standard padlock secured the gate. Jade gripped the chain to break it.

Harry said, "I've got it. No need to break anything. Or make any noise." He pulled out a small leather pouch and in thirty seconds the lock popped open. Harry stepped back and swept a hand to the open gate. "After you."

"*Sabelotodo*," she said with a shake of her head. She placed a finger to his lips. "*Silencio*."

They moved down a narrow passage between the small building and an eight foot brick wall. At the back of the building an open space contained three company pickups, two battered dumpsters, and a storage container in the corner next to the wall. Jade pointed to the top of it.

Harry looked up the eight feet to the top, then at Jade. Hands out, he shrugged the question.

In answer, Jade stood next to the container and locked fingers. Harry took a deep breath and stepped onto her hands. Effortlessly, she boosted him up so he could almost step right onto the container's top. One leap and Jade landed beside him.

From the corner they looked into the mansion's back yard, seeing manicured grass, a profusion of flowers, and a fountain by a swimming pool surrounded by a stone patio.

Even with Harry's mortal vision he could see that the sliding doors into the house were open. He scanned for security cameras, finding none.

He whispered, "No cameras. Can you sense any vamps?"

"Three, I think. Maybe one at the front."

"Won't they sense you?"

"Yes, if they are paying attention. They are not expecting us, but we are expecting them."

"Door's open."

They dropped into the yard. Using the flowers and plants as cover, they crept along the wall to the corner of the patio. Weapons ready, they waited several minutes.

Seeing no movement, Jade whispered in his ear, "Four. I think three in the kitchen. Other, not sure."

"Let's go. If The Girl gets here before we get them out...."

On full alert they moved to the sliding doors where they waited against the wall. They heard heavy footsteps approach down a long stone-floored hall. The footsteps stopped in the kitchen. A German accented voice said, "She has landed. She will be here in one half hour. Be ready. Check down."

Two voices, male and female, said, "*Si, señor* Jost."

The footsteps receded. Jade darted a look, then indicated that Harry should go in first, then duck to the right next to the glass door.

Harry wasn't wild about that idea. With vamps inside shouldn't a vamp with a chance to survive go first? When he hesitated, she emphatically pointed to the right, grabbed his arm and guided him through.

Realizing she had a reason for him to duck right, he did just that. He felt the tug of a blade ripping his jacket. He spun to confront his attacker, but Jade had already struck off the vamp's hand and jammed her blade up under his chin far enough to pierce the top of his long–haired head. The poor guy never had a chance to utter a warning.

Jade dragged him outside and laid him on the stone patio, then entered the house. They were in a formal dining room with a table set for twelve. Many old paintings hung on the vertically striped multi-colored walls. Gold statues on carved marble pedestals guarded each corner. A wide hallway led to the front door. A swinging door on the left led to the kitchen. Jade headed that way.

With one finger she gently opened the door enough to peek through. Harry felt Jade tense. Anger flowed off her like a hot wave. He knew she was going to barge in, so he gripped her arm in warning.

Her glare warned him most emphatically not to fuck with her. Harry had been around enough vampires, including his lover Justine, not to be intimidated by a vampire's fierce glower, at least up to a point. He stared right back at her while moving his hand palm down.

Her anger turned to surprise that a mortal would not back down. Harry swiveled his head while keeping eye contact and used his finger to indicate the whole house. Jade didn't like it, but she got the drift. Though she didn't need to breathe, she sucked in a deep breath, squared her shoulders and slowly pushed the kitchen door open.

The vamp sitting at the kitchen table with his back to the door paid attention only to his cell phone. He wasn't the only one in the kitchen, as Jade realized as soon as she stepped into the room. From behind the kitchen door a large tattooed hand grabbed her and threw her to the floor. He stomped the hand that held her machete and kicked the blade away.

"*¿Quien diablos eres tú?*" he asked in German accented Spanish, full of distain. He chuffed and offered his own answer. "Some local slut vamp looking to steal something."

The young vampire jumped to his feet. He held a machete and his cell phone. "Jade?"

"Roberto," she replied with a sneer. She may have been down, but she still had a few moves. Spinning around, she slammed the back of the German's legs with her knees. His legs buckled. She jumped up and struck his head with her elbow.

Turning away from the big vamp, she confronted Roberto, a Hispanic vamp of about 20 with long dark hair pulled into a tight ponytail. "*Tú eres el traidor.*"

Harry didn't need a translator to know what Jade said, and that she was pissed.

Jade stood two feet away from Roberto and let loose a torrent of Spanish. "You told them where the safe house was. You betrayed your Family. Coco and Sarah are full dead. Tomas, your cousin is full dead. Others, too, Jorge and Ozzie. You killed them." She pushed his chest, forcing him against the wall. She poked his chest continuously as she spat, "Why Roberto? Why? The Guerro Family took you in when you were a Young Blood feeding on drunks and druggies and being hunted. We saved your ass and gave you a home. Gave you a Life. And now you betray us. *¿Por qué traidor ingrato? ¿Por qué?*"

"You gave me Life? One of you *took* my life. I was going to college and one of you killed me and left me."

He slapped her hand away. "Yeah, you took me in and gave me a new Life as an errand boy and a janitor in one of your clubs. I told you I wanted to study electrical engineering, and you laughed. These guys promised to take me out of this shit hole to where I can study and get an education. I've had two lives and the Guerro Family has ruined both of them."

He swung at her. She easily dodged and slammed him back against the wall, this time holding a knife at his throat.

"You stupid kid," Jade said.

"I hate all of you. I hope they wipe you out. And I made sure they took Jorge's head. He was the one who killed me."

"You ungrateful little shit. Don't you realize you had years to prove yourself, then years, decades, to study whatever you wanted. That's finished now."

The German vamp had stayed back and watched the two, ignoring the mortal in the doorway. He must have read Jade's body language or felt some vampire vibe that spurred him to action. Blade raised, to Harry's perception, the German appeared instantaneously next to Jade.

Jade snarled, "Jorge was my friend."

"Jade, behind you."

Too far gone in her rage, she sliced halfway through Roberto's neck.

Harry had no choice. He shot the German vamp in the head—a kill shot, even for a vampire.

Jade turned to see him fall, threw a glance at Harry, then pushed her blade through to Roberto's spine. *"Traidor!"* With both hands on the knife she cut through the bone. She jerked the knife out and stepped back. Roberto's body slid down the wall. As he hit the floor, his head toppled off to land between his legs.

Jade, still quivering with rage, stared at the head, then nudged it with her foot. *"Estúpido."* Lips still twisted, she glanced at Harry, who kept his expression neutral. *"Gracias."*

Harry nodded, then, "Look out!"

Jost, the head vamp, charged through the other kitchen door from the hallway and ran full speed into Jade. Both of them tumbled through the dining room door, knocking Harry on his ass. They slid across the floor until they slammed into the sliding door. In an instant they sprang up fighting.

Harry struggled to his feet and tried to follow the fight. He held his weapon with two hands, searching for an open shot at Jost. The kicks and punches were a blur. They destroyed several chairs as paintings and a mirror crashed to the floor.

Jost got in a strong kick to Jade's chest. She flew over the big table, landing with a crash of cutlery and fine china as she slid off.

Harry thought he had a clear shot. Jost saw him raise the gun. He flung a heavy china plate like a Frisbee before Harry could fire. The plate hit Harry's shoulder with incredible force. It shattered, slicing into his arm and sending tiny shrapnel across his face. The blow numbed his arm and the gun fell to the floor. Harry followed it to his knees.

Back on her feet, Jade flung two plates distracting Jost long enough for her to run around the table, smash into him and slam him against the wall. But he was tough. He spun her around and held her against the wall while he punched her body.

Harry had a clear shot except at his head. Fighting the pain, he picked up his gun with his left hand. Unsteady, his vision blurry, he aimed at Jost's legs and fired.

Even for a vamp, getting shot with a .38 is a painful experience, and a distraction. Jade kneed Jost in the crotch and punched his head with her fist. Harry slid her machete across the floor. She snatched it up and without hesitation or ceremony cut off Jost's head. The only way Harry could tell she was hurting was that it took two swings to do it.

Jade slid down the wall to sit on the floor next to Harry. "I might have to start carrying a gun."

Eyes closed, holding his bleeding arm, Harry said, "They do come in handy sometimes. Even against you guys."

"That hurt?"

"Yep."

Jade knelt beside him. She gently turned his head to face her. He turned away just enough to signal his reluctance.

"Come on, mortal. After tonight, you don't trust me yet? I'm not going to make you do a funny dance or make chicken noises. You need to be in good shape when we find your girlfriend or she will be pissed at me. Look at me."

The vampire's ability to look deep into mortals', and sometimes other vamps', eyes and "Glamour" them could be a curse or a blessing, depending on how it was used. Something like hypnotism, it could make a subject do anything, whether or not they would ever consider doing it on their own. Relieving pain was one of the blessings.

Harry looked. Immediately Jade's dark eyes captured his full attention. All else faded except for a voice in his head saying, "You do not hurt. You feel no pain. Your arm does not hurt. Your face does not hurt. You have no pain." The pain slipped away as if he had taken a hit of the good stuff.

The world faded back in.

"Come on, partner. Let us go rescue your damsel in distress."

✳ ✳ ✳

"If we hit that door right next to the hinges it should split like my high school prom date when that slut May Snikerson promised to put out."

Simone lowered her head and gave her a top-of-the-eye look of incredulity.

Justine shrugged. "I was a good girl back then."

Simone grabbed the front of Justine's T-shirt. "Not like the bad girl you are now." She gave her partner a quick but thorough kiss.

"Bad is better. Shall we kick that freakin' door?"

They readied to kick, Justine high, Simone low.

The sound of a gunshot filtered into the room. They froze, listening with all their vampire power. Somebody yelling. Bumps, bangs—furniture breaking. A cry of pain. Harry? More noise, another gunshot.

"The door, now."

They hit the door just where they planned. The door was tougher than they thought. It cracked, but held.

*"Merde!"*

"Well, shit. One more time."

They moved back to get a good run at it. Before they could take a step, the muzzle of a shotgun stuck through the peephole. Justine and Simone jumped to the side as the barrel swung right, fired, swung left, fired.

"Stay away from door," a German accented voice ordered.

Justine and Simone looked at each other, silently communicating the way they had come to do. Justine held up one finger, two, three. They charged the door. Justine grabbed the shotgun barrel and yanked it in as far as it would go. Simone peered back through the peephole. She signaled *now*. Justine thrust the gun back out of the hole. By the surprised groan it hit somebody hard. The gun clattered to the floor outside.

Immediately they kicked the door. Still hanging tough, it bent enough to swing wide open, banging against the wall and revealing one vamp on the dirt floor with a dent in his forehead.

Justine charged through the doorway. Simone grabbed her and dragged her back just as a machete blade swung down where her head would have been.

Letting go of Justine, Simone rushed through and attacked the lean vamp who held the machete. With her experience, few could best her. However, lean of body and face, this man also had a lot of experience.

Despite the dent in his head, the vamp on the floor also had experience and no desire to fully die. When the lean vamp managed to back Simone close to him, Denthead rolled toward her and hooked her leg with his foot. This disrupted her focus and knocked her off balance. Lean vamp landed a kick that sent her down. A quick slice and she would be done.

Denthead rolled the other way and grabbed the shotgun, swinging it up as Justine was about to pounce.

Within two seconds, two things happened. Jade smashed into Lean vamp and skewered his head before they tumbled to the dirt. A second later the blast of two shots filled the narrow passage. Harry's first shot hit one of the hands holding the shotgun. His second shot made a small hole on one side of Denthead's skull and a larger one opposite.

Jade nodded her approval. With one swipe of her blade she separated Lean vamp's lean head from his lean body.

In the sudden silence Justine said, "Harry."

"Justine."

In a blink she was with him. She touched his injured cheek. "You're hurt."

"Yeah, but still alive."

"Pain?"

He shrugged. "Jade glamoured it away, but it's wearing off."

Gently she held his face then kissed him, soft and easy, the kiss of a lover thankful their beloved is alive. She looked deep into his eyes and glamoured the pain away.

Jade said, "No time for that. The Girl is in country and coming here right now. We need to leave here, *¡ahora mismo!*"

A minute later they were packed into Jade's car. She drove quickly through the city's wakening streets. Holding hands, Harry and Justine sat in the back shoulder to shoulder, knees pressing against the front seats. Nobody spoke until Jade stopped the car by a waiting business jet.

At the gangway Simone spoke to the pilot who immediately disappeared into the cockpit.

Jade, ignoring Justine's slightly jealous glare, hugged Harry. She hung on a bit longer than seemly, in Justine's view. Smiling, Jade shook hands with Justine.

"Harry's a good man. Take good care of him."

"I will. Be careful, The Girl is a ghost. A vengeful ghost. You cannot detect her. She'll be pissed to have missed us."

"We will be careful, those of us still alive."

Simone stood next to Justine. "*Merci* for your aid. We hoped for a quiet in and out visit. We apologize for the loss of your people. Contact Claire at the Vampire Family Council."

✳ ✳ ✳

The Girl walked through the house followed by male and female vamps who came with her, plus an angry and scared local vamp who had driven them from the airport.

The Girl wore sneakers, blue jeans, and a black cotton blouse under a light jacket. A five foot tall waif with short black hair, she could be a teenager from anywhere. She wasn't. Over a hundred years old and bred to be a servant, she was one of the most dangerous vamps anywhere. She was skilled and ruthless, but her danger came from the power of serving Rubicon, who took her on after Justine killed her previous master, Sinakov, for the second time.

Rubicon was an incredibly wealthy thousand-year old vampire with the desire to take over the world. Now that he had captured the powerful witch Teresa, Justine's best friend, he could use her magic to breed a race of Sunwalkers—vampires who could walk in sunlight without burning.

The Girl had only one other desire besides serving Rubicon. She wanted to kill Justine.

With her foot she rolled one of the bodies over. Jost, one of her favorites. The Girl had no sympathy for him. If he let himself be fully killed, then he was no use to her.

She caught a whiff of a scent. Nose in the air she inhaled deeply, sorting out the various scents. A female vampire scent was strong on him. But it was another that made her walk around the room sniffing, sorting the various odors. She knew that smell too well. A male mortal—Harry, Justine's lover.

The thought of both of them enraged her, making her lose the tight control she held on herself. She kicked a chair, then another one. She pounded the heavy mahogany dining table with her fists until it cracked apart.

The female vamp moved close to her with the hope of calming her down. The male gently gripped her shoulder and shook his head. He knew better.

✳ ✳ ✳

Justine had killed her previous master—twice. She had decapitated him and left him to burn, revenge for raping and killing her daughter. The Girl had dragged her master's body and head to safety where she reattached his head, a practice rarely done and never completely successful. If they did come back to life, their minds were never the same—sometimes blank, sometimes with large memory gaps, always with an unpredictable personality change.

The Girl had taken care of him and shepherded him across country for help. Harry followed them and almost killed her. In the end Justine finished The Girl's previous master and Rubicon took The Girl into his service. She would do anything for the ancient vampire.

Rage spent, besides an almost disinterested kick, she barely noticed the two bodies in the basement. She stood by the broken door and inhaled the scents of the cell. For certain—Justine and Simone. She contained another burst of rage, adding it to her simmering hatred. Life was long for vampires. Justine and Harry would be found, and though she preferred a quick kill, she hoped to have the time to make them suffer before their final demise.

"Do we know where they are?"

The driver, who had been on his cell phone, said, "They had a plane waiting, *Señorita*. It take off maybe ten minutes now."

"Where are they going?"

"Not sure. *Estados Unidos*?"

"Can we catch them and shoot them down?"

"*Señorita?*"

The Girl turned and glanced at the bodies. She appeared to take a deep breath. "Never mind. I know where they will appear." To her two followers she said, "Clean up this place." To her driver she asked, "Where's my room?"

# Chapter 6

Simone had been quiet during the flight to Palm Beach, Florida. Justine and Harry had been too busy being together to notice. Simone had to smile at them, two ordinary lovebirds, holding hands, whispering and giggling. Some of that had been relief at having survived, again, but they really did love each other, and had accepted the dangers of a relationship like theirs.

Her smile was bittersweet. Their little touches and looks reminded her of a time during World War I when that was her. Walter Meir was her lover in the year before the Great War broke out. He was only thirty, but smart and mature. Somehow, his youth melded perfectly with her 300 years.

He was lean and blond with the requisite piercing blue eyes. A casual observer might think him a stern, maybe even cruel, man. Underneath, though, he cared deeply for his country and for all people, German or not, rich or poor, disabled or prime specimen, ugly or beautiful, like himself and Simone. Both thought they'd be together forever.

They tried to ignore the war. But Germany called him, and he went. Though Jews were not treated as badly then as under the Nazis, they were still restricted in the rank they could obtain. Being a good German, Walter Meir changed his name to Konrad Rinman.

Simone, heartbroken, fought for France, eventually joining the French underground.

✵ ✵ ✵

Simone sat in an upholstered chair at a small conference table with Justine, Harry and Claire, the head of the East Coast headquarters of the Vampire Family Council. Mortal, Claire had proved herself a friend of vampires and an able administrator.

Claire had run into Harry while he tracked The Girl and her maimed master Sinakov across the country. A nurse, she helped Harry survive one of his encounters with The Girl. With Harry in no condition to drive, she drove him to Fort Lauderdale. When the previous Headquarters were destroyed, she found herself in charge.

"Grace?" Justine asked about the very powerful witch who had taught Teresa how to use her magic.

"She says Teresa's location is blocked from any spells. She can't break through. If… if you can narrow it down to a certain area, she may be able to go there and break through. You got any ideas?"

Simone slouched in her chair with her feet up on another. Outwardly, she looked like she didn't give a damn about Teresa's location. She didn't have as long or as close a connection with Teresa as Justine, but she and the witch had their own solid bond. Simone wanted to find Teresa every bit as much as Justine did.

"Europe has been Rubicon's home base for the last few centuries. But he has been all over the world."

"He has houses and castles and businesses all over Europe," Claire said. "The Families have been checking them out with not a hint. He probably has a "Secret Laboratory" somewhere. No hint about that either." She leaned back and sipped from a beer bottle. "So, with all the trouble in Columbia, did you find out, 'Where is where?'"

"We did," Justine said. "But I'm not sure it'll help."

Claire leaned forward. "Justine, a shitload of Guerro vamps, not to mention mortals, died down there. It damn well better mean some damn thing."

Justine glanced at Simone. Simone shrugged and nodded. "Meir knows where is the weir."

"Who the hell is Meir?"

"Not a clue. We assume weir means a small dam—"

"I know what a freakin' weir is. How didWhere is where' get to be whatever?"

Justine shrugged. "Three different languages and a lot of alcohol."

"Ya think? So, Meir. Any ideas? Simone, you've spent a century or two in Europe. Simone?"

Startled back from old memories, Simone took a few seconds to remember what Claire asked. "*Non. Non.* I do not know any Meirs," she lied.

Elbows on the table, Claire massaged her eyes with her fingertips. "Okay, the German Böhm Family is centered mostly in the north, Frankfort and Berlin. They say they have a contact in Stuttgart who says he may know a vamp in Basel, Switzerland who used to work for Rubicon. Nobody else is talking. Apparently, Rubicon has quietly put the word out to keep your mouth shut about him."

"So why would this guy in Basel talk?" Justine asked.

"I don't know. Why don't you go there and find out?"

Justine and Simone looked at each other, communicating wordlessly. Simone shrugged. "Why do we not?"

✳ ✳ ✳

That afternoon, welcomed by two hostesses—Katherine, a tall, thirty something vampire and Suzy, a diminutive, blonde mortal—they boarded a private jet run by the Council. Used to ferry vampires long distances, it had upgraded window shades. Each premium leather seatback had a large video screen that played movies and could also be programmed to see outside. Vampires couldn't go outside for more than ten minutes without feeling the burn, but many liked to watch the clouds, sunrises and sunsets and the sparkle of light on the ocean during daylight.

Justine and Simone settled into the second row of thirty first-class seats—two seats per row, very plush. Justine sat by the window, Simone on the aisle. They had a divider with a small tray and cup holders between them.

"Harry would have liked this," Justine said.

Harry, still a cop, had to go back to work. Plus, as they were moving closer to Rubicon's territory they thought they might have to move fast at some point. Harry, not quite a hundred percent, didn't put up much of an argument.

"Perhaps one day he will be allowed onboard."

"Don't start."

Five other passengers also took their seats. A middle-aged Chinese couple, both exceptionally attractive, nodded pleasantly to them.

"I am Chi Jing and this is my husband Sang. Have you taken this flight before?"

"No," Simone said, returning Chi Jing's smile.

"It is very comfortable, but somewhat boring. I hope they have a good movie." They took seats in the third row on the opposite side.

Three boisterous young vamps sat in the last rows.

Justine had watched them check out her and Simone and the Jings. "Ready for party time?" she asked Simone, who just shook her head and rolled her eyes.

As the plane leveled off Justine heard the click of unreleased seatbelts from the three men. They moved into the lounge area and sat at two of several tables and bench seats along each side of the plane. A small bar was set up in back with four seats with seatbelts.

Justine glanced back. One of the vamps—mid-twenties, dark hair hanging around a flat face with close set eyes and a twisted mouth—stared back at her. *Bad news there,* she thought. The Chinese woman caught her eye. With the slightest of motions she indicated the three New Bloods. She had the same bad feeling. Justine nodded her understanding.

With a pleasant smile Suzy offered them wine or blood. They all took wine.

"So," Justine said when they had settled in with their wine. "Who's Meir? You know something."

Simone hugged herself and stared at the ceiling.

"I knew a man whose mother's maiden name was Meir. We were… close. I thought we'd be together a long time."

"He was a vamp?"

*"Non.* Mortal."

"You were in love with him. What happened?"

"World War I. He loved me, but he loved Germany more." She looked down with little shakes of her head. "When the archduke was assassinated, we knew war was coming. We planned to go to Switzerland, but he was persuaded to join the German army."

"Persuaded?"

"German nationalism. Walter chose to defend his country rather than come with me. Plus his mother's family was Jewish. He wanted to make sure they were seen as patriotic. His mother's maiden name was Meir."

"What happened to him?"

*"Je ne sais pas.* I never heard from him again."

"You're not thinking this Meir is your Meir, are you?"

"It is unlikely. There are many Meirs. But this man is in Basel. Where we were to meet."

"So what if this guy is your guy? You going to settle down in a little chalet and raise sheep for the next century or two?"

"And leave you on your own, *chère*? I do not love him anymore." Simone studied her hands in her lap.

"You sure?"

*"Oui, non.* There have been others since then."

"Like Fin?"

*"Oui, comme* Fin."

"And… others?"

Simone settled into her seat then rolled her head toward Justine and flashed a smile full of secrets.

"Don't give me that little secret grin of yours. We've got at least four more hours before we land. Plenty of time to tell me about your boyfriends, and girlfriends."

Simone barely got started when the three young male vamps pushed into their passenger space.

The Flat-faced one scowled down at Justine. Pretty Boy, slender with short blond hair, grinned down at the Chinese lady. The burly one, a bit older with lank black hair and tattoos visible on his hands and neck, stood against the door used by the attendants.

Pretty Boy said to the Chinese lady, "That old man able to satisfy you, babe?"

"I am most satisfied."

"I bet I could do better."

"I bet you could not."

His smarmy smile turned mean. "We'll see." He was way too full of himself to recognize the warning in the Chinese couple's eyes.

Flatface favored Justine with a yellow toothed smile.

In a thick British accent he said, "You ladies look like you could use some satisfyin'. Don't cha-think, Klaus?" he asked Burly.

"*Ja*. Maybe take three of us."

"Yea. Three rides for your last ride."

"Only three? Who are you, the three stooges?" Justine said with a humorless smile.

"Ah, Justine and Simone, don't matter who we are. You won't have the heads to remember us when this flight ends."

Simone said, "Ah, Rubicon."

"How did you find us?" Justine asked as she sat up in the seat, the hand pushing her up out of sight at her side.

"Rubicon has eyes everywhere, luv."

"In the Council, I assume. Who was it?"

"You just gonna have to die without knowing, luv," Flatface said, drawing out a well-worn machete.

"Well, I know it wasn't you," Justine said. "You aren't smart enough to do that."

Flatface snarled, "I'm plenty smart. Smart enough to know I'm getting off this plane alive and you ain't."

"No you're not. It's the other way around." Justine leaned forward to get out of her seat, exposing her neck.

Flatface wasn't in a good position to make a clean strike at her neck, so he struck forward with his blade, aiming to stab her neck instead of slicing it.

Ready, Justine jerked back, grabbed his hand and yanked him hard so he lay over her and Simone's lap. At the same time her hidden hand drove a slender stiletto into his gut. Simone snatched Flatface's knife from him while jamming her own small blade into his arm.

Justine had planned to gut the vamp with a quick flick of the blade, thus putting him out of commission long enough to handle the others. But, Klaus, quick despite his size, grabbed Flatface and dragged him off Justine before she could inflict a more serious wound. Then he came after her with just his beefy hands.

He clutched her blouse and yanked her out of the seat, punched her head, then whipped the stiletto from her hand. Justine punched him back and instantly they were at it.

The narrow aisle limited Justine's use of her black belt martial arts skills. Nevertheless she easily held her own until Klaus landed a solid fist to her jaw, driving her backward where her heels tripped on Flatface crawling down the aisle. Stunned, she fell back on her ass.

Klaus, smarmy smile still on his full lips, drew out his long blade. Standing in the aisle with Justine at his feet, he raised the blade to split her head open.

Standing between the seats, Simone swung out and sliced off Klaus' machete hand, a good distracting move. Hand and machete dropped toward Justine's head. Slowed by the narrow space Simone still snatched the machete up inches from Justine's face.

Pretty Boy, who had been standing back sipping wine while watching his partners attack, cried out when he saw his buddies go down. He attempted to draw his blade as he backed away, his pretty face grimacing with fear rather than anger.

It switched to surprise as Chi Jing tightened a garrote around his neck. "Now I will be satisfied," she said into his ear. She tightened the wire slowly. When the wire reached bone she yanked it hard. The garrote made a snapping sound as it cut through his spine.

Klaus didn't hesitate. Outnumbered, his only chance was to draw a gun from his waistband and shoot them all in the head before they could rush him.

Justine threw Pretty Boy's head at him. Klaus easily swatted it away, but the distraction was enough for Suzy to come through the door and smack his head with a stainless steel serving tray. Taken by surprise he whirled around. That gave Simone an opening to jam her knife up into the back of his skull. She wiggled it around enough to make what might have been a survivable injury into a fatal one, even for a vampire.

Everyone watched Klaus crumple, shudder, and fall still.

"Well, okay," Justine said.

"Not quite, I think," Simone said. She stood in the aisle with her foot on Flatface's hand, still holding a knife similar to the others. She took the weapon then flipped him over on his back.

He tried to grab Simone's leg. She stabbed his arm with her machete.

He tried to hook Justine's leg with one foot. She kicked his leg away then straddled him with her blade pressing on his throat.

"Once again, who sent you to kill us? Rubicon?"

His nose and mouth wrinkled. "Rubicon do not speak with the common people."

"Who does speak to the common people?"

"Who do you think?" He spit to show his distaste. "That Girl."

Justine glanced at Simone who showed no surprise. "Why don't you like The Girl?"

"Take orders from a girl. *Eine verdammte Schweizere Hündin.* Not right."

"I agree with you on that. Where is she now?"

"*Ich weiß es nicht.* Back I think."

"Back where?"

"*Schweiz.*"

"Where in Switzerland?"

"Let me stand. I tell you."

"You tell me and then you can stand."

"*Nein.*"

"Justine, be..."

Flatface yanked his hands from under Simone and Chi Jing's feet. He swooped his arms between Justine's, forcing her blade from his neck. Continuing the motion, he grabbed her head front and back, intending to twist it and break her neck. Half a second and she'd be in for a long rehab.

But Justine was quick, too. She ducked the knife under his arms and jammed the blade to the hilt under his chin.

He froze but for a faint quiver. His eyes fixed on her, his lips attempted to form a smirk. Unable to talk with a knife through his throat and in his brain he managed to form the words, "*Sie geht zu...,*" before his eyes glazed over in real death.

Justine knocked the truly dead hands away and sat up. "Shit, shit, shit. What did he say?"

Chi Jing dropped into her seat. "He said, 'She went to….'"

"Bastard. Well, that was fucked up. Guess I should have pulled that knife out."

Simone took her arm and helped her stand. "He was not going to tell you. He probably didn't know."

"So we learned nothing."

Chi Jing said, "There was one thing he said. *Eine verdammte Schweizere Hündin.*"

"Which means?"

"A damn Swiss bitch."

"That's fairly specific, if he wasn't playing us."

"*Chère*, it is something."

"Right. So what happens now, here?"

Suzy cleared her throat. Not looking the least bit freaked out, she stood by the door to the cockpit holding the tray across her chest. She pointed a finger at the boarding door. "Out the door," she said almost apologetically.

"How high are we?" Simone asked.

"Thirty-one thousand feet."

Justine stroked her chin. "Won't that suck us out if we open the door?" Justine had been dumped into the water with an anchor dragging her down a couple thousand feet. It had taken her days to climb out. The thought of falling thirty-one thousand feet into the middle of the Atlantic Ocean with the possibility of sinking to the bottom and having to walk a thousand miles to land did not appeal.

"Not likely you all would have to worry, but we'll tie a rope around you. It'll be fine."

"You've done this before?"

Chi Jing asked, "Would not the pressure drop hurt you?"

"Oh, no problem," Suzy said with a dismissive wave. "I wear an oxygen mask."

Justine shrugged. "Well, okay. Who gets to open the door?"

As if on cue the door to the cockpit opened. Katherine came through and surveyed the scene. "Ah," she said. "We have received a special message from the Council for Justine and Simone. But I see you have already gotten the message."

Suzy, wearing a heavy jacket and oxygen mask, tended the ropes secured to a sturdy hand rail. Justine wasn't going anywhere near the open door. While she and Chi Jing and Sang watched from behind a row of seats, Katherine pushed open the boarding door while Simone threw the three bodies and heads out.

Suzy used a handheld carpet cleaner to clean the vampire blood. Katherine came out with four wine glasses for the four remaining passengers.

Her chore done, Suzy flashed them a smile. "Please enjoy the rest of your flight."

# Chapter 7

The vampire who met the plane at a private airfield just outside Stuttgart, Germany looked about twenty-five, but he'd been a vampire for ninety-two years. Justine had been a vamp barely a year. She still had to take a minute to process that an apparent kid had lived longer than she. He had short sandy hair, a square chin and icy blue eyes. He was good looking and polite to just shy of being smarmy. Justine disliked him at first sight.

"I am Franz Heisman," he said in English with a faint German accent. "I hope you had a pleasant flight?"

"Yes, uneventful," Chi Jing replied with a sly smile for Justine and Simone.

"Yes, very good. Welcome Madame Chi Jing, there is a car waiting for you."

The elegant Chinese lady nodded to Justine and Simone, "Good luck in your quest."

The two vamps nodded back. Simone said, "And you also."

As Chi Jing and her husband climbed into a waiting car, Franz said, "So, you must be Simone and Justine. I am here from the Böhm Family to guide you. I understand you wish to talk with Johan Brandt."

"Yes," Justine said, wanting to get on with it.

"It is almost daylight. It will take at least one hour to arrive at his house. We have secured rooms for you at a most comfortable hotel with all the amenities for our kind."

Neither one wanted to wait, but without a word between them, they agreed it was probably a prudent option. After all, travelling for vampires could be as exhausting as it was for mortals. They hadn't had any real down time for two days.

Das Nachthotel, an anonymous five story block on the Northeast side of Stuttgart, sat on Sigmaringer Straße where fields ended and the city began. They had separate rooms with a connecting door. After baths and a change of clothes they lay together on Simone's bed sipping blood they found in the small refrigerator and heated to a perfect 36 degrees Celsius. Though the windows were very well blacked out they could feel the sun rise.

"What do you think about Franz?" Justine asked.

Simone stretched out, eyes closed, the mug of blood resting on her chest. "I do not think anything of Franz. He is an errand boy."

"I still don't like him."

"He is cute."

"True…I still don't like him. Didn't you say you'd spent some time in Germany?"

Simone finished her blood and set the mug on the bedside table. *"Ja."*

"Were you ever here in Stuttgart?"

*"Ja."*

"So you know the city."

"That was one hundred years ago. Is not the same."

"We could ditch Franz, find our way without him."

"Justine, we will not ditch Franz. It is daytime. Sleep."

*"Mais oui,* mom."

The noise that woke Justine was not a usual sound. It was daytime—cars passed, people walked and talked, sometimes coughed or sneezed. These were everyday sounds, easy to ignore even for the acute hearing of vampires. This noise was subtle, unexpected, barely audible to Justine's subconscious alertness.

*The click of a door lock turning.* Fully alert, she stared at the bedroom door. Nothing, no movement, no sound, no person on the other side.

*The delicate swish of a door opening.* Her bedroom door.

*A tingling on the back of her neck*—another vampire close by.

She touched Simone who woke instantly. At the connecting door Justine listened then slowly depressed the lever and pulled open the door.

*Swish and tiny thump of a door closing*—her door.

Justine rushed through her empty room to the hall door, yanked it open and scanned the hallway. She saw nobody except Simone at her own room door.

"Are you hearing things, *chère?*"

"Yes. Somebody in my room."

"Perhaps to steal your virtue."

"You took that a long time ago."

Back on the bed Simone said, "I think we must be careful, now. Rubicon—."

"And or The Girl."

"—will know what happened on the plane. They will be looking for us."

Justine sighed an all too mortal sigh. "Somebody should just kill that girl."

# Chapter 8

Hands in her pockets The Girl stared through the one way glass at Teresa Diaz strapped on an operating table. That woman had caused The Girl a lot of trouble. Her master, Rubicon, needed Diaz for his experiments and had sent The Girl to get her. She'd been successful, but at some cost. She had no desire to return to New Orleans or the bayou.

Teresa struggled as she always did, physically and magically. A forty-two year old, big-boned woman about six feet tall, if she got loose it would take several attendants to subdue her. But it wasn't merely the woman's physicality that required the straps. The Girl, barely five feet in heels, if she ever wore such things, a waif with unruly hair, was a very dangerous Ghost vampire. If it came down to it she could take Teresa in a fight, of that she had no doubt. But if Teresa had full control of her magic…?

Teresa was a very powerful, though mostly untrained, witch. That was why a sorcerer always stayed in attendance when samples had to be taken.

Juno, Rubicon's chief sorcerer, had created the original spell that prevented Teresa from using her power. Juno or his assistant, Gerhart, had to be in the magic room to maintain the spell just in case Teresa managed to take control of her power.

Although carved out of the interior of a mountain, nobody doubted that Teresa could, and would, destroy the laboratory if her power broke the bonds of the spell. It hadn't, yet. But it could. The Girl thought they should take more precautions.

But The Girl was in no position to insist. Her master, the thousand year old Rubicon, had not been happy that Justine and Simone had not been killed on the plane or taken in Columbia. The failures had not been directly her fault, so she had *one* more chance to capture or kill the two.

That order was not only Rubicon's desire. For her, it was personal, an obsession. She had history with those two, and planned to end it.

Raised to be a servant like her father who trained her, she eventually served Stephan Sinakov, the head of the Sinakov vampire Family. Sinakov, in some sort of ritual, killed Justine's daughter. Justine did not just cry and move on. She searched for the killer and persuaded Simone Gireaux to make her a vampire.

In the end Justine took Sinakov's head as his mansion burned. The Girl saved him and reattached his head. Harry, Justine's lover, had tracked them across the country to where Justine, in front of Rubicon, had finally killed Sinakov for real. Rubicon had become The Girl's master. Her duty to her new master—take Teresa and end Justine and Simone.

# Chapter 9

Minutes after sunset, five kilometers west of Stuttgart, Franz turned the Mercedes off the main highway onto a narrow paved road. It wound through wooded hills broken by jumbles of grey boulders.

"For thirty years no man is allowed to live in this area," Franz said. "But *Herr Brandt's* family has lived here for over one hundred years, so they let him stay."

"How do you know he knows where this Meir lives?" Justine asked.

"I do not know. It is in the Council's records somewhere."

They rounded a corner. A small clearing appeared, entirely bounded by trees except for a ten meter swath of sloping rock. A chalet style house with faded white cement lowers and a weathered brown-stained wooden upper portion backed up to thick trees and rocks.

From behind a sliding glass door that opened onto a second story deck, a figure watched them exit the car.

"Secluded much?" Justine said to herself as she scanned the surroundings. "Does Superman know about this place? Could have saved himself a lot of work instead of hollowing out that mountain."

Simone scowled at her and playfully punched her arm. To Franz she said, "Does he know we are coming?"

Franz glanced at the pine needle covered ground. *"Nein."*

*"Wunderbar.* Shall we see if he will open the door?"

Keeping an eye on the man watching them from the deck, they approached the heavy wooden door and knocked.

Justine held back. She wasn't wild about being surrounded by unfamiliar woods. A warm breeze stirred the trees enough to hide any movement of the watchful beasts hidden behind every trunk. The back of her neck bristled with their gaze.

The door opened revealing a man in his fifties. He was thin, almost gaunt, with black hair, and a crutch to make up for the one leg that had been cut off mid thigh. He looked each one in the eye and asked, "Are you here to kill me?"

This was not the greeting they expected. The three visitors had no answer until Simone stepped forward and said, "Herr Brandt, we believe that after the war you knew a man with the last name of Meir. We need to talk with him. Do you know where he is?"

His eyes opened wide at the mention of Meir, but then his shoulders dropped and his head bowed, making tiny side to side shakes. Herr Brandt was an unhappy vampire. The three felt disappointment radiate from his slumped shoulders like a heavy mist settling over them.

Justine stood behind the others casting all her senses into the surrounding dark. "We should go inside, now."

Franz said, *"Herr Brandt, dürfen wir reinkommen?*

They did not wait for Brandt to invite them. Inside, Brandt, using his vampire strength, climbed the stairs one step at a time. The upstairs living room and kitchen were wood paneled with heavy wood furniture. A picture window beside a door that led to the front deck had a partial view down the valley. Two windows were open on either side wall.

Brandt stood at the far end of a chintz-upholstered couch. *"Was willst du?"*

Franz said in English, "What we want, Herr Brandt, is to speak with a man named Meir, whom I believe you know."

"Why do you want to speak with him?"

Justine said, "He may have information we need."

"What information?"

"The location of a particular cave."

"Ah… *ja…* the cave," he whispered.

Franz waited behind the couch. Excited, he asked, "You know where it is?" He leaned forward, hand by his ear to hear the reply.

*"Ja."*

Justine stood closest to Brandt by the front of the couch. She took a step toward him. "Where is it?"

Reflexively he stepped back. His crutch caught on the rug. He began to fall backwards.

Justine reached for him. She grabbed his jacket and caught him from falling.

*"Dank—."*

The high powered bullet came through the open side window unhindered. It entered the right side of Brandt's head, leaving a relatively small hole. It came out the left side creating a large hole and taking half his brains with it. A killing wound, for a vampire.

Still holding him, Justine glanced out the window. Full dark had settled in, but she saw movement in the trees heading toward the back of the house. "There," she said, and dropped the now dead forever Johan Brandt.

Justine and Simone didn't wait to go down the stairs. In seconds they had leaped off the balcony. They raced around the house, then stopped at the bottom of the stony slope. Extending their vampire senses they listened and scanned the woods and rocks.

They heard a faint scrape of rock and a whispered curse.

They had no need to speak—a quick flick of a finger was enough. They bounded up the boulders, Justine on the right edge, Simone on the left.

A couple hundred feet up the slope Justine held still, detecting the assassin, a young vampire. She sensed, more than saw, his movement. She definitely heard the gunshot and felt the pain and tug of the bullet catching the calf of her right leg and knocking it back. She couldn't help but utter a tight cry of pain as she dropped to one knee. Aware that she was exposed, she rolled off the boulder. A second bullet whizzed past her head.

A surprised cry, the clatter of a rifle falling on stone and the sounds of a struggle brought a satisfied grin to her lips. Rocks tumbling on rocks, a deep thump that shook the ground and an unrestricted scream wiped it away.

"Simone?"

"*Ca va.*" Simone called. "You?"

"Got a hole in my leg, otherwise fine." Pain already fading, Justine climbed up to Simone. A cry of horror and a short string of German cussing greeted her.

"Oh shit."

The assassin could only be seen from the stomach up. The rest was crushed by a five foot boulder.

"He can't survive that, can he?"

"*Oui*, it is possible. But, his body is crushed too much to repair, even if we could remove *le grand rocher.*"

"That sucks. We can't leave him like that, though he probably deserves it."

"No, we cannot."

"Well, fuck."

Simone knelt beside him while Justine retrieved the rifle.

"*Sprechen sie Englisch?*"

"Yes." His voice was a rough whisper. His eyelids fluttered.

"You are American?"

"Was. German now."

"Why were you sent to kill the old man?"

"I can't survive this, can I?"

"Not intact," Justine said.

His eyes followed the rifle. "If I… tell you, will you… finish…?"

Simone laid a gentle hand on his chest. "Yes."

"Who sent you to kill Herr Brandt?" Justine asked.

"No one. Sent to… to kill you."

"The Girl sent you?"

"Rub… icon sent. Angry I fail…."

"Does not matter now."

"No. Hurts."

"I'm sorry," Justine said.

Simone backed away.

A grimace of distaste on her lips, Justine pulled the trigger.

✳ ✳ ✳

Back at the chalet, Franz was not alone. A second car had parked next to theirs. Wary, Justine mounted the stairs, while out of sight from the main room Simone leaped up to the balcony.

In the main room Franz casually leaned against a small bar while sipping a beer. He watched a woman keeling beside Brandt's body, her head bowed.

"Hello," Justine said as she and Simone entered the room.

"The shooter?" Franz asked.

Justine drew a finger across her throat.

"Rubicon?"

Justine nodded and pointed at the woman.

"Tilda Hoffman, his mortal granddaughter."

Tilda sighed heavily, patted her grandfather on the chest and stood up to face the newcomers. She was an attractive sixty something, tall, tanned and slim with the same broad shoulders and facial features as her grandfather. She was not at all intimidated by three vampires.

"Franz here told me what happened, but he was not sure why it happened. Can you tell me?"

Justine traded looks with Simone then said, "I'm sorry for your loss."

"Don't be. But continue."

"Well, the assassin, who was a vampire and is now fully dead, was trying to shoot me or Simone. The rug caught Herr Brandt's crutch. He fell, I tried to grab him. The bullet hit him instead of me. Why should I not be sorry?"

"He has wanted to die for years. He hated being a vampire and hated having one leg. And, as he told me many times, he hated being too weak to kill himself."

Simone said, "That explains something. When he opened the door he asked if we were there to kill him. He was disappointed when I said no."

"Yes, he asked me many times to end him." Tilda wiped a tear from her mostly unlined face. "I loved him, I wanted to help him, but I could not do it."

After a minute of silence Tilda hunched her shoulders then let them fall as she blew out a deep breath. "I could use a beer." She found a beer behind the small bar and took a big swig. Resting her elbows on the bar she said, "Two questions. Why would someone want to kill you? And why are you here?"

With a look between them Justine and Simone agreed to lay it all out. Justine sat on the edge of the hard cushioned chintz couch.

Elbows on knees, hands clasped, Justine said, "Do you know who Rubicon is?"

Tilda sat on a straight back chair opposite Justine. "I have heard of him. A very old vampire, *ja?*"

"Yes. He's planning to take over the world. To do that he has kidnapped a very good friend of mine. I... we want her back. Then we'll stop his grandiose plan to take over the world."

"Why your friend?"

"She is a powerful witch. As is her daughter who he has also kidnapped."

Not wanting to believe a word, Tilda studied each of them. "And he wants to kill you so you won't rescue your friend."

"Yes. Among other reasons."

"Hmmm." She drank the rest of her beer and held the empty out to Franz for another. "How and why did you find your way here? My grandfather hadn't left this house for years."

"We had the name Meir," Justine said.

Tilda gazed into the past. "I knew of a man during World War I whose family name was Meir. Apparently he had changed his name to fight for the Germans. Jews were not very popular then."

"We believe he may have grown disenchanted with the Germans

and deserted, switching back to Meir after the war."

"So how did you connect Meir with...?" She inclined her head toward the body just behind her.

They all looked at Franz.

"I don't know, really," Franz said as he stared at the stone fireplace. "The Family Council must have dug through their archives and made the connection. Maybe a report when he lost his leg?"

"Would this house be mentioned in that report?" Justine had settled into the couch, arms crossed, feet on the sturdy wood coffee table.

"Very possible," Tilda said. "This house was part of a network for refugees and downed pilots during World Wars I and II. From here they went cross country to France and were handed over to the Alice Network who took them to safety. There were vampires here then."

"And your grandfather was here?"

"Yes. Yes. He helped as much as he could. He saved a lot of lives."

"Jewish lives?"

"Yes," Tilda said, adamant. "Jews, gypsies, Polish, English, American, German. He helped anyone who needed it."

"Tilda, how did he lose his leg?" Simone asked. She sat across the small dining table, elbows on the table, chin propped on fists. Her attention never wavered.

Tilda leaned back, planting her feet on the coffee table. She thought a bit, chuffed, shook her head.

"Toward the end of World War I a German defector, a vamp, came through. He was an officer, but didn't like what the Germans were doing."

"He deserted."

"Yes. For some reason he and my grandfather became quick friends. He stayed around for several months. With his abilities, he could track down lost refugees. Also, he could warn if German patrols were close. He was an engineer, built tunnels. He helped expand a cave in the rocks behind us where our guests could hide. It caved in years ago. They went off to build a tunnel somewhere. There was an accident, I think. My grandfather lost the leg and the only way to save him was to change him. That's what I was told."

Simone, her voice carefully neutral, asked, "What was this man's name?"

Tilda's lips twitched in thought. "I do remember. Grandfather talked of him often, sometimes with affection, some—."

"Tilda. What was his name?"

The mortal's eyebrows, and heartbeat, rose as she recognized the power of a vampire's request.

"Walter Rinman."

Simone's mouth opened, but it took a couple of tries for her to whisper, *"Mon Dieu. Mon Dieu."*

Justine leaned forward catching Simone's gaze. "Meir... is... him?," she asked quietly.

"Who?" Franz asked, trying to catch up.

Much quicker at figuring things out, Tilda said, "You think Walter Rinman is the Meir you're looking for?"

"Yes."

"And you knew him before."

*"Oui,"* Simone said, falling back to her native language as she struggled with the implications. "Before *Guerre Mondiale I nous... nous devions quitter l'Allemagne pour la Suisse. Mais..."* She looked out the window to the past. "He wanted to fight for his country. I never saw him again."

"Why would he pick the name Meir? It is a Jewish name."

"His mother's family's name was Meir. What true German would change his name to a Jewish name?"

"So we are searching for this Rinman who changed his name back to Meir about a hundred years ago after World War 1."

"It seems so," Justine said. "Tilda, do you know where he is now?"

"No, but his daughter might."

# Chapter 10

"Daughter? Adopted, I presume."

"Yes. He married a mortal woman who had a daughter."

Simone gave Justine a look. It was unlikely she and Harry would ever really get married, but her look was to remind Justine that the option was on the table. Justine sent her an eye roll.

Justine said, "Okay, so who is this woman and where is she?"

"Her name is Hedy Duchene. She is American, but has lived in the EU for many years. She is a nurse at the Stuttgart Hospital."

"Are you in touch with her?"

"Not for maybe two years. She only came to this house once about three years ago when she was in Stuttgart for some special training. There was a huge explosion and building collapse at the time. She helped and the hospital hired her." Tilda leaned back and finished her beer in one gulp. "A year later I saw her at the hospital. We talked for five minutes. That was all."

"Will you go and find her tomorrow?"

"One thing I remember, she only works the night shift. Living with a vampire she liked the night."

"What do you think?" Justine asked Simone.

Simone shook herself as if waking from a dream, or a memory. "Cell phones work here?"

"No."

"Sunrise soon. We wait until evening and go find Hedy Duchene." She glanced at the body. "Your grandfather. Does he need to be buried or…?"

Tilda turned and looked down at the body. "No. He wanted to be blown-by-the-wind dust. He wanted to be free of the inconvenience of one leg and the tedium of living too long. There is a way to a flat section of the roof back there. He liked, yearned, for the freedom to roam the world in the sun."

Justine stood up. "Come on, Franz. Help us get him to freedom."

While Tilda waited on the rooftop for the sun to turn her grandfather to dust and the morning breeze to catch him up and sweep him to freedom, the three vampires prepared to sleep. Franz took a small guest bedroom in the back. Justine and Simone settled in the living room, Simone stretched out on the couch and Justine curled up in a recliner.

"We need Harry," Justine said. "This daylight waiting sucks, as well as wasting time."

"Will he be able to come?" Simone asked. She hadn't liked the idea of Justine and Harry, a mortal detective, being together, let alone falling in love. But he'd proven himself several times to be brave and resourceful, even taking on The Girl. They'd become friends.

"Well, if I could call him I'd ask him. We're not that far from a big city, why can't we get a freaking cell phone to work?"

"You were a real estate agent—location, location, location."

"Oh shut up."

Simone laughed then turned thoughtful. "How did that assassin know we would be here?"

Justine caught Simone's quizzical gaze. "Hmm. *We* didn't know."

"Only Franz."

"And whoever told him about Brandt. It was supposed to be a secret. Need to know and all that."

*"Peut-être devrions-nous lui parler?"*

"If that means we should interrogate the little weasel, I agree."

They marched down the hall and entered the small bedroom.

*"Il n'est pas ici."*

"The window's open. An easy jump."

"A cell phone may work up the hill."

Justine poked her head out the window. "It's daylight. But it's cloudy, and the trees are thick next to the rocks."

Simone gripped Justine's arm. *"Écoute.* Listen."

For several minutes they stood together by the window, focusing on the outside sounds.

Finally Simone said, "Someone comes through the trees quickly."

"I hear him. Was that a German swear word?"

A minute later Franz jumped into the room. He took a couple steps before he felt the two other vampires waiting on either side of the window.

"Reporting in?" Justine asked.

Franz spun around, handgun in his hand. Backed up against the bed Justine and Simone were only a few feet away, too close to cover both. He pointed at Justine.

"They are looking for you."

"Who?"

Franz's mouth twisted into a dismissive sneer. "Rubicon and The Girl. They are coming. You cannot get away."

"Who is coming. The Girl?"

"*Nein.* A team. They will take you to her."

Simone asked in a calm reasonable dangerous voice, "And you will keep us here until they come, *oui?*"

Franz's jaw clenched as he suddenly recognized his danger. He shifted his aim to Simone. "*Ja,* they are come quickly."

Justine said, "Do you expect to be alive when they get here?"

He swung his gun at Justine.

Moving at her full vampire speed, Simone swung the machete she'd been holding behind her back. The flat of the razor-sharp blade smacked the gun from his hand. Justine caught the gun before it hit the floor. Simone pushed him back onto the thick, red and white checked poof that covered the bed.

Justine held her blade to his throat. "Is this all about us, or do you want to find Meir also?"

"I don't have to tell you anything."

"If you want to live you do."

"If you end me Rubicon will angry. He'll come after you."

"Do you want to think about what you just said for a minute? Like, why are *you* here?"

Franz took a long moment to think and a short moment to realize, once again, his danger. Considering the sting of Justine's blade on his throat, he really only had one choice.

"They want to discover if anybody knows where is entrance to the tunnel."

Justine and Simone glanced at each other.

"And where is this tunnel," Simone asked, smooth and uninterested.

"I don't know." Justine added a bit of pressure to her blade. "I was told anybody who knew would know what I meant."

"You climbed the hill to use your cell phone, yes?"

"*Ja,* yes."

"What did you tell them?"

"Brandt was dead, the assassin was dead and you were alive."

"What about Tilda or Hedy Duchene?"

"Yes, Tilda. Only that she might know a woman who knew where is Meir."

"You did not say the name of Hedy, correct?"

"*Ja.*"

Justine grinned. "You wanted to find out the name and be the hero."

"*Ja, ja.* Now will you leave me alone? I know nothing more."

Justine, wearing a rain jacket with the hood up, climbed the narrow stairs up to the roof. Tilda sat on a weather-worn bench watching the last of Brandt float away on a steady breeze. "Tilda, we have to leave here, now."

She swiped away a tear. "What do you mean we have to leave?"

"There are some bad people coming and you know stuff that they want to know. You will tell them, and then they will kill you. So come, now. They are on their way here."

"But they can not—"

"Yes, they can. Come now."

Tilda studied Justine's earnest face, glanced at the remaining dust, and said, "Out of my way then." At the bottom of the steps Simone waited with Franz's body. "What happened here?"

"We will explain later, *Madame,*" Simone told her. "We must go *rapidement.*"

Simone led her through the house to the front door while Justine placed Franz in the rooftop sun. When Justine joined them she said, "Listen."

"Two cars, coming fast. Is there another way out of here?"

"There is a trail that was used in World War II, but much of it is open to the sun now."

The two vamps communicated wordlessly. The coming vehicles would have mortals, but surely a few vamps, well equipped and experienced. They had no choice but to take the trail.

Quickly they found a hoodie for Simone and hats for both. Tilda, an experienced hiker, led the way into the trees where they connected with the overgrown trail. A couple hundred meters along, she said, "Stop. There is a cave right up the hill. It is not deep, but is hard to find. Refugees used to hide from the Nazis there."

"If they find the trail they will catch up," Simone said.

Leaving no trace, they left the trail and climbed through tightly packed trees and boulders. An egg shaped boulder about three meters high half embedded in the slope appeared above them. Tilda led them around one side. She pointed to a half rotten log standing on end leaning against the junction of rock and earth.

"Move that log over," she said. "I am not as strong as I was."

Justine easily slid it aside.

Tilda took a flashlight from her small backpack and crawled through the opening. "Move that log back when you are in."

Inside they crawled back two meters to a space about eight meters long, five wide and two high. There was a well used wooden table and two matching stools. A large slab of rock had crushed one of two metal cots with thin ancient mattresses and moldering blankets. Stone rubble buried a chair rough-made of bark covered branches.

Tilda dropped onto a stool, leaned against the stone wall and crossed her ankles. "Now we wait."

Justine and Simone found more or less comfortable spots deeper into the cave where they couldn't be seen from the entrance. Like Tilda they stretched out and tried to relax while keeping an ear open for any approach.

Voice low, Tilda asked, "How long have you been together?"

"A year, more or less," Justine said.

"I would have thought longer the way you work together."

Justine favored Simone with a crooked smile. "Sometimes it seems like centuries."

"For you also, *chère*?" Simone said returning Justine's smile.

"*Très* funny, *chère*," Justine said. "But I'm glad we are together. Otherwise I'd probably be dead dead or wish I was."

Simone stretched out her hand and gripped Justine's. "On the path you were going, *oui*, you would have been dead dead. I am pleased you are not."

"Me too."

"So who are you looking for?" Tilda whispered, leaning forward with elbows on knees.

"We are looking for a witch who...." Her voice faded off as Simone held up a hand for silence.

All held still, their attention, and weapons, focused on the hidden entrance to their little den. The two vampires listened to the searchers, one vampire and two mortals, talk. They had entered the house, found

Franz, and were discussing what to do.

Simone's German wasn't as good as it used to be. She squinted as she concentrated on the faint voices. She pointed at the searchers, at her eyes and spread her hands wide. They were going to search the whole area.

A minute passed, maybe two. Nobody in the cave moved an inch. Then, closer—"*Diesen Weg. Ich rieche sie.*"

Tilda heard. She pointed to her nose then pointed outside and swept her finger to indicate that the vamp was following their scent and that might lead them to the cave. They traded glances. There was nothing they could do but wait. They did not want to kill anybody else, although they would if they had to. Maybe the false trails they had had time to leave would be enough to cause the vampire to think they were gone.

They waited, not moving, not talking, just listening. The mortals tramped through the trees, occasionally calling out. One came within two meters of the cave. Justine and Simone raised eyebrows, knowing that if that had been the vampire he would have detected them.

Finally the searchers moved away and fifteen minutes later the women heard doors slamming and the crunch of tires on gravel. In a short, whispered conversation, they agreed to wait until sunset, just in case.

They were sure the searchers had left, though Justine still had that lingering tingling on the back of her neck. Simone lay next to her, but they were so familiar with each other they automatically dismissed each other's vibe. That vamp must have been very old for his sense to linger so long.

It being daytime, Simone and Justine dozed off and on. Wide awake, Tilda thought of Brandt and how she'd miss him, but was also glad that his unhappiness was over. Tears fell for him rolled over her bittersweet smile. She dozed a bit. When she realized they had an hour and a half to wait she took a paperback novel from her voluminous purse and moved close to the entrance for some light.

The excitement of the day made the suspense of the book seem tame and dull. She dozed again.

Justine thought of Harry. It would be much cozier with his warm body next to her cold bones. He also had that cop turn of mind she suspected they might need at some point. Though silence was called for she checked her cell phone; no service. Not surprising, as they were surrounded by rock.

Eyes half closed she watched Tilda settle by the entrance with her book. Justine shook her head. Here she was immortal, though only for a year or so, and when was the last time she had had time to read a book?

She knew—the night before she left for Columbia. She and Harry had finally had some time to themselves. That afternoon they had lovely slow sex to last for how long, they had no idea. They no longer used phrases like, "As long as I live," "Forever," "Until death do us part." Technically, Justine was already dead, Harry was not. Unless Harry let her change him, he would grow old and die.

Justine felt the warmth growing behind her eyes, tears that she could never let go. Being a vampire had many perks, but being able to release a cathartic tear was not one of them. She massaged her eyes in an attempt to rub away the heat. She barely felt the prickle across the back of her neck.

She ignored the feeling. It was only Simone.

A sound—a twig falling, a displaced pebble, the rustle of cloth against rock—came from outside.

Justine's eyes popped open, shattering her mind's eye vision of Harry. Oh. Shit. She waved at Tilda: *get away from there.*

"Was?"

"Get back from… ."

A sudden burst of light, as someone ripped the log away from the entrance, interrupted her warning. An arm, followed by a crew cut blond head, reached in, grabbed Tilda's arm and dragged her out of the cave.

Tilda's scream galvanized Justine. A second after Tilda's foot disappeared, Justine dove out of the cave.

The vampire, with an arm around Tilda's neck, stood three meters away. He pointed a large semi-automatic pistol at Justine. He fired as she dove out and rolled to the side.

She did not allow the sting of the bullet along her thigh, only centimeters from her previous wound, to stop her. Two bullet wounds on the same leg in one day. *A first for everything.* With no close cover she knew the next bullet would do damage, as would the next and the next until she was incapacitated and the big vamp could take his time shooting her in the head—for real death.

Feet against a small boulder ended her roll. Immediately she launched herself at the intruder. Another bullet tugged at the heel of her shoe as she launched herself at the vamp's legs.

He was strong and solid and quick. He jumped aside. Justine's body flew past him, but she wrapped her arms around his legs and twisted.

He fell forward, landing on Tilda.

"Ow, damn it! Get off me." Tilda rammed her elbow back into his ribs.

The blow did nothing but cause him to spit, *"Sterbliche, Schlampe!"* He still held his gun. He swung it up to point at Tilda's head.

Justine knew he was going to kill her. All she could do was grab his leg and yank. The gun went off, shooting wild. Justine drew her machete ready to slice through his neck. But he rolled over and aimed the gun at Justine's head. From four feet away, he couldn't miss.

Justine's last thought would have been about Harry, except Simone kicked the gun from the vamp's hand then swung her blade through his neck.

Justine froze, well aware how close she'd just come to real death. "I guess I get to bonk Harry one more time. He thanks you."

"He is welcome." Simone helped Tilda to stand. "Do you know this one?"

Tilda winced at the severed head. "I have seen him before. Local. I do not know his name."

"I'd say he works for Rubicon. We should put him in the sun and get the hell out of here."

"Agreed," Simone and Tilda said.

Still on full alert, they put the body up on the rocks where the sun would turn him to dust. While Tilda closed up the house, Simone and Justine inspected Franz's SUV in case the searchers had left an explosive surprise. Finding none, with Tilda in the driver's seat they drove down the dirt road headed for the Krankenhaus Stuttgart.

# Chapter 11

The nighttime hospital hall was quiet as Tilda led Justine and Simone to the third floor nurse's desk. *"Bitte, ist Hedy hier?"*

*"Sind Sie Familie?"*

*"Nein.* A family friend. Do you speak English? Somebody she knows has died."

"Ah. Yes, I speak. She is with patient. She will be here soon. Please wait." She pointed to a row of chairs. *"Bitte."*

Justine smiled her best ex-real estate agent smile. "Has anyone else asked for her today?"

The nurse's eyes narrowed as she studied the three. "Why, may I ask?"

"We are meeting a friend here. I just wanted to know if they had been here."

"Ah. *Nein.* I mean no." She waved toward the chairs. "Please, sit. Hedy be here soon."

They sat.

Justine, in the middle, asked Tilda, "You think Meir is in Switzerland. How far is that?"

"Bern is about three hundred kilometers. I do not know where exactly he is."

"How far is three hundred kilometers?"

"Really, Justine, you Americans should catch up with the rest of the world. About a hundred and ninety miles. Three to four hours by car," Simone said.

"Can you drive us?" Justine asked Tilda.

"No. I cannot drive you. Maybe Hedy will? The Council?"

Simone said, "I do not think we can trust the Council at this time."

"No, I suppose not."

Justine looked sideways at Simone. "Claire?"

"Let us wait to hear this Hedy."

Justine nodded and joined the others: legs extended, ankles and arms crossed, the universal waiting position. Though their eyes seemed closed, the two vampires were on alert, scanning with eyes and ears for any enemies.

Justine thought about Teresa. What had happened to her? Was Rubicon using her like The Girl said to create vampires that could walk in the sun? Was she even alive? Yes, she must be. No magic could block that from her. Teresa's power and their connection was too strong.

And what of Teresa's daughter, Antonia? Pregnant by a vampire, something universally considered impossible. The baby would have been born by now. What was it—human, vampire, a hybrid? If Rubicon was successful in creating his Sunvamps they'd be an unstoppable army, easily able to take over the world.

Before she could begin to consider the consequences of that, her highly tuned hearing picked up the faint squeak of sneakers heading toward the nurse's station.

A nurse stopped at the station and filed some paperwork. The station nurse pointed toward the three women looking at her.

The nurse studied each woman, trying to place them and figure out what they wanted. The three stood, studying her in return.

Nurse Hedy Duchene was more handsome than beautiful with short hair and intense blue eyes in a square face. Her narrowed gaze steadied on Tilda. With a resigned sigh, Hedy moved to meet them. They spoke in German.

"Tilda, *ja?*"

"Hedy."

"These your bodyguards?"

Tilda raised one shoulder, dropped it. "Yes, but soon to be yours."

"Oh?" She inspected the two vampires. They maintained neutral expressions.

"Brandt is dead," Tilda said. Hedy raised an eyebrow. "Really dead."

Simone gripped her arm. In English she said, "Come with us. We will explain, but you are in danger."

Hedy attempted to step back, but Simone's firm grip held her in place. She glared down at Simone, ten centimeters shorter and nine kilos lighter. She knew better than to struggle against a vampire wearing an *I-mean-business* face.

"Who killed Brandt?"

Tilda said, "An assassin who was trying to kill her." She pointed at Justine, who wore a *who-me?* face.

Simone glanced at the desk nurse. "Not here."

Still holding Hedy's arm, she led Tilda and Hedy down a corridor to an unoccupied waiting room.

Justine, eyes on her cell, walked a few meters behind them. She stopped and leaned against the wall as she dialed a number.

"Claire, Justine. We have a problem."

"Justine, the only problem you have is that I've had a hundred problems today and now I'm lounging with my feet up and half of a large glass of wine in my hand, attempting to keep my promise to myself that I would not listen to one more problem today." Justine almost didn't need the phone to hear Claire's deep sigh of resignation. "What?"

"Well, actually there's two problems."

"Of course there are. What's the easy one?"

"Franz is dead, he betrayed us, led a Rubicon assassin to kill me, but he killed Brandt instead. He's dead. So is a local heavy duty vamp. We're with Brandt's granddaughter, Tilda, who has just connected us with Hedy, Meir's daughter, who might or might not voluntarily lead us to Meir who may or may not tell us where the secret back door is. They'll be looking for us and will find this hospital soon enough. Your problem is there's a spy for Rubicon in the Council. Your problem is you need to find who it is because otherwise you, and us, can't trust anybody."

"Okay," Claire said, dragging the word out as if she didn't quite believe any or all of what Justine just said. "And the real problem?"

"We may need transport and accommodations in Bern, Switzerland. Or, in that area. Soon."

"You need to get your priorities straight. Hang on."

Justine leaned casually against the wall. Down the hallway she saw Simone and the others enter a stairwell door. The station nurse ignored her.

Claire said, "Call this number. They'll get you a vehicle. It will cost you a few hundred marks, but you can trust him. He'll give you an address in Bern. Got it?"

Two men approached the nurse's station. No nonsense vampires.

Justine barely whispered, "Gotta go."

As quietly and as fast as she could, Justine ran down the hall. She looked back from the stairwell door. The vamps and the station nurse all looked at her. Door closed, she shouted, "Simone. They're here."

She pressed her back to the wall beside the door. The door burst open. The first vamp charged through. Justine grabbed the second, swung him around and slammed a knee into his gut. He doubled over and she slammed an elbow on his head. She figured he'd be down for at least five minutes.

The first vamp made it halfway down the stairs before he realized what had happened. He leaped up to the landing, grabbed Justine and threw her down the stairs. She came to a jolting stop against the landing wall.

She shook her head, and wobbled a bit as she stood, just in time to see vamp one race down the stairs and jump, aiming his feet at her head. Justine was shaken up, but still quick enough to spin away. His feet hit the concrete wall hard about two meters above the floor. Justine heard the crack of a bone. She helped him fall to the landing with a hard fist to his chest and a hand smacking his head to the floor.

Justine shook herself to make sure she was in one piece, then started down the stairs.

At the first landing she heard a scuffing sound behind her. The first vamp was tougher than she thought. He came full speed down the stairs, rammed into her and slammed her against the wall. It hurt. She felt like she'd had the wind knocked out of her.

With one arm against her neck, he pulled a hunting knife and tried to stab her. Using her well-embedded Kung Fu training, she blocked the strike with one hand while jabbing his throat with her fingertips. He uttered a gurgling sound and retaliated with a head butt that broke her nose. That really hurt.

She gripped his knife hand. He had his arm tight against her throat. She tried to use her free hand to punch his ribs. He lowered his elbow enough to block the power of her punches. They were at a stalemate. Then Justine forgot the pain of her nose and remembered the one classic move that always worked on mortal or vampire. She shifted her body a bit, then jerked her knee up, hard.

First vamp grunted, then let out a low moan as he dropped to his knees. He wasn't done yet. As he went down he struck out with the knife and stuck her just under the ribs. Justine flinched but she wasn't done, either. She yanked the six inch blade out, intending to jam it into his skull, finishing him for good. But then there would be a body which someone would find, raising a lot of awkward questions. Until he turned to dust in sunshine, he was just another suspicious corpse. Instead of his head, she jammed the blade into his back beside the shoulder blade where he couldn't reach it.

Simone appeared beside her. "Justine, *ca va?*"

Justine spit and leaned on the wall. "Not as pretty as I used to be, but, okay."

Simone grabbed Justine's chin and examined her nose. Without warning she grabbed the nose and gave it quick tweak.

"Ow."

*"Maintenant, tu es aussi jolie* as before. *Allons,* we must go."

The vampire at their feet groaned and began to rise.

"These guys are tougher than you think."

"Ah. *Oui.*" Simone kicked him against a wall then smacked his head with her fist. He moaned and fell silent. *"Allons, chérie.* She put an arm around Justine and they quickly exited the hospital.

# Chapter 12

Hedy, Justine and Simone sat in Hedy's car, a three year old VW Golf, across the street from Krauss Autowerkstatt, an auto repair garage on the outskirts of Stuttgart. Hedy sat at the wheel, head down, lips pursed, thinking. Before leaving the hospital Tilda had explained what Justine and Simone were after and the reason they were after it—or her: Teresa.

Though Brandt had lived in seclusion for many years, his death mattered to Tilda and a few others. Plus she had a job to go to. Hedy had agreed to drive them to the garage while she considered their request to find Walter Meir. She didn't know his exact location. He tended to move when the paranoia that Rubicon's vamps were coming for him hit. However, Hedy did have a number to call if needed.

Did she need it? It had been about three years since she came to Stuttgart to find Brandt. Their parting had been at best neutral. Walter didn't want her to search for Brandt, thinking it would revive interest in him and lead people to him. Which, she thought, is actually happening.

Before that day she would have said this was her new home, she was happy and had new friends. But driving down to Krauss Autowerkstatt and sitting across the street in a three year old VW Golf, listening to the two vamps talking about rescuing their friend and the consequences either way, she thought about her own life. Would she go to such extremes to rescue any of her new friends? Probably not. Would any of them do so for her? Probably not. If she never saw them again—so what? Really, she was alone most of the time. Lately she'd been thinking of her stepfather, missing him. And her mother, too.

Sitting there, staring at the garage, Hedy realized that despite all the patients, doctors, and nurses, she was lonely, and bored, and missed the Alps, and that choosing to go with Justine and Simone would change her life—maybe end it, but definitely change it.

"Okay, we go to Basel. And then to…." She threw up her hands and looked each of the vampires in the eye. "Please remember, I am mortal with all their frailties."

It was only minutes to sunrise when they knocked on the office door. A few seconds passed before the locks clicked and the door opened.

"*Kommen Sie*," said a thick muscled vampire, with a trimmed auburn beard on a round face. He closed the door and stood with hands in the pockets of stained blue pinstriped coveralls. He looked each of them over, saying nothing.

Hedy said in German, "These two are friends of Claire from America. She called?"

"*Ja, ja.*" He continued in English. "A car to drive to Switzerland for the vampires."

"And me."

"And you are?"

"Hedy."

He smiled a greeting. "I am Jacob." He pointed at each woman. "Welcome, Hedy. And you must be Justine and you Simone. How is Claire?"

Justine, wary now about everyone, asked, "How do you know Claire? I don't believe she has ever been to Germany."

"Come," Jacob said. He led them through the garage itself to a fastidiously clean break room. "Do you drink coffee?" He pushed some buttons on a large, gleaming, complicated plumber's nightmare of a coffee machine. "Wine seems to be the vampire's drink of choice, but coffee is my drink. Addiction may be a better word." He opened the doors to a large upper cabinet stocked full with different coffees. "Columbian, Haitian, Honduran, African. Some of the mechanics stay here because of the coffee." He chuckled at his own joke then turned a raised eyebrow to the women. "Coffee?"

Hedy raised her hand. "*Ja, bitte.*"

Justine shrugged and raised her hand.

"Espresso?" Simone asked.

"Espresso! *Ja, ja.*"

After the machine finished clunking, hissing and pissing, they settled around a spotless black Formica table.

"Claire?" Justine asked again, mistrusting of anybody, vamp or mortal, so affable in the morning.

Jacob sipped from his huge coffee mug, sighed, and said, "We met after the Council's base was destroyed. I was sent to help establish the new one." He looked deep into his mug. "I know you two were there when it happened. That it was you they were after."

Hedy watched as Justine and Simone traded *is-this-going-to-be-a-problem* glances. Obviously, what Jacob said was true.

"I was very good friends with Jasmine and her boy, Lenny. I miss them." He didn't try to hide his accusatory tone.

Simone leaned forward, hands clasped around her espresso cup. "We are sorry, Jacob, for what happened. We had no intention but to save our lives and the life of our mortal friend."

"The witch, Teresa, who you now wish to save again."

"Yes."

Jacob kept his gaze on the table as he sipped his coffee. "I know you did not mean for them to die. Because Claire trusts you and says rescuing your friend is important, I will help you. But I still blame you. More 'I'm sorrys' will not change that."

Justine said, "Thank you, Jacob. We can't bring them back, but rescuing Teresa could save many lives, vampire and mortal."

Jacob studied each of them, judging their sincerity. Finally he forced a smile. *"Mehr Kaffee?"*

"Sorry it's so late," Justine said.

"I've learned that the night time is the right time," Harry said.

"Where'd you learn that?"

"From a beautiful and mysterious lady of the night who's now going to tell me what the hell is going on."

"Your line is still secure, right?"

"Yes," he said, drawing it out to signal fact and question.

"Sorry. We were betrayed by someone on the Council. I can't trust anything, or anybody, not anymore."

"Rubicon is after you?"

"Big time. He sent an assassin after me. But he killed the wrong vampire." She didn't bother to mention that it was a pure accident she was still alive.

"The assassin?"

"Dead dead."

"Simone?"

"She's fine. Probably listening in through the walls."

"Where are you?"

"Holed up in a car repair shop waiting for night before driving to Switzerland."

"You have a lead?"

"Possibly."

A silence followed. Personal conversations did not come easily to either one.

"Are you working on any big cases?"

"Nothing special. The vamps seem to have settled down for the moment. Darwin is a big help."

"Good. Say hi. Are Bailey and Susan talking to you?"

"Susan, yes. Bailey...."

"I miss you," Justine said.

"I miss you. I can come over there if you need me."

"Not yet. It's just too dangerous. I know you can take care of yourself, you've proved that many times. We have no real plan. We're just playing it by ear. When we get something solid, I'll call. Okay?"

"Okay. The Girl?"

"Haven't seen her yet, but she's around, on our trail. If I see her I'll tell her you said, 'Fuck you.' Or 'Hi' anyway."

"You do that. Then shoot her in the head."

"You got it. I love you, Harry. Be careful."

"I love you, Justine. Tell Simone to take care of you."

"I will."

Justine stared at her phone for a minute. If it wasn't for Teresa she'd be happily home in Harry's apartment waiting for him to come home and kiss her.

She sat on a bare single bed in a spare room with two beds, a table with two chairs and heavy blinds on the single window. While she was talking, she'd pushed the blinds aside and watched normal life pass by.

For a moment, the heat of unsheddable tears built up behind her eyes. Normal life. One with Brittany still alive and happy and with a future. One with no vampires or witches or plots to rule the world. A happy world. But with no Harry or Simone or Teresa being an awesome witch.

Well, it was her choice to become a vampire and there were some awesome perks to being a vamp, like being immortal, with enough time to make it all right.

Or, eyesight that could see the man sitting in an anonymous Mercedes sedan across the street. He kept his eyes on the garage, taking pictures of every car that came or went, occasionally using small binoculars to study the building, look into every window.

Though she sat five feet away from the window in a dark room, Justine pulled back out of his sightline. Peeking back, she saw him talk on his phone, nod, and disconnect. He studied each side of the building, put on a black cap and sunglasses, and walked casually toward the garage.

He was looking for something and it didn't take a great leap to know that she was it.

She raced down the narrow back stairs and told Jacob what she'd seen. In rapid German, he fired off instructions to one of the mechanics, named Lukas. Then, in English, he said, "We will take care of this. You must return up. He must not see you."

"But if he knows Hedy's car he—"

Jacob gripped her shoulders to make her listen. He grinned and said, "No worries, mate," in a very bad Australian accent. "We will take care. Now you must go up." He steered her to the stairs. "Up. Up."

Justine managed a quick look in the back before she went up. The mechanic strolled across the back lot toward the side entrance. About ten cars were parked in the lot. Most were customer's cars, but some hadn't moved on their own power for an unknown length of time. Along the back was a simple three car garage. Jacob had parked Hedy's car in there.

Upstairs she filled in Simone and Hedy about the Mercedes guy and where he was heading. They moved across the hall to a room with a window overlooking the back lot. They huddled together, peering through the blinds like school girls checking out the hunky grounds guy.

The mechanic, tall and muscular and casually holding a large wrench, approached the interloper. They spoke for a couple of minutes then Lukas led him to the garage door where they'd hidden Hedy's car.

"What the hell's he doing?" Justine gripped Simone's arm. All three sucked in a collective breath. As Lukas rolled up the door the tension drained from them. Hedy's Golf had been replaced by a black BMW sedan on blocks with its hood up.

"That's not my car."

"When did they move it?"

"Where is my car?"

"I think this Jacob knows what he is doing," Simone said. "Good for us."

Mercedes guy looked at the other cars and finally shrugged and shook his head. On his way out he made sure to check the vehicles in the shop. Once he was out of sight they moved to their room and watched him cross the street and get in his car. As he looked at his cell to make a call, Simone raised the window an inch. He studied the upper windows as he made the phone call.

Simone crouched by the window, ear next to the opening. Mercedes guy spoke for about a minute, shaking his head at the beginning of the call and nodding at the end. He drove away.

"Could you hear what he said?" Hedy asked.

"We must leave, *maintenant*!"

# Chapter 13

"He did not see your auto, but he thinks we were or are here. More people are coming."

Before they had a small travel bag packed Jacob appeared at the door. "I am most sorry, ladies, but you must leave us. More of his people may come."

"More *will* come," Simone said.

"Ah. You heard his call, yes?"

Simone nodded. "I think they will be coming soon."

"*Ja, ja*. We are ready for you. Come."

"Where is my car?" Hedy asked.

"It is hiding."

In the shop, Jacob led them to a Lexus sedan with the trunk open. "I am sorry, but you must ride here for a short time. Hedy, you may ride with Thomas."

"Looks cozy." Justine flashed a leer at Simone.

Simone bumped shoulders with her. "Ah, *oui, chère*. We have been in closer quarters than this."

"Ladies, *bitte*."

Justine rolled into the carpeted trunk. "How long in here?"

"Not long. Thomas will take you to another more suitable vehicle."

Simone rolled in. Justine wrapped an arm around her. They both grinned.

"Take care of my car. It is a good one. Wherever it is."

Jacob pointed to the end of the garage. Hedy's Golf sat high on a lift, its roof almost touching the ceiling, invisible from the outside.

"Clever."

"That is why you paid me fifteen hundred marks. You must go, now, please."

✵ ✵ ✵

Hedy put the seat back a couple of clicks and tried to stay awake. She was used to working nights, but she was also used to having been asleep for six hours by this time of day.

"How far do we have to go?" she asked Thomas, glad to speak German again, though she had been raised in England until she was eighteen.

"Only ten minutes." He made a right turn onto a tree-lined, two-lane secondary road. "Have you known these vampires long?"

Hedy chuffed, "Since nine o'clock last night."

Thomas glanced at her. "Yet you travel dangerously with them."

"An old vampire called Rubicon has kidnapped a witch friend of theirs to help him take over the world."

"I know of Rubicon. Very dangerous."

"*Ja.* Maybe I should have gone back to the hospital. It is boring and safe."

"Maybe, but did not two vamps come to the hospital, looking for you? I don't think you would have enjoyed the encounter."

"No, probably not."

Indecision ran circles around her brain. Her job wasn't really boring. It dragged occasionally, maybe, but she helped people and that gave her much satisfaction. Life outside of work gave her little satisfaction, though. There had been a boyfriend about a year ago. He had wanted kids right away, married or not. As compensation she could remodel his kitchen and bathrooms any way she wanted—apparently, so she could spend all day cooking for him and the kids when she wasn't puking from morning sickness. Somehow that relationship actually lasted six months.

There hadn't been anyone since. She had no real ties to the area, except her job which was expendable as far as she was concerned. Hedy really wanted to see her family—mother, stepfather, brother—whether they got along or not. Still, she should—

A black SUV zoomed past, then darted in front of them, cutting off Hedy's thought. Thomas had to stand on the brakes and swerve off the street into a dirt parking area for a small local park. Two men, wearing military style clothing—boots, gray pants and bullet proof vests over dark shirts—stepped out of the rear doors and began firing at Thomas and Hedy.

They flattened themselves on the seats as spider web holes appeared in the windshield. Thomas grabbed a gun from under the seat. Hedy had the gun from Brandt's house.

The shooting from in front of the car stopped. More shooting came from behind.

Justine spooned with Simone in the plush trunk, her face nestled in Simone's dark hair, her right arm across the older vampire's stomach. They had been lovers when Justine was a New Blood discovering the joys and challenges of being a vampire—before Harry. And maybe a time or two after. Justine inhaled her friend and maker's familiar scent—a subtle combination of floral and an ancient musk comprising old dirt, old ashes and a hint of fresh blood. Simone laid a hand on Justine's.

Justine knew that neither of them liked being in the trunk, not knowing where they were going, with no control, trusting a man who should be trustworthy, but who they didn't know, at the mercy of the sun.

Justine closed her eyes and for a moment replayed her life since she got that call about Brittany. Her desire for justice, meeting Simone, learning the ways and rules of vampires. Finally getting blood justice. The search for Teresa's daughter, Antonia. The killing of Sinakov for the second and final time. The Girl and the taking of Teresa.

A bump shook her back to the present. "Do you think Teresa is alive?"

"*Oui, chère.* We would know if she was not. She waits for us."

"I know. Not that it's not nice and cozy in here with you, but how far do we have to go to get out?"

"*Peut être* ten—"

The car slewed to a stop. Justine heard gunshots, felt them smack into the windshield. Another vehicle screeched to a stop behind them. They had their weapons ready when the trunk popped open.

A quick peek and Simone rolled out and ran to the right. A half second after her, Justine rolled out and ran left. Both fired back at a SUV and four military style gunmen firing at them.

❋ ❋ ❋

Hedy glanced up when the shots stopped. Two men wearing bullet-proof vests carefully approached. She thought *Fuck it,* leaned out the side window and shot the closest man. Her first shot hit the vest.

He jerked back, then, firing, managed one step forward before Hedy's second shot hit him just above the knee.

Thomas shot at the other attacker, but he was right-handed firing out of a left side window. He threw open the car door to get a clear shot. He succeeded, but so did the other guy. A bullet hit Thomas just below his collar bone. He grunted and slumped sideways. The other guy stumbled and advanced to finish him.

Hedy pushed open her door and shot Thomas's shooter four times, before a bullet from behind gouged a shallow trough across her shoulder.

Ignoring the sting from her shoulder she looked to Thomas. Barely conscious, he grunted, *"Du fährst."*

*"Mich? Scheisse."* Ignoring the shooting behind her, Hedy grabbed Thomas by his coverall and dragged him across the seat. She slammed the passenger door, ran around and slid behind the wheel. With the engine still running, she jerked the gear shift into reverse and stomped on the gas.

✳ ✳ ✳

Justine shot one of the attackers within seconds. The other man had ducked behind an open door, but he came up with an automatic rifle.

Justine ran for cover from the sun and the automatic rifle firing from behind a parked car. To her left, totally exposed, she spied a woman with a baby carriage frozen in shock. To Justine's right the man tracked her with the rifle. She had no doubt that the man would not hold fire because of the woman.

Justine ran to the woman, probably seeming to appear out of thin air. Keeping herself between the shooter and the woman, she wrapped an arm around the woman's waist, grabbed the carriage handle and rushed to the cover of a concrete wall. Bullets left puffs of dust inches from her feet. "Stay."

A quick check on her remaining ammunition, and Justine darted out of cover and ran a zigzag course toward the shooter. She was fast but not faster than a bullet. One caught her below the knee. She stumbled and fell face down. Her gun spun out of her grip.

She looked up into the muzzle of the rifle. He couldn't miss. He grinned at her. Then a bullet hit the back of his head taking a chunk of that grin off his face.

Simone grasped her arm and pulled her up. "Come, Justine. We must go."

Her leg wound still hurt dand the sun heated her skin. "Yeah, it's getting hot any way you look at it."

A shot sounded. Simone grunted and fell to one knee, holding her side.

Justine also fell to a knee. She could see the shooter she wounded before. He lay on the ground, his bloody hand aiming at them. "Well, shit." She stretched out, groping for her weapon. Before she reached it, the sedan's motor revved up and Hedy backed  over the man, stopping hard against the SUV's front tire.

"*Komm schon. Wir müssen gehen. Allons. Nous devons aller.* Come on. Come on. We have to go!" Hedy yelled.

Justine and Simone looked at each other, grinned, and helped each other into the back seat.

Hedy rammed the transmission into Drive, hit the gas, spit gravel as she swerved around the first SUV and raced away.

# Chapter 14

"Thomas needs a doctor. A hospital," Hedy said over her shoulder. Her pain fast receding, Simone leaned over the front seat and checked his pulse and the wound. There was a lot of blood which she managed to ignore.

"A hospital will ask questions we don't want to answer," Justine said.

"There is another way to save him," Simone said, staring at the blood staining Thomas' coverall.

"No, you can't turn him without his permission."

"He will probably die before we find a hospital."

Hedy pulled over by a petrol station. "I am thinking of Brandt. Maybe he would rather not be changed. I don't know him. Can't you heal him without changing him?"

Simone sat back and hung her head. "It does not work that way."

If it did, there had been many mortals, some she had loved, she could have saved over the centuries.

Justine pulled out her cell phone and handed it to Hedy. "Call Jacob. He'll know." She reached through and pressed on his wound. "We won't let him die. He'll have to make the choice, like Brandt. Right, Simone?"

Simone shook herself and pushed those needless deaths back into the shadows of her mind. *"Oui, oui.* Call quickly."

Together they laid Thomas on the back seat. Simone ripped open his clothes to expose the wound. It was close to his heart with no exit wound.

"Don't you dare lick his blood," Hedy ordered.

Simone and Justine locked eyes. It had been a thought. Holding her gaze, Justine raised her chin, recognizing where Simone had been in those few quiet moments.

Simone managed a tight smile. "You might have saved some, also."

"Jacob says hospital," Hedy said. "One kilometer east. We are going. Drop Thomas off quick and go." She made a hard left turn. "His wife and brother will go there."

Justine said, "So he'd rather die than be changed?"

"I think most people would if really offered the choice."

Simone took Justine's hand. Justine had begged Simone to change her. She wanted blood justice for what was done to her daughter. She had not cared what happened after. It was way too late to second-guess her choice, but Simone saw that Hedy's words had dug deep.

A gentle shake of Justine's hand brought her attention back to the present. Simone offered her a softly sympathetic smile as they communicated in their usual silent way.  Finally Justine tilted her head and let a resigned smile creep onto her lips. She raised her shoulders in a *too-late-to-change-now* shrug. They were at the hospital.

Simone held Thomas in her arms and ran through the door, *"Hilfe! Ich brauche Hilfe!"* When someone noticed, she laid him on the floor and ran out. As Simone jumped into the sedan, Hedy tore away.

They headed east then turned south.

"I need to rest," Hedy informed them. "My shoulder hurts like hell. Ideas?"

They agreed. They all needed to regroup. Though they wanted to head south to Basel they headed east. Outside a small town they found a motel snuggled into a grove of trees, far from any main roads.

Simone slipped on a jacket to hide Thomas's blood and her torn blouse. Inside she smiled at the slender fifty year old woman at the front desk. The woman's overbite gave her return smile a slightly creepy feel. "Do you have a room with two king size beds?"

*"Ja,* we do. Do you have identification?"

Simone leaned over the counter and grabbed the woman's head, forcing her to look into her eyes. Five minutes later she came out and said, "Around the back."

An hour later the women had cleaned up and tended to wounds. As a nurse Hedy carried a bottle of Tylenol in her purse and a small first aid kit. With a little glamour for the pain Simone tended the wound on Hedy's shoulder. Hedy ate a protein bar and now slept curled up on one of the beds.

Simone and Justine lay on the other bed. Though they could stay awake for days if necessary, daylight and the absence of immediate danger drew them to sleep.

Before succumbing to sleep, Justine asked, "I wonder what's happening with Teresa right now?"

# Chapter 15

Teresa's body arched against the restraints. She felt as if gravity was being sucked from her insides. Every muscle tensed as she instinctively fought to retain the power being torn from her.

Exhausted, she wanted to give up. Fuck it. Let them have the magic to make their super vamps. But she had one thing they didn't know or care about. She had a secret that gave her hope. Not to mention a perverse streak of giving deserving people shit.

She forced her eyes open enough to observe Gerry struggling to keep Dr. Reich's magic sucking spell working on her. His wide set eyes glistening, he liked to watch her suffer. A smug little man with a smile no better than a grimace on his small mouth, he thought he was a big time sorcerer, but he didn't know as much he thought he did. He couldn't even grow a descent mustache.

Back on the Bayou he had almost been the one to capture her, but she had punched his face and gotten away. He had not forgotten it was her fault he missed his chance to be the hero of the day.

Knowing Teresa's power was much greater than his, maybe greater than anyone's, it gave his ego a boost to be able to hurt her as he monitored the spell that sucked out her magic. However, he didn't know that by focusing on her pain and not the spell, he left her an opening to siphon off a tiny bit of the power leaving her and store it somewhere undetectable in her body, perhaps along her spine behind her liver.

Due to Juno, Rubicon's powerful, clever and tame sorcerer's suppression spell, she could not use that power yet. But someday she'd have a chance to break through Juno's spell and use it to free herself and the other women. Teresa was a good witch. She had no desire to hurt anyone, although she did consider turning to the dark side after she had the chance to rest and replace her stolen magic.

That little secret stash gave her hope that she could escape. But she also hoped that Justine and Simone would rescue her before that. She didn't need any magical power to know they would be coming.

"*Genug!*" Gerry barked.

Within a few seconds the pull on Teresa's body tapered off. With a moan, her muscles slowly relaxed and she settled onto the gurney, barely able to lift her hands against the restraints.

*"Genug!,"* Gerry repeated, mopping his sweaty brow with a clean rag.

The wide door to the spotless white, antiseptic ten by ten meter room banged open. Two male vamps in blue scrubs entered.

"Take them first," Gerry ordered. Wearing a hate filled smirk, he stood over Teresa and added in heavily accented English, "Teresa does not mind waiting."

Trading scowls, the vamps moved away from Teresa.

Teresa found enough energy to say, "Hey Gerry. Fuck you."

He hated when she called him Gerry instead of Gerhart, which of course was why she did it. Gerry sucked air through his teeth and raised his hand to strike her.

"Uh, uh." Teresa flashed him a malicious grin. "Your master may be watching."

Gerry growled like a little yapper dog, spun and stomped out of the room. "Bitch."

Teresa let her head roll to the side. Forgetting her own pain for a moment she watched as the vamps wheeled out the ten women strapped to gurneys. They were all part of an experiment to confirm that with the magic power extracted from Teresa vampire sperm could impregnate mortal eggs without destroying them. The intention: to create vampires that could walk in sunlight.

Her energy level close to zero, Teresa lay on the spare but comfortable bed in her cell. In two hours she might be able to move to the toilet. After recovering from previous "magic sucks" she had moved the bed close to the bars. She might not be able to move, but she could talk.

The next cell held another witch, 35 year old Condi Maba from Sierra Leone. They also experimented with her.

"It go bad today?" Condi said, her accent oozing sympathy. She'd been through the same harsh treatment.

*"Si."*

"Gerry in charge again?"

*"Si."*

"Someday, luv, we get dat bad guy. I think Paul Nix want to help. Dey almost kill him every day. Ten year old and dey do that to him."

Teresa breathed deep to store up the energy to speak. "Are there more like us here?"

"I do not think so. Others too smart to be caught."

Teresa managed a small chuff. "If Juno is dead would the spell disappear?"

"I don know. Is a very powerful spell. I only make myself animal, maybe do small things. Not big time *bruja* like you, my friend."

"Big time, but know nothing."

"We kill him, we find out."

"They guard him close. They know if we get loose…."

"Yes, yes, that is the problem is it not."

*"Si, Si, el problema."*

Teresa plunged into sleep with a brief thought of Justine and Simone, and strangely enough, Harry.

# Chapter 16

Harry zipped up his jacket against an unusual chilly night breeze. Even Dawson, a centuries old vampire friend of Simone's pulled his jacket tighter. They stood on the beach by the Oceanside Pier with a vamp called Günter who stood a few feet away while speaking rapid German into his cell phone.

Günter stood six feet tall. Eighty some years as a vampire hadn't marred his good looks. He was a member of the Sulwaytup Family which had wiped out the unloved Sinakov Family and taken over their business, *Transport Francaise*. He had known Meir years ago when he first ran from Rubicon. Günter didn't know exactly why he was running, or where he was now. But he had a friend in country who did. Neither of them had any love for Rubicon and so had helped Meir hide.

Günter disconnected, then frowned at the device for a few long seconds, as though deciding whether to continue on or walk away. Harry and Dawson also frowned as Günter approached.

"*Bitte*, your cell phone." An order, not a request.

Harry handed it to him and watched as he entered a phone number.

Günter handed it back. "This is the number of a man who knows where Meir is. He will not tell me, or you, where on the phone, only in person. Rubicon is still looking for Meir. He screens thousands, millions of cell phone calls, looking for him. Do not say his name, or mine, or anybody's."

Harry studied the number, a different configuration than US numbers. "If I can't say names how will your friend know what I want?"

"Tell him you are from Photographic and you are looking for Möwen, that is Seagulls in your English. He will tell you what to do."

"Exactly why is Rubicon so interested in Meir?"

"I do not know, exactly. He knows something he should not."

"He'll only tell me in person?"

"Yes, when you arrive in Switzerland call that number. Remember, no names."

"I guess I'm going on vacation again."

"Harry, be very careful. You are known and respected in our world, your name will be on his long list. We have not spoken of it, but I believe you sunk one of his yachts, with him on it." Günter's dark eyes sparkled with amusement.

"Oh, that. He probably hasn't forgotten about it."

"Probably not. Go safe, Harry." Günter gave a quick nod to Darwin and walked away.

Harry stared at his phone wishing Justine would call. She needed to know about this guy and no names and seagulls—and that he missed her. With a sigh he stuck his hands in his jacket pockets and said, "So, how do I get to Switzerland without using my name?"

Darwin told him. Laughing, he said, "Almost makes one want to be a vampire, doesn't it?"

Harry paced his apartment, a burner phone to his ear, waiting for an answer.

An unfamiliar female voice said, "Family Council."

Suddenly slightly paranoid, he didn't want to use any names, but he wasn't going to talk with anybody else. "I need to speak to Claire."

"She's not available. Can I help you?"

"Yes. You can make her available. This is important. Wake her up if you have to."

Silence, then, "Name?"

"Is this a secure line?"

"Very."

"Fred Mann from California. Tell her two women may be in trouble."

"Wait." Silence.

Harry paced a bit faster—front door, spin, into the kitchen, spin, repeat. He really wanted to talk with Justine, but they'd agreed that he wouldn't call in case it would put her in danger. He only knew she was on her way to Switzerland.

"Fred Mann, is it?" Claire asked.

"For the moment, yes. No names. Recently I have reason to be paranoid about such things."

"Only recently? What can I do for you, Fred?"

"I need to get to Switzerland ASAP. With proper papers and, if possible, no official scrutiny. I'll explain in person."

"You're at home now?"

"Yes."

"Hold on."

Head bowed, Harry stopped pacing in the middle of the kitchen. A couple of minutes later Claire said, "Be at LAX by six o'clock." She gave him a name and where to meet. "Somebody will meet you there. Be safe."

"Have you heard from… the others?"

"Last I heard they were safe."

Harry stared at his phone. Maybe they were safe then, but things could go real wrong real fast in the vampire world.

He knocked on Bailey and Susan's door.

Bailey opened the door. "Harry." She looked right and left. "No… youknows with you?"

"It's okay. Just me."

Inside Susan, wearing a light robe over striped pajamas, joined them. She put her arm around Bailey. "Hi Harry. Keeping Vampire hours now?"

Through his grin he said, "Seems like it. Sorry to disturb you, but I'm going out of town. Can you keep an eye on my place, water my plant, collect my mail. The usual things."

"Where to?" Susan asked.

"It's best I don't say."

"For how long?" Bailey wanted to know.

"I don't know. A few days, a week."

"I feel safer with you here."

Harry touched her arm. "I feel safer with you guys next door. But, it's important."

"This has to do with Justine, doesn't it?" Susan said.

"Yeah."

"Will you see her?"

"I don't know." Harry grimaced and shook his head. "I don't know what or who I'll see." A deep breath. "I don't really know what will happen. I'll do my best to come back so you'll feel safe."

Bailey hugged him tight. "You'd better. Good neighbors are hard to find."

Susan gave him a quick hug. "Be safe, Harry. Say hello to Justine, and, if you need anything…."

"Thanks. You guys be safe too. Don't invite any strangers in."

Harry packed a small bag and slept a few hours. He made a cup of coffee, locked his door and went down the steps to his car. He got into the car, oblivious to who else was in the parking lot just outside his range of vision.

# Chapter 17

Bailey couldn't sleep. She'd dozed a bit while spooned with Susan, but after an hour she was wide awake. She untangled from Susan's arms, went to pee, then got a glass of water. She wandered about the apartment, hugging herself tightly and clutching the glass, ending up at the front window.

Curtains open six inches, she gazed at the nighttime view: a bit of ocean to the left, another apartment building to the right, a few stars in a cloudless sky, the parking lot. Her heart rate jumped as she peered down both ends of the second floor walkway.

Vampires. Bailey still couldn't quite wrap her mind around the fact that vampires were real. If Susan and Harry, and even Justine had merely told her they were real, she wouldn't have believed them. But she'd seen Justine's vamp face up close. Seen what she could do. Seen her face return to normal. She had to believe. But it all still freaked her out.

A bartender since she was fifteen, she'd seen some shit, although beheadings were new. Her father had owned a roadhouse bar just outside of Tulsa that tended to get rowdy on Friday and Saturday nights. He kept a shotgun, a pistol, and a baseball bat under the bar. A shotgun blast tended to cut through any mayhem and calm the belligerents down.

The bat got the most use. A tap on the head got even the drunkest drunk's attention—especially when some guy got handsy with his daughter. Unfortunately the bat was no match for the bullet that took him down.

Bailey's mother had split three years before, so, not yet eighteen, she took over the bar. She liked bartending, but she was no businesswoman. A year later she sold the bar and lived with her mother in New Orleans. A year later she lit out and eventually ended up at the Sundowner. She missed her father, but had one thing to remember him by: that old, worn, dented, slightly blood stained bat which she kept by the door, just in case anybody but Susan got handsy.

She heard Harry close his door and watched him go down the steps, carrying a small bag to his car. A touch of anxiety made her shiver and pull her robe tight. Before vampires became a reality she wouldn't have thought much about him leaving, but now….

Still, as she watched Harry, she remembered a time when she snuck out late to go joyriding with a couple of girlfriends and thought she got away with it. Next day she found out her father had watched her go from the apartment above the bar…just like she was watching Harry now. Her fond smile of remembrance vanished when she saw somebody running toward Harry.

# Chapter 18

arry threw his bag on the passenger seat, slid into the seat of his Mustang and buckled his seatbelt. He set his coffee in the holder and inserted his key. Just before he turned the key the driver's door swung open.

A hand reached in.

Instinctively, Harry leaned away and swung his left arm up to block the hand. Twisting his body, he grabbed the hand and slammed it back. A grinning vampire face came into view. "You helped to kill our master," the vampire said, his voice rough like a long time smoker. "You also will die. Come with me." He easily pulled his hand out of Harry's grip.

Harry didn't have much leverage, but his fist smacked the vamp's face hard enough to force him to step back.

Harry reached for the key to start the engine. The vamp grabbed his arm and tried to yank him out of the car. The seatbelt did its job and held Harry tight. Harry couldn't get to the key, but he did have a machete placed between the seats. He reached for it with his right hand.

But the vamp had come prepared. He pulled out a flip knife, flicked it open, and sliced through the seatbelt. Harry tried unsuccessfully to grab the steering wheel as the vamp yanked him out of the car and threw him to the asphalt.

"What do you want from me?" Harry asked.

"You took our master's life. Now we want your life."

"I didn't kill Sinakov. He deserved it, anyway."

"We know who took him away from us. The Girl will take great care with your Justine." His grin turned his face into a truly grotesque visage with distorted jaw, hatchet nose and black eyes. "Get up."

Harry knew he could not outrun a vamp, so he charged. He ran straight at the vamp and hit him low, wrapping his arms around the vamp's legs. To Harry's amazement the vamp went down, landing on his butt. If he'd had his blade Harry might have been able to score a minor strike, giving him about two seconds to land a critical strike and actually survive the encounter.

However, he did not have the blade. All he did was piss off the vamp.

The vamp grabbed his head and twisted. Harry grasped his hands and rolled with it. So did his assailant. On top, he said, "Fuck the others. I want to feed on you now." He bent Harry's head sideways, exposing his neck.

Head caught in a vise grip, Harry fought, arching, twisting, every muscle exerting full force. None of that helped. Harry could do nothing except watch the distorted jaws open and the two fangs descend. Images of Justine flashed through his mind… before she was a vamp, her marriage to the idiot who cheated on her, seeing her to tell her he was dead, again to tell her that her daughter Brittany was dead, trying to keep her out of trouble, his first sight of her as a vampire—strong, angry, beautiful—the sight of her as she emerged after days underwater—strong, confident, beautiful. He would miss her, but knowing she would miss him made him sad.

But thinking of Justine in those last few seconds, he knew she would never give up. As the toothy jaws lowered to his neck, Harry jerked his head to the side and headbutted the jaw.

The vamp pulled back. "Mortal. Think you're tough."

Before Harry could come up with a snarky retort, he heard a sharp *whack* sound and the vamp's head jerked to the side. Stunned for a moment the vampire emitted a very mortal sounding, "Ah, fuck!" He shook his head and turned to see what had happened.

Those few moments were enough for Bailey to shout, "Let go of my neighbor, you freak," and whack his head again.

While Bailey stood over the vamp ready to smack him a third time with her father's baseball bat, Harry pushed to his feet, which made him dizzy, and reached into his car. With his machete he stood, a bit unsteadily, over the hurting but quickly healing vampire. Surprised—though not really—he glanced at Bailey. Her eyes were huge and her breath came much too fast. Nevertheless, she nodded.

With two strikes he took off the vamp's head. Immediately he looked around for any witnesses. Bailey stood frozen, staring at the head. "Bailey, thank you. You should go back up."

"He, he was already dead, wasn't he?"

"Yes he was. And you saved my life. Go. I'll take care of this."

"… Okay."

As Harry dragged the body behind his car Susan ran up to Bailey, wrapped arms around her. "Come on, baby. You did good. You okay, Harry?"

"Besides some damage to my manhood, yeah." He picked up the head and dropped it out of sight on the other side of his car. He went to Bailey and gently removed the bat from her grip, handing it over to Susan. "I'm going to call Darwin. You two should go home. He may want to talk to you."

Fifteen minutes later Darwin arrived with a vamp and a mortal assistant.

"Nicoli Rostos," Darwin said, after he'd rolled the head over with his foot. "One of the old Sinakov stalwarts."

"I thought the Sulwaytups had wiped them out."

"A few survived, this one went into hiding. The Sulwaytups have been rooting them out. Nicoli here might be the last one."

"He was really after Justine. If there are more they know where I live and maybe about Bailey."

"*Si, si.* We will keep them safe."

Harry glanced up. Bailey and Susan, arms around each other, were watching from their window. He nodded toward them. "I told them you might stop by for a chat."

The two assistants gently closed the van doors on Nicoli Rostos.

"You know where to take him," Darwin said. "*È una bella notte.* I'll walk from here."

Harry shook Darwin's hand. "Thanks. I have to go. I assume I have a plane to catch."

"You are welcome, Harry. You have been a great help to… us. Even if it is not your jurisdiction."

A few hours later, as he strode down a corridor to meet whoever he was going to meet, Harry's cell phone beeped. "Darwin, what is it? Are Bailey and Susan okay?"

"They are fine. Günter is dead. Tortured. Rubicon may know about your plan. Be careful, *mio amico.*"

"Well, shit," Harry muttered as he walked toward a man walking toward him.

# Chapter 19

Justine listened to Hedy in the bathroom. It was late afternoon with the sun still up. She had slept longer than planned. She and Simone had intended to switch off every three hours to keep watch. Though vampires could go days without sleeping even they could succumb to no immediate danger and a comfortable bed.

"I'm starving," Hedy said from the bathroom door. "I saw a restaurant down the block. I'm going to eat." She said it in a way that suggested she was going to stuff herself, calories be damned.

"You look different."

"Hair, makeup, glasses, and I borrowed your jacket."

"Looks good on you. Don't make a spectacle of yourself by eating the whole menu."

"I won't." She started to turn away, then turned back, glancing at Simone asleep next to Justine. "Are you… hungry?" She took in a deep breath and blew it out. "I'm all in at this point. It's unlikely I still have a job, even if I still wanted it. I would like to see my mother again. And my stepfather. He was good to me. And, if this Rubicon is trying to do what you say he's trying to do, the least I can do is help find your friend and prevent the Sunvamps from taking over the world." She cocked her head in question and held out her wrists.

Justine smiled and said, "Thank you, Hedy. We need all the help we can get. We will try to keep you safe. And no, we do not need to feed now. But I'm sure you do." She gestured toward the window. "We should move on as soon as we can."

"Yes, I agree. I'll only eat half the menu."

She was at the door when Simone, who hadn't moved except to open her eyes, said, "Hedy, I am pleased you are with us. If you could find the bus and train stations and schedules that will be a great help."

"I'll see what I can find."

"Train station?" Justine said. "I hate buses."

"Right."

After Hedy left Simone rolled to face Justine. "Hate buses?"

"It's a long stupid story from twenty years ago. I'll tell you sometime on a tropical beach with a large glass of wine. So what do we do with the car? Know any chop shops around here?"

Barely a minute before the night train left, Simone joined Justine and Hedy in a half filled compartment. Hedy and Justine sat on either side by the window. A school girl in her uniform blazer and skirt sat on Hedy's side by the door. A man in his mid-twenties slouched next to Hedy with his earphones on and a history book he took from a backpack on the floor between his feet. An elderly man with several shopping bags sat straight up across from the girl with arms crossed and eyes closed. Justine saved a seat next to her for Simone.

Not knowing what languages the others spoke, Justine asked in English, "All set?"

"Yes."

Using a voice low enough that only Simone could hear, she asked, "Where?"

"Parking lot, shopping center, two kilometers away."

Justine nodded then nodded at Hedy. Hedy shrugged, *oh well.*

"We'll buy you a new one."

Two talkative business men in their fifties entered and took the two available seats, one by the old man, one next to the girl who held tight to the backpack on her lap. The fact that the compartment was filled made no difference to their boisterous conversation.

The train lurched forward. The men kept talking. It didn't take long for the man next to the girl to try and include her. She clutched her backpack tightly as he became more insistent. It was obvious to everyone but the two men that she was not interested. Their shaming stares had no impact.

Justine emitted a low growl as she watched. After all, they needed to keep a low profile. Even when the man poked the girl's leg she sat tight. Then he went too far. He gripped the girl's leg. Both men laughed when she flinched. His hand moved up, pushing her skirt.

Justine turned to Simone. "You speak the language."

"Do you think the language will make a difference?"

Justine stood up, pulling her cap down, and strode the two steps to stand in front of the man. "Stop that."

*"Was geht dich das an,"* he said, without removing his hand.

Justine didn't know what he said but assumed it was something like, "Fuck off, bitch."

Low profile or not, Justine wasn't letting that go. She reached down and gripped his wrist. At first she pulled gently. He resisted, his sneer saying *you can't move me, woman.* Justine flashed him a *you-think-you're-hot-shit?* grin, and lifted his arm up, placed her hand inline with his and squeezed, hard, curling his fingers into his palm.

He tried to take back control from her, but it was like his hand was set in concrete.

"Hey." His friend stood up and tugged at her arm.

She let him pull for a few seconds, then let go of the hand and pushed the second guy into his seat like an inflatable doll.

Justine caught the fist that swung at her, grabbed the arm and twisted it back while pressing her thumb against the back of his hand, forcing him to lean forward until he almost fell out of his seat.

Still holding him she relaxed the pressure so he could sit up.

In German, Hedy said, "Mister, I don't think she wants you to touch that girl, or any girl, again. Do you understand?"

He made another attempt to get loose. Justine pressed her thumb a little harder.

The second businessman spoke some English. "Let him go."

"Does he understand?" Hedy said.

The two businessmen spoke for a minute, the one angry, the other level and reasonable, while Justine slowly increased the pressure. Finally the handsy one nodded.

Hedy said, "You must apologize to the girl."

There was another conversation between the two men, then another nod of compliance.

"He will apologize. Let him go."

Justine released him and stepped back.

Handsy rose up swinging. She easily blocked him and popped him in the eye. Then she grabbed his head in her hands and stared deep into his eyes. She released him and stepped back again.

Dazed, he stood unsteadily and stared at nothing. His friend roused him and led him toward the door. Handsy stopped and bowed to the girl. "*Fräulein, ich entschuldige mich dafür, Sie berührt zu haben. Es wird nicht wieder vorkommen.*"

With the two men gone, the tension in the compartment eased. Justine looked at the old man. He looked back as if he wanted to say something, but didn't. The younger man studied the book lying flat on his lap, glanced at Justine, then turned to Hedy.

Justine sat next to the girl. Over her shoulder she asked, "What did he say?"

The girl said in British accented English, "He said he was sorry and it would never happen again."

"You speak English," Justine said.

"Yes. My mother is from England. Thank you, that was amazing what you did. I should have done something, but I was scared. I'm not very brave."

"It's okay to be scared. If there's a next time I don't think you will be scared. You will be brave."

Still a little freaked out, shy, and a little intimidated by Justine, she said, "Thank you."

"Martial arts, kiddo. You get good at one and you can handle an asshole like that."

"You think so?"

"I do."

The girl smiled, nodded, and looked through the glass across the corridor and out the window at the night passing by.

Justine plopped into her seat beside Simone.

Simone, amused, shook her head at her partner. "You need to look in your English dictionary for what 'low profile' means."

"You would have done the same thing."

"I have seen men put to death for less than what he did."

"Huh. I thought about it, but, you know, low profile."

Justine stretched her legs out and slumped in her seat. Hedy and the younger man beside her, whose name was Zeke, were having a pleasant conversation in German. Simone and the girl had a low conversation in German and English with a bit of French thrown in. The old man beside her didn't seem inclined to talk in any language. Justine thought that with all the advantages of being a vampire—enhanced senses, superior strength and speed—why couldn't she have superfast language learning? Maybe that was what immortality was for.

Justine closed her eyes and let the words flow around her. Harry often crossed her thoughts. How were Darwin, Bailey, Susan? She'd call him when they were able to talk freely.

The girl got off the train, then the old man. He had never said a word. Apparently Zeke was going to Zurich, back to college. Other passengers came and went and the train continued on through the night.

# Chapter 20

It was nine at night the next day, a Wednesday, when Justine and Simone surveyed the street from the second floor of the Hotel Hoffsteader. Hedy wasn't with them now, she had things to do.

They had arrived in Zurich about midnight then took a taxi to the Hotel Hoffsteader. Zeke had suggested the place to Hedy, saying it was cheap and didn't ask questions. They'd checked into room 404. There they cleaned up then left through a back entrance. A circuitous route took them to the back door of the Estelle 2 Hotel, directly across the street from the Hoffsteader. They were only accosted once by a couple of drunk young guys who wouldn't take *nein* for an answer. Simone easily shut them down.

Simone and Hedy checked into the Estelle 2 using one of Simone's many identities. Justine was almost six feet tall, blonde, beautiful, and memorable. Maybe a haircut, a brunette dye job and a slouch would make her less noticeable. Wearing a wool cap, she snuck in the back door and joined them in room 207.

Hedy got some solid sleep, thanks to a bit of glamour help. First thing in the morning she left for breakfast and a few errands. She returned a couple of hours later, then left again.

From their window, Simone and Justine had a clear view of room 404 in the Hoffsteader. They identified three people down on the street, mortals, who seemed to be watching who went in and out. It was unlikely any vampires would attack before nightfall. Too many people, as well as the sun, out and about.

A bit after ten o'clock they saw a light go on in room 404 and three people searching the room. Standing back from the window, on full alert, they watched.

"Good call," Justine said.

Simone had been listening to Hedy and Zeke's conversation on the train. She understood German better than she let on. Three times he had mentioned a "she" with no mention of who "she" was.

"It is important to do a good job for 'her.'"

"'She' suggested the Hoffsteader Hotel."

"Funny, I don't remember meeting 'her.'"

Simone suspected who "she" might be and thought some caution might be called for.

They could feel the presence of two vamps in room 404. But three people moved about the room. A form appeared in the window, scanning the street.

*"Merde,"* Simone muttered.

"Fuck. We knew she'd come around at some point," Justine whispered.

The Girl, who didn't seem to have any other name, stared straight at them.

"Time to go." Justine grabbed up a jacket and headed out the door, Simone right behind. At full speed they descended the back stairs, went down the alley and turned left at a cross alley, coming out onto a side street. Already they felt the two vamps closing on them.

With no particular plan and little traffic, vehicle or pedestrian, Justine and Simone ran. Two blocks up, one across, one up, three over, they managed to keep ahead. But they gained little ground.

They came out on a busy tree-lined street that arced around the Lake Zurich waterfront. Passing by were a bus, a few cars and a large delivery truck. With seconds to decide, Justine pointed. "The truck."

In moments they caught up to the truck and leaped to the top. Ignoring the dirt, they lay flat and rode out of sight. A kilometer later, with no sign of pursuit, they dropped off the truck and quickly moved down Seefeldquai along the waterfront. Screened by a small growth of low growing trees, Justine and Simone sat on a bench looking at the moored boats.

"Your cell is on?"

"Yes." Justine checked anyway.

"We wait here then."

After a few minutes contemplating the sky, boats and water, Justine asked, "Do you think The Girl will find us?"

"Not before Hedy, *j'espère.*"

"I think it's time she told us exactly where we're heading. If The Girl gets her, she'll talk. Then The Girl will kill the mother after she tells where Meir is, then she'll kill Meir and we'll be fucked. And not in a good way."

A minute passed. Simone said, "If it should come to it, could you kill Hedy to prevent The Girl taking her?"

Justine had to think about that. She liked Hedy. The woman had saved their asses more than once. She'd left everything and put herself in danger to help two vampire strangers find a witch and save the world from being taken over by some super vamps which she had no real evidence actually existed.

"It would be hard. You?"

*"Le même mon chère. Le même."*

"The same what?" Hedy said as she sat next to Justine.

"Nothing," Justine said. "Vampire stuff. Any trouble?"

*"You* are asking *me* that?"

"The car."

"Got a car, waited, tracked your phone, here I am. We should toss these phones."

Justine and Hedy tossed their new phones into the water.

"You two were moving fast for a few minutes. Somebody chasing you, I assume."

"We'll tell you later." Justine and Simone traded looks, communicating in their wordless way.

Simone rose, and hands in pockets, walked in a circle ending in front of Hedy.

"Hedy, The Girl is here. She searches for us now. This is dangerous. We will protect you best we are able. But it is possible we will fail. If she takes you, you *will* tell her about your mother and she *will* go to her and make her tell where is your stepfather and they will find him and kill you all. It is time you tell us where we need to go."

Hedy studied the two, avoiding their dark stares.

"What happens after I tell you?"

"Then you come with us and show us where it is, then help us find Meir. After that…." Justine spread her hands out. *Whatever you want.*

"You could glamour it out of me right now."

*"Oui,* we could."

"You can walk away anytime," Justine said.

"After I tell you."

Justine lifted a shoulder and nodded.

Hedy looked around for eavesdroppers. "458 Maxstrasse, Zwinglac. It's close to Basel."

Justine stood up, rolled her shoulders and stretched. "Where's your car?"

They walked quickly along the wide, treed shoreline space. They passed a spa of sorts built over the water, offering massages and hot tubs as well as bicycle and small watercraft rentals.

Simone said, "Do you feel it? There is a vampire in the area. Not close, maybe in one of the buildings there."

"I feel it, too. Distant, but different, somehow."

"Not so distant, Justine," a voice said behind them.

The three spun around, though Justine and Simone knew by the voice who spoke.

The Girl. A dangerous girl, a very dangerous girl.

"I have been searching for you."

Justine's hand went to her blade. "Why?"

"Justine, do you really have to ask why I would search for you? And Simone, you helped her kill my master, so you are guilty, too." She pointed to Hedy, "I don't really want you, Hedy, is it? I only want what you know."

"*Ce n'est pas possible,*" Simone said.

"Ah, but it is possible." She raised a finger above her head. In an instant three burly vamps appeared behind the three women and grabbed Justine's and Simone's arms. They fought to free themselves, but the men were vamps, bigger and stronger. They held tight and even Justine's Kung Fu training couldn't help her break free.

The third vamp held Hedy's shoulders. After a token struggle, Hedy relaxed and waited, working on an idea.

Finished struggling, Justine squared her shoulders. "So you're still Rubicon's little errand girl."

The Girl may not have broken five feet in height but she acted as if she was seven feet tall. She walked up to Justine and slapped her. "I work with him, not for him. I can do with you what I want." She swung her hand as if to slap her again, stopping an inch away. Justine flinched. The Girl grinned.

Simone asked, "What now, Girl."

The Girl pointed to the spa. The three burly vamps shoved their captives down to the deck leading to the spa building, where The Girl kicked open the door.

Inside, The Girl struck Justine's stomach, then smacked her head with her fist. She was small, but still packed a punch. In the seconds it took Justine to recover, the vamp holding her pushed her against a support post, then gripped her hands from behind and pulled her back against the pole.

Simone's vamp held her to one side. Hedy unobtrusively kept herself to the other side where she could clearly see Justine's vamp.

Machete now in hand, The Girl paced back and forth in unrestrained triumph. She smacked Simone with the flat of her blade. "Ha!" She flicked a cut down Simone's cheek. "Ha!" Finally she sliced Simone's leg with a flourish. "Ha, ha!"

She strutted around the open area, glee evident in her wide open eyes and wild grin. She poked Justine with her blade repeatedly. "Oh Justine, I've dreamed of this, having you here like this. Now I'd prefer to have more time to make you suffer as I suffered." She made two more pokes, an inch deep. "But I can't wait. I have someplace to go." She poked at Hedy's body. "Where Hedy tells me to go after I have given you the final death. My Master will be pleased to know that you and Simone will no longer be a nuisance."

The Girl poked at Simone. "Watch, Simone Gireaux. You will be next to lose your head."

"I do not believe so." Simone leaned back against her captor and kicked The Girl in the chest, sending her skidding across the floor.

She rolled up to her feet and ran at Simone. "You are right. You will be first."

"Hey, Girl. What's the matter? You afraid of me?"

Just as she was about to swing at Simone's neck, The Girl spun to face Justine. A malicious sneer distorted her lips. "I am afraid of no one." With obvious intent she strode toward Justine, blade held high.

The burly vamps did not consider Hedy a threat. They hadn't thought to search her for weapons. The vamp holding her only had his hands on her shoulders, his attention on The Girl. When The Girl advanced on Justine, Hedy knew it was time to act.

She reached into the purse that hung across her chest and drew out the handgun she'd retrieved from the car attack. She pointed the gun back and shot her vamp in the leg. The noise filled the room. A second later she shot the vamp holding Justine in the head.

Freed, Justine met The Girl with another kick to her body that sent her hard against a steel I-beam support. Justine grabbed up a blade and ran at Simone, who bent over, allowing Justine to strike off her vamp's head.

Before the head hit the floor Justine turned to The Girl, who was just gaining her feet. Focused on The Girl, she didn't see Hedy's vamp toss the mortal aside and rush Justine. He collided with her, picked her up and threw her down hard.

Justine felt as though she'd had the wind knocked out of her and her head cracked with a hammer. A kick in the ribs rolled her on her back. Though hurting, she braced for the next kick. It never came.

Simone had snatched up the blade Justine dropped and rammed it into and out of the vamp's head.

"The Girl!" Justine cried.

Simone spun around. The Girl wasn't there.

Hedy sat against the wall by the door. "That way," she said, pointing toward the back of the building.

Simone raced past a counter and down a passage through the building. The crash of a door being kicked open led her all the way back to an outside walkway with a wooden railing. She stopped in the doorway, checking left and right. The Girl had vanished. A slight scraping sound gave her a split second warning. The Girl slammed into her back, driving her through the door and up against the railing. Simone managed to twist about and hit the rail backwards. The Girl punched her stomach and tried to push her over the rail.

Because the Girl stood so close Simone couldn't get in a good swing, so she hammered the diminutive girl with the butt of the machete.

The Girl dropped, rolled away and came up with a small knife. Simone held her blade in front ready for the attack. The Girl considered, then raised her arm to throw.

"Stop!" Hedy shouted from the corner of the walkway, gun pointed right at The Girl.

The Girl spun and flicked the knife at Hedy.

Hedy fired.

The blade sliced Hedy's arm.

The bullet caught The Girl in the shoulder.

Simone saw the opening and stepped forward to swing.

Hedy still held the gun. Simone's blade swung at The Girl. The diminutive vampire had no choice. She leaped over the rail and vanished into the water.

Simone and Hedy leaned on the rail and searched for Rubicon's servant. Night and shore lights reflecting on murky water defeated even Simone's augmented eyesight. The Girl could be five meters away or five hundred.

"I don't suppose she can drown, can she?" Hedy asked, knowing the answer.

"Most unfortunately, she will not."

Simone could not help but think of Justine trapped for days a thousand feet under water. She survived. The Girl would, too. "Come, we must go. Can you drive?"

"To get out of here and on the road, it will take more than an impossibly thrown knife to stop me."

# Chapter 21

Through an unmarked door Harry entered a wide, antiseptic hallway with six single office doors on the right and windowed double doors on the left which looked out on a loading area and the tarmac. His footsteps echoed as he strode toward the last door.

He didn't hear anything; it was more like he felt a slight change in the air pressure. He glanced over his shoulder and saw a man wearing a cap, both hands in a suit jacket's pockets. Ordinarily he wouldn't think anything about it, but recent events made him suspicious of everyone.

The man walked quickly, his footsteps silent. As Harry reached the sixth door the man called out, "Harry Frazier."

Harry turned. Was this the guy he was supposed to meet? "Yes." He had a gun in his carry-on bag, not particularly accessible. That might have been a mistake.

The guy looked up and down the hall while reaching behind his back.

Yep, a mistake.

Harry threw his bag at the assassin then rushed to follow it. Harry had faced down bad guys, vampires and even The Girl, he could fight if he had to. The bag slowed the man down a second—long enough for Harry to block and grab the hand with the gun and jam his shoulder into the guy's chest.

But he missed the long slim knife blade in the guy's other hand.

The assassin, tough and fast on his feet, raised his hand to plunge the blade into Harry's neck.

Harry could do nothing but think, *Sorry, Justine. I love you.*

A hand reached over the assassin's shoulder, interrupting Harry's final thoughts of Justine. Another hand reached over the other shoulder. Both hands grasped the knife, forced it around and jammed it deep into the would-be assassin's eye.

Gun in hand, Harry spun away expecting to have to shoot the new assailant, only to find a six foot plus African American man holding the assassin up.

"Quick, into the office."

By the ease with which he carried the dying man through the door, Harry knew him for a vampire. He snatched up his bag and followed.

Inside the spare office, the vamp yanked the blade from the assassin's eye and closed his elongated jaw over the bleeding wound.

Harry's first cop instinct was to get his gun and arrest the vamp. The assassin had been a mortal, after all. However, he'd also been about to kill Harry, so the vamp had saved his life. He'd been around vampires enough not to be queasy about seeing one feeding. Still, he turned away and considered what the attack meant.

Rubicon was serious about making Harry dead, even though he knew next to nothing. Was it because of what he might discover? Was it because he and Justine were together? Or maybe simple revenge because Harry sunk his mega-yacht? Or maybe because Justine and Simone, and now him, were coming after Teresa and that would hurt his grandiose plan of world domination with his hybrid sunvamps? Best guess was all those reasons.

"Fred Mann?"

Harry had a quick thought. His attempted killer had called him Harry. Did that mean he didn't know about Fred Mann? That would be good. Maybe Fred Mann could travel anonymously, and with any luck, safely.

Harry blew out a deep breath and turned around. "Yes." He looked at the body, slack and pale on the floor. "I should arrest you for that, but you did save my life, so I'll let you go with a warning."

"Appreciate it. I'll take care of a… disposal."

"I don't want to know. You are…?"

"Lennox. You got a gun?"

That was the right name. Still wary, Harry said, "In the bag."

"Good, keep it there."

"What about security?"

"I'm your security. Here's your ticket and boarding pass. And a Fred Mann driver's license."

"That was quick. First class, too."

"Hey, you know us vamps. We can move quick if we need to. Passport will be at the other end."

Harry glanced at a security uniform jacket draped over a desk chair. "You work security?"

"Yep."

"Daytime?"

Lennox put on the jacket and a matching cap. "Regular hours is nighttime, but I'm here daytime for special needs, ya know."

"Yeah, special needs, sounds right at the moment."

"Hey, man. Anybody who's going up against Rubicon is special needs. Come on, we got a plane to catch."

Lennox guided Harry through a door at his end of the hall, leading into a narrower hall, then though a small door into an open bay where baggage was stacked on trailers at one end and loaded on conveyer belts at the other. At the end of the bay they left the cover and mounted an open air stairway.

Lennox studied the early morning marine layer of clouds then gave Harry a fake grimace of fear. They came out on one of the gate concourses. Two gates down Lennox walked up to an attractive blonde gate attendant.

"This guy is special needs. Take care of him, will ya, Wendy?"

She locked eyes with him and showed a sly smile. "You know I will, baby."

"He ain't got time for that, but I do." He turned to Harry. "Good luck, Fred. You gonna need it." He nodded at Wendy and walked off.

# Chapter 22

Teresa lay on her bunk, hands behind her head, mentally trying to gauge the magical power she felt she had stored up. She felt it deep in her body, somewhere behind her heart. The thing was, it felt the same now as when she first realized she could save a little as she was drained of her power to boost one vampire sperm to fertilize one mortal egg.

At first she thought the women receiving her magic were volunteers, maybe paid to carry a baby for some barren couple. But, a few times she had had a chance to talk with the women. They were not volunteers. Most were abducted, raped by a vampire, and forced to carry the resulting child. They had been glamoured into acceptance and obedience.

It had only been months since she discovered she was a witch. She'd had some training from Grace, perhaps the most powerful witch on the globe, but she knew she had much more to learn. Now, the suppression of her power and plight of the women sat heavy on her chest. Frustration made her teeth grind and her hands clench into fists. Teresa was a good witch; she had no desire to hurt anyone. But right then, power or no power, she'd have gladly beat the crap out of Gerry or Juno, Rubicon, if she had the chance, and Dr. Reich, the brains behind the vile science experiment she was caught in.

Dr. Ferdinand Reich was a brilliant if infamous scientist. As a graduate student at Heidelburg University he stole a freshly dead cadaver and attempted to reanimate the man. Forced to drop out and never mention the incident he became a research assistant at a biotech company. There, he used an unauthorized lab and equipment to attempt to create supermen and women. His experiments resulted in one death, three hospitalizations and his status of unemployable. Then he met a man who smelled of dirt and age with unlimited money and an offer of his dream job with no restrictions.

The bangs of doors opening and shouts and cries cut through her thoughts of mayhem. She rolled off the bed and strode to the bars.

Paul Nix screamed and thrashed about on a gurney pushed by a vampire attendant.

Gerry, clutching his ubiquitous clipboard, yelled at the boy, *"Halte den Mund, halt den Rand, Halt die Klappe!"*

The boy did not shut up. "Let me go. I want to go home!"

*"Halt den Mund, Sterbliche!"* Gerry snarled, then slapped the boy.

Paul cried out.

Gerry slapped him again. *"Halt den Mund! Halt den Mund!"* he screamed as he hit the boy with his fist, pounding his head and chest.

Condi yelled, "Halt, Gerhard, halt. He is only a boy."

Gerry paid no attention.

Teresa shook the bars. *"Pinche cabrón.* He's just a kid."

Gerry ran out of steam, but not anger. He stalked over to Teresa and stopped two feet in front of her. He could barely speak through his anger, frustration and insecurity. "You do not tell me what to do. You are prisoner. You are a no power witch. You do what I say to you."

"You want to beat up somebody, open this door and try me." Teresa rattled the bars. She had broader shoulders, ten inches, and twenty–five pounds, none of it fat, on him. "I do what you say because of those guards, not because you say it, *pequeña perra.*"

"You would not beat me up, guard or no guard."

"Oh, *si?"* Teresa reached through the bars, grabbed him by his white jacket and yanked him hard against the bars. Her other hand punched his face.

*"Wachen! Hilfe!"*

The two guards—one vamp, a kid who never spoke, and one mortal—wearing sidearms and batons, looked at each other, shrugged, and went, not quickly, to Gerry's aid.

"Release him," the mortal said with a *sorry-I-gotta-say-it* tone.

Teresa punched Gerry again.

The mortal, a regular guy in his thirties, casually poked her face with his baton as a warning. Teresa punched Gerry again. The guard poked her hard enough to draw blood and get her attention.

Gerry whimpered until she let him go. As the guard who brought Paul in led him away Gerry started cussing in German while he shook a-you'll-pay-for-this finger at her.

*"Pinche cabrón,"* Teresa muttered.

"I am sorry I had to hit you so bad," the mortal guard said to Teresa.

"Your arms and head hurt very bad, yes?" [who is speaking this line?]

"Yes. I hurt all over. Let me see the boy. I'm a nurse. He needs some help."

The mortal guard glanced at the boy's cell, thinking. He looked at the teenaged vamp, who was the regular guard who stood by the entrance and never said a word. The younger vamp nodded.

"I won't try to escape. You need him in good health to do the shitty things you do to him."

The mortal guard studied her face. "I believe you will only help him, but it is worth my life if I let you out." He looked away and shook his head. "Somebody will see. You cannot see, but there are cameras. I am sorry." The teenage vamp shrugged sorry, as well and followed his partner to the door where he took up his usual post.

Condi asked, "Teresa, are you okay?"

"Yes. The phrase, whinny little bitch was made just for Gerry."

"That is true, but he will not forget."

"It was worth it. How is Paul?"

"Hurting. Scared. We have to get him out. He will die."

"Yes. Yes. Getting to Juno is the key."

"That will not be easy," Condi said.

"But not impossible."

"You speak true, my friend. We be ready for any chance. You say you have friends who try to rescue you."

"Yes. I know they will be coming. But I don't know when. Where the hell are they?"

# Chapter 23

"Hello."

"Hello. Bailey?"

"Nope. This is Susan. Justine, is that you?"

"Yeah. I'm trying to get Harry, but all I get is voice mail."

"Oh, I'm sorry. Harry is gone."

"What? Gone? What do you mean, gone? What happened?"

"Oh, Justine, sorry. I didn't mean gone like… well, you. He left, yesterday."

"Where did he go?"

"He wouldn't tell us. Said it was too dangerous."

"Dangerous for you guys? Susan, what the hell happened, or is happening."

"Oh, yeah, he said not to use names or places because somebody might be listening."

"Who?"

"He wouldn't say, but it probably had something to do with you."

"Damn. Well it's no stretch to figure out who he's talking about. Did he say how long he'd be gone?"

"He thought a few days, maybe a week. Course he almost didn't make it."

After an exasperated silence, Justine said, "And what the hell does *that* mean?"

"Oh, yeah. He was getting in his car when a, ah, vampire attacked him."

"What?"

"He's okay. Bailey saved him."

"Bailey? Our Bailey, saved Harry from a vampire?"

"Yeah, we're all surprised, not the least her. Smacked him around with her father's baseball bat until Harry took the top off, if you know what I mean."

"Yes, I know. Why did he attack?"

"I'm not sure. Bailey's oldest nighttime customer said it was a local thing. Something to do with a vamp you killed twice."

"Fuck, I thought we were done with that. Bailey's okay?"

"She's working through it. Me too, I guess."

"Yeah, I get that. If you ever hear from your neighbor tell him to call me. I don't care who's listening."

"Will do."

"Okay. Thanks to both of you for being good neighbors and good friends. Be careful, okay?"

"You too. Whatever you need."

"Did you hear that?" Justine asked Simone.

"*Oui.*"

"I didn't," Hedy said from the back seat. "What's up?"

"Harry left home careful not to tell anyone where to. As he left a vampire attacked him, and his neighbor saved him with a baseball bat. And he said that Rubicon could be listening so no names or locations by phone or computer."

"That last part is not good. With his money he probably has better equipment than most governments. Do you think Harry has a lead on this secret laboratory?"

"Don't know any other reason he'd leave like that."

"So what do we do?"

"Go see your mother."

Zwinglac turned out to be a farm town made up of a loose assortment of houses and barns in rolling hills about fifteen kilometers south of Basel. It was surrounded by broad swaths of pristine farmland mingled with patches of dense trees just beginning their autumn turn. 45 Maxstrasse turned out to be on a winding paved road barely wide enough for two cars to pass.

The house, square, two story and white with a red shingled roof, nestled in a small depression. Its nearest neighbor lay about a kilometer away.

At about four in the morning, lights off, they turned into the short driveway up to the house and stopped. Car windows open, Justine and Simone scanned for danger.

"I'm getting nothing, yet, something."

"*Moi aussie.* A vampire was here, but when, I do not know."

"My mother knows some vamps," Hedy said. "I want to go in there, now."

Hedy slowly drove up the packed dirt driveway and parked heading out. She led the way up three steps to an open wooden porch. With a key from deep in her purse, she unlocked the front door.

Simone lightly gripped her arm. "Is she going to shoot us if we go in?"

"Maybe. She's an early riser."

"*Si'l vous plait*, allow us to enter first. The Girl is a ghost, remember."

"You think she might be in there?"

Justine said, "You never know with that one." She indicated she was going around back then pointed to the key in Hedy's hand. Hedy selected a different key and Justine slipped away.

Simone waited ten seconds then pushed the door open.

Inside, she scanned the large living room, noting the white walls and the spare but modern wood furniture. Stairs on the right led to the second floor. After the stairs the room opened up to the right, out of sight from the door.

Simone cocked her head then pointed to that area. She stepped forward.

"Stop! *Wer bist du? Was willst du?*" A light flicked on revealing Hedy's mother in a dark blue robe, aiming a double-barreled shotgun at her.

"Mom, it's me, Hedy."

Mom swung the gun to cover Hedy. Squinting, she leaned forward to study her face.

"Mom, put your glasses on. It's me."

The gun didn't waver. "You sound like her, but you look different."

Just then Justine reached around Mom, making sure she didn't pull the trigger as she lifted the weapon from her hands.

"Oh!" Mom tried to spin away, but Justine held her firmly.

Hedy came up to her mother and took her hands. "Mom, it's okay."

"She's a...."

"Yes she's a vamp, and a friend."

Her mother looked Hedy up and down. "It is you. Again? You cut your hair and lost some weight. And no makeup."

"I haven't had much time, or desire, to glam myself up lately." Justine stood beside Hedy. Simone stayed back, wary. "This is Justine and that's Simone. We've been traveling together. This is my mother, Lily Duchene."

Lily studied the two vampires up and down. "A pleasure to meet you. I don't have any blood to spare, but I do have coffee." She turned and walked into the kitchen. Smiling, the three women followed.

They sat on stools at a raised breakfast bar while Lily made coffee.

"I don't know where Konrad is," Lily said, more to herself than them. "I told you."

"Mom, why did you say that?"

The older woman's brow furrowed as she studied the wood floor. "Didn't you ask about that?"

"No, mom. I never mentioned Konrad."

"But…."

Simone broke the silence. *"Merde."*

Hedy said, "What?"

Justine, "I noticed it too. Are we too late?"

Simone swung off the stool and walked around the counter. Hedy started to speak, but Justine laid a hand on her shoulder.

"Lily, you are familiar with glamour?"

"Yes."

"I believe you were glamoured, maybe a few hours ago. That is why we get a faint feeling that a vampire was here. I would like to glamour you. I may be able to recover what you said and who you said it to. Would you allow me to do that?"

"You want to reverse glamour my mother?"

Justine said, "Can you really do that?"

*"Je le pense.* Maybe. May I try?"

Hedy said, "If someone was here before us and glamoured you into forgetting they were here, we need to know. And you were right, this is about Konrad. He knows something Rubicon does not want us to know. It's very important."

Lily looked each of them in the eye, Hedy last. "You're not going to look at any other stuff in my head, are you? Private stuff."

Simone grinned. "I will try not to see your 'private stuff'."

"Good. I wouldn't want to embarrass my daughter."

Hedy just rolled her eyes. "Mom."

Justine had a thought. She held up a finger to get their attention. She pointed to her ear then around the room. The others got it—a listening devise could have been left behind.

"Why don't we sit over there," Hedy said, pointing to a kitchen table with four straight back chairs.

While they moved about they did a quick search, under counters, furniture, lights and shelves. They found a listening device under the counter they'd been sitting at and another under a table in the living room.

Using voices so low neither the mortals nor the devices could hear them, Justine and Simone discussed a plan.

Seated face to face by the table Simone held Lily's head close and stared hard into her eyes. Neither moved except for Simone's lips quivering, emitting an unintelligible murmur. Nothing else happened for half a minute.

Simone sat back and asked, "What is your name?"

"Lily Duchene."

"Lily, were you visited by a vampire earlier today?"

"I… no."

"Do you know where your husband Konrad is?"

"Yes."

"Where is he?"

"He is in Leysan."

"Where is Leysan?"

"Up the mountain from Lausanne."

"Do you know how to contact Konrad?"

"No. Before, he went into town and called me. This place is new."

"You have no way to contact him?"

"No."

"Lily, you are no use to me, or anybody."

Simone raised a finger. Justine pressed a pillow up against the listening device under the counter.

"You did very good, Lily. Now tell me where Konrad really lives."

"I don't know."

"Who does know?"

"Peter Raza knows."

Simone looked up at Hedy.

"I know him. A long time friend. Konrad trusts him."

"How do you contact him?"

"Call him."

Simone looked to Hedy for confirmation.

Hedy shrugged and nodded.

Simone leaned forward and took Lily's head in her hands. "Lily, you will forget all that we talked about." Simone removed her hands and leaned back. She nodded at Justine who removed the pillow.

"She does not know anything."

"Leysan. We'll have to go there. How many vamps can there be in a little mountain town?"

"Sunrise is about five hours. We should go now."

*"Oui,* once we leave she will not remember us."

Quietly Justine placed a stool under the listening device and stuffed the pillow up tight against it. They all moved to the front door and made leaving noises. Once the door shut, Justine pulled off the device in the living room and crushed it with her fingers. The other they left to make listeners believe normality had returned.

"So Mom, how do we contact Peter?"

# Chapter 24

Claire met Harry at the airport. He almost didn't recognize her. She wore her new authority well, he thought. The last time he'd seen her, she was the newly appointed mortal representative of the Vampire Family Council, a bit dazed and unsure of herself. Now, she stood tall, wearing khaki trousers, a dark blue golf shirt and top of the line sneakers. Her short blonde hair had been fashionably cut to frame her oval face with its pale blue eyes and sharp nose.

She flashed him a relieved smile. "Harry, I mean Fred, I'm glad you made it in one piece. I heard what happened at the airport."

"I'm glad, too. I was expecting the plane to blow up at any time."

"Well, I hope your next flight will be a bit more relaxing. You can tell me everything on the drive to my office."

Outside her office in Delray Beach, Claire and Harry sat in her car. "So you're supposed to call this guy in Switzerland and he'll take you to Konrad Meir who knows the back way into Rubicon's secret lair, yes?"

"That's what I was told. And warned that Rubicon might be listening in to our conversations, emails, etcetera."

"Our communications are as secure as they can get, but specific cell phones such as yours and Justine's and Simone's may not be."

In Claire's modest office, located in an unpretentious commercial building, Harry took a seat facing Claire over her computer and paper laden desk.

"You sure this room is secure?"

"I had it swept this morning. You're getting paranoid, aren't you?"

"Two people have tried to kill me in the last twelve hours, I have no doubt Rubicon's minions will try again and again while I'm on some sort of secret mission to save the world, and I don't know who to trust. I'm entitled to my paranoia."

"Do you trust me?"

Harry leaned elbows on knees and massaged his temples. "Mostly. Ask me again in a few days, if I survive."

"Right. I have made my European colleagues aware of the situation.

You'll be met at the Geneva airport. They'll help you on your way, but you'll be on your own, mostly. Ever been to Europe?"

"England, about fifteen years ago. Three days working with Scotland Yard."

"So, no. Your flight doesn't leave until seven thirty tonight. Switzerland's  not hard to figure out, but I have someone who's well acquainted with the country. She'll give you some information about getting around."

"Will I have time to take a nap?"

"Sure." She removed a large brown envelope from a locked drawer and pushed it toward him. "You are now Fred Mann. Passport, drivers license, credit card, gun carry card, Swiss currency, and a few other things."

Harry checked all the IDs. The pictures weren't too bad. "If they run this passport, what will they find?"

"You're Deputy Chief of Security at a San Diego tech company. Single and taking a quick vacation before becoming the Chief of Security. It will pass."

"You did these fast."

"You know those vamps, Fred, they can move fast if they need to."

"I do know that. Thanks for your help, even if I am only a mortal."

"You're on unofficial-official vampire business. Undercover. Nobody wants sun-walking hybrids running around." Her lips twitched as she considered how much to tell Harry. "The Girl is after Justine and Simone. She almost caught them in Zurich. They're traveling with a mortal woman, Hedy Duchene. She is Konrad Meir's step-daughter, I think. They may have a lead to Meir. Maybe you're looking for the same lead. In any case keep a low profile. With all communication suspect, watch what you say."

During a lunch, Greta, a thirty-something woman with rosy cheeks, gave Harry some basic information about Switzerland—money, transportation, languages. He was grateful for the information, but his new paranoia kicked in when she asked for the third time—insisted really— where he was going. Even though he didn't know where he was going, he didn't reveal that. Paranoia—he trusted no one.

After he got a couple of hours sleep, Claire drove him to the airport.

"First class again? I thought I was undercover."

"You are. Economy was sold out. If you weren't you'd be on a private jet."

"Ah, poor me. If you hear from Justine… I don't know what to tell her. Really, I don't think Rubicon is likely to catch any of our calls. But I've been wrong before."

"I think it's best to assume he's listening."

"By the way, how much do you trust Greta?"

"About as much as I trust anybody. Why?"

"She seemed very interested in where, exactly, I was going. She also emphasized how reliable the Swiss communications system is. Emphasis on its security, as if I should have no concerns about using it."

"Huh. You think a bit of your paranoia is kicking in?"

"My paranoia is running full on."

"I'll check her out. You'd better go. Good luck, Fred."

Harry had no trouble boarding the plane. As before, he had a guide to take him around security to the gate. Nobody died. On the plane he found first class more than comfortable. He settled in, determined to get some sleep and not think about mad vampires and world domination. Or about Justine or Simone or Teresa. He'd give his paranoia a rest.

Largely unsuccessful, he did get a few hours' sleep when fatigue, mental and physical, took over after a surprisingly good meal. But most of the time he spent staring out the window, ignoring the starry night and three-quarters moon.

For a while Harry managed to put away his paranoia and think about Justine rather than vamps, though in reality it was impossible to separate the two. They'd been through a lot together as a vampire/mortal couple, which Harry still had to convince himself was real and true at those rare times when he was relaxed. Setting aside his completely understandable paranoia seldom lasted long.

Automatically, he kept a wary eye on the passengers and flight attendants. One or the other of the couple across the aisle always seemed to be glancing at him, as if sizing him up. A man behind him seemed to be working too hard not to be noticeable on Harry's frequent trips to the toilet. One pretty attendant seemed a little too attentive, her smile not quite reaching her eyes. Harry half expected the plane to blow up any time.

The plane landed in Zurich intact and on time. Harry delayed before disembarking. He had acclimated to the plane, almost accepting that nobody on it wanted to kill him. Now he readied himself to enter a new and unfamiliar environment where he knew somebody wanted him dead. He sucked in a deep breath and walked up the ramp.

As he left the ramp and entered the building he checked the cell phone Claire had given him. He stopped when he read the text message: *Talked to Greta. Trust NO ONE!*

Paranoia ramping up again, he followed the crowd to customs, where he passed through easily. In the area for waiting family and friends, he saw a man in a dark suit holding a sign with his name on it. He walked past the gate and exited the airport.

# Chapter 25

Hedy's and Lily's phone calls failed to connect with Peter Raza. He was at the top of the ski slopes preparing for the skiing season. Though there was a gondola lift, he and several others elected to stay at the top for four or five days running instead of using the lift twice a day. Hedy said that it wasn't unusual. The male staff used the pre-season time as a sort of vacation where they could say and do Man Stuff.

"No big surprise," Justine said with a chuckle. "I've been on a few women's weekends where we did and said Women's Stuff."

Smiling, Simone added, "That is nothing new. Even before I was changed, men and women gathered together and I believe 'talked smack.'"

"Well, I can talk smack with the best of them," Lily said. "But it's some ungodly time in the morning so I'm going to bed. It's too late for you to leave now. Sleep until sunset, then you will have plenty of time to get to Davos."

Hedy hugged her mother. "I've missed you. I'm sorry this is such a short visit."

"Oh Hedy, I've missed you, too. When this nastiness is over you will come and stay for a long visit."

"I hope so."

✴ ✴ ✴

Though the three were on high alert for most of the trip, they enjoyed an uneventful drive to Davos. Lily had reserved two rooms for them in a small, inconspicuous hotel. They checked in with no problem and climbed two floors to their rooms. After confirming their plan for the next day, Hedy entered her room and quickly got into bed. Sleep did not come easily.

She thought of her mother, strong, yet alone and a target. She loved Konrad, wanted to live with him again. Hedy had seen them together and knew that he loved her, too. For her safety, he had chosen to live alone. Her mother understood, though she didn't like it.

Hedy promised herself, and her parents, they would be together once again… assuming, that is, they all survived.

Justine and Simone did not go to bed. It was a clear autumn night, cool, bordering on cold. The winter crowds had not yet descended. Though they could easily endure the chill, they donned long coats and went for a walk.

When Justine stepped outside she sniffed the air. Finally, at least for a little while, she felt free to enjoy autumn scents—cold, clean air, the residual smell of restaurants, the perfume of a young woman walking with her man. And… there, just under it all, Harry. Stopping, she sniffed again and spun around, searching each of the few pedestrians.

*"Quoi, Chèri?"*

"Harry, I thought… I smelled him. It's gone."

"You are worried for him, as am I. I believe we know that he can take care of himself."

"I know he can, but I miss him."

*"Oui, je sais que tu le fais.* Claire said he had a lead on Meir. Perhaps we will meet him there." Simone took Justine's arm. *"Venez, mon ami.* It is a beautiful night. Let us walk about as two mortals on holiday with no cares. Perhaps have a drink, perhaps feed. Possibly we will soon have no time for such frivolities."

Justine shrugged and gripped Simone's arm. "If…."

"You have doubts, *chère?"*

Justine bumped shoulders with Simone. "Not a one, *chère.* Not a one."

# Chapter 26

Hedy woke early. While sipping hotel room coffee, she skipped makeup and dressed in a turtleneck sweater, trousers and sturdy shoes. In a restaurant next door she had a big breakfast of eggs, potatoes, sausage, and good coffee.

She thought of checking in with the two vamps, but didn't. They all knew what her task was and there was nothing they could add or say to help. Besides, the sun was up and she figured they probably needed their sleep, too.

Hedy drove to the lift station and caught the first Jakobshornbahn 1 gondola. She shared the gondola with three ski resort workers, a family of six hikers from France, and a middle-aged couple from England, all riding up to the Jakobshorn mountain peak. Just before the doors closed a man of about forty, easy to look at with dark hair escaping a dark cap, got on the gondola. He wore sturdy boots, jeans, and a dark blue hoodie. From his air of confidence, Hedy figured him for a manager of some sort, maybe on his way to check on the work at the top. Another time she might have chatted him up, but saving the world took precedence.

Once the gondola started to rise she caught Hoodie studying her with intense eyes that reminded her of snake's eyes, sending a thrill down her spine, not in a good way. She managed to nonchalantly turn away, though her breath was catching and her heart rate matched the rising gondola. She'd been bitten by a snake at eleven years old, nothing poisonous, but ever since she agreed with Indiana Jones: no snakes.

Her first thought was *Vampire!* But the sun streaming through the window illuminated his face. Were his eyes yellow? She caught her breath. What if Rubicon's vamps who can walk in the sun were real and this was one of them? Why would he be heading for the top of the mountain on a cloudless, sunny day? A test drive to see if he blended with the mortals? If so, he needed to change his eyes. Or was he following her to find her connection to Meir? Or was he actually just a manager, not dressed for pick and shovel jobs, going up to check out the work? Or was he just some guy with an unfortunate eye disease taking a day off? After a few minutes of near-panic attack she relaxed enough to breathe. She'd keep one of her plain brown eyes on him, even though he was just standing there. He was easy to look at, after all.

Gazing out at the constantly unfolding mountainous landscape, Hedy felt a small twinge of jealousy for the hikers. In her twenties and thirties, she had been an accomplished hiker, traveling throughout Europe to test herself on demanding trails. She recalled the freedom of that time, open space and no cares, no vamps, no worries about the end of mortal life as she knew it. Only the independence of the mountain whether she traveled with others or alone.

As the gondola approached the landing midway up the mountain, Hedy sighed deeply. Now there were vamps and cares and worries. Now there was a real danger that the world as she and these workers and hikers knew it would end.

A short walk brought her to the Jakobshornbahn 2 gondola, a 1.2 mile ride to the top of the mountain. The workers and the French family went in another direction. In the slightly smaller gondola designed to carry sixty people, the other passengers retreated to separate corners. Eyes, as Hedy thought of him, crossed his arms and dropped his head as if taking a brief nap. The middle-aged couple nodded and smiled at Hedy, but all were silent as if waiting for something to happen.

The landscape opened up as they rose. Peaks twenty or thirty kilometers away became visible as well as Lake Davos northwest of town . The land below the gondola was rocky and sparsely treed. Ahead, a long line of densely packed evergreens followed the cable's route.

The couple, all smiles and bonhomie, approached Hedy.

"Do you speak English?" the woman asked in German accented English.

Wary, Hedy said, "Yes."

"Have you been on this gondola before?"

"No."

"Oh, good. Come with us. There is an amazing sight approaching. You can only see it from the other side."

"I'll catch it on the way down."

"No," the man said. "It is better now." He backed up his opinion with a semi-automatic pressed against her ribs.

They each gripped one of her arms. "Who are you meeting here?" the woman asked.

"Robert Smyth."

"Why?"

"Why do you think?"

The woman punched her, a quick jab to the cheek.

The man jammed the gun against her ribs. "Be smart, not a smartass. Who?"

"Robert Smyth, who else would it be?"

"Why are you going to see him?"

"He's my boyfriend and I haven't gotten laid for two weeks."

"What's your name?"

"Sam Roberts."

The man snorted. "No, no. You're Hedy Duchene and you are looking for someone to help you get to Rubicon. Tell us who you're meeting and you live. Don't and you die."

"Fuck off." Hedy thought she was doing a good job of playing it cool, but she didn't want to die. Not right then, anyway.

The woman, who had a surprisingly strong grip on her upper arm, said, "She's not smart enough to talk. Let's finish this."

"Perhaps a closer view of the trees will convince her."

They dragged her to the door.

"What about him?" Hedy jerked her head toward Eyes.

The woman said, "Oh, he attacked you, you know how men are, and we had to push him out."

The man slid open the door.

"So you're going to push me out to kill me, right?"

"Unless you tell us what we want."

"So, self-defense," she muttered. A moment later, "Oh my God!" Suddenly weak-kneed Hedy bent forward, twisting to her left, forcing the woman on the right to step close to the edge. Out of sight of the assassins Hedy reached into her purse for her gun. "Oh, I'm better now."

She straightened up with a jerk while swinging her arm behind the woman. It was an awkward angle for her, but the woman got the idea when Hedy pressed the gun against her back. "Can you fly, bitch?"

*"Arrêtez. Suffisant!"* Eyes shouted.

"No, not enough." Catching the assassin by surprise with a full swipe of her hip, Hedy bumped the woman to the edge of the door and kicked her out.

She barely noticed the scream drowned out by the man's gun firing. She felt a slight sting along her ribs. Jamming her weapon against his stomach, she shot him. He staggered back against the door's edge. As he fell out the door he grabbed her jacket and pulled her with him. With nothing to grab onto Hedy fell forward. She was going to fall and die.

Then she stopped as if she'd hit a wall. The man held on for a second before Hedy smacked his hand with her weapon. His grip failed and he fell. For a few seconds she hung suspended over the abyss. Then, it felt like somebody grabbed the waistband of her trousers and yanked her back. She sprawled across the metal floor, coming to rest against the opposite wall.

*"Madame."*

Hedy shook her head, shutting her eyes against the dizziness. Then she gasped, her eyes popped open and her body tensed, ready for another attack.

*"Madame, vite!"*

Eyes lay on the floor, blood staining his shirt.

Ignoring her own pain, Hedy crawled to him.

"Oh, damn it. I'm sorry. I'm a nurse, let me help you. Wait, how did you...?"

"Never mind. You are with the two vampires, yes?" he asked, with a slurred French accent.

Hedy gaped at the man. How could he know?

"Quick!"

"Yes."

"They... assassins sent by Rubicon. ... After them long time. Discovered they were sent to kill someone. Did not know it was you."

"Who sent you?"

"Vampire Family Council. Trust nobody. Rubicon must be stopped. I must go."

Go? No, let me help you."

He ignored her. Instead he reached out toward the door and grasped at the air. Though he lay five feet from the door he slid smoothly up to it.

Wide-eyed, Hedy watched him slide. "How...? Did you pull me...? You're a witch."

He answered with a grin while he pulled himself farther out. "I prefer sorcerer."

*"Merci.* Your name?"

*"De rien.* I am Lucien."

"Hedy."

"Trust no one, Hedy." With that he tumbled out of the gondola.

Hedy scrambled to the door. She saw him falling toward the edge of the trees, but not fast—more like floating. He disappeared into the trees.

She sat against the wall. "What the fuck just happened?" she said aloud. She'd just killed two people, professional assassins yet, been saved by a witch, no, sorcerer, and though he was badly wounded, she saw him float down to the ground. *Breathe, Hedy. Breathe.*

The slight rumble as the gondola rolled over a pylon broke her concentration on *what-the-fuck-just-happened*. She hauled the gondola door closed and stood at the front to watch the top station approach.

She expected questions when she stepped off, but only received a welcoming smile from the attendant.

*Don't trust anybody.* She left the station and walked toward the restaurant. Outside, she appeared calm, composed, a tourist gawking at the dazzling scenery. Inside she was tight and frizzy as if fighting a mild electric shock. It wasn't only the altitude that made it hard to breathe. *So, find Peter, get the hell off the mountain and disappear.* If Peter could still be trusted.

# Chapter 27

In a hotel lobby Harry bought a phone taxcard to use instead of coins. The lobby had a public telephone booth. He dialed the number he'd been given.

"Hallo."

"Hello, do you speak English?"

"Yes."

"I was told to call this number when I arrived in the country."

"Who are you?"

"My name is Fred. I am with Photographic. I am interested in Möwen."

A male voice with a German accent said, "Rent a car. Go to the Etzel Kulm restaurant. It is near Pfäfflkon at the south end of the lake. Remember, you are a fan of Maynard K photographs. They close at nine."

The voice had spelled the restaurant and town's names. Harry hoped he got them right. Keeping a watch for people who seemed interested in him, he walked two blocks to an Alamo car rental. Using the Fred Mann credit card Claire gave him, he rented a VW Golf for a week. He wanted to ask directions, but thought better of it. He knew how to read a map.

He only made one wrong turn before he got onto the A3 road that took him south close to the long Lake of Zurich. He let himself enjoy the half hour drive through the picturesque countryside of well-tended fields and many white houses with red roofs. From his higher elevation he had good views of the lake and the mountains farther south.

Certain that he hadn't been followed, for that half hour Harry allowed himself to relax his guard. Who would be interested in boring, conventional Fred Mann?

He did worry about Justine. He missed her. She and Simone had survived some shit together. For someone who willingly died to become a vampire, she was quite a survivor. He thought the whole *no communication—somebody might be listening* thing was a bit much. But Rubicon was a thousand years old, he probably had learned a few tricks in that time.

In any case… blue sky, a warm autumn day, gorgeous views—plenty of time to worry later.

GPS knew the way to Etzel Kulm. Harry turned off on the 8, then off that to go through the small town of Feusisberg. From there GPS led him up narrow roads winding through densely packed trees to a hilltop clearing, where the restaurant, a three story block that could easily be mistaken for an office building, commanded magnificent views of the lake and mountains.

Harry surveyed the interior of the restaurant—wood floors, tables and chairs set by large windows where diners could enjoy the view. For those jaded by the view, central tables and booths were available. A family of four and a young couple still in honeymoon bliss were the only customers, it being close to three o'clock. Seeing no hostess, Harry seated himself by a window where he could watch the customers and anybody who approached the restaurant.

An attractive waitress came to his table. *"Guten nachmittag. Was kann ich dir bringen?"*

"Ah, hello? Do you speak English?"

"Yes, but I think not too good."

"You sound good to me."

"Thank you. What may I get for you?"

"Just coffee and something to eat. I was told that sausage with fried potatoes was good."

*"Ja, yes, Bratwurt mit Bratkartoffeln,* very good."

While she got the coffee Harry looked around the room. There were many large photographs of the scenic wonders of Switzerland on the walls.

When she returned he asked, "You have nice photos on the wall. Do you have any by Maynard K?"

A slight twitch of her eyebrows was her only reaction. "I am not sure. I will ask."

Sipping the very good coffee he watched her disappear into the kitchen. Through a small window he watched her speak with a man who could have been her twin, if he were thirty years younger, with longish light brown hair, wide-set eyes and about two weeks of beard.

Five minutes later the man brought the food out. He set it on the table then sat across from Harry.

*"Mange,"* he said with a French accent. "Is good."

This was the voice that had told him to trust no one. But hunger combined with the aroma rising from his plate persuaded him that it wasn't poisoned, so he ate. It was good.

"What is your name?"

"Fred Mann."

"It is not." He waved that comment away. "It matters not. I am Anton. Why are you here?"

"You don't know?"

"I do, but I want to hear from you."

Leaning on the table, arms crossed, Harry knew he'd go no further unless he told the truth. One had to trust someone sometime.

"I am here to find someone who will help us retrieve a friend held by Rubicon and stop him from taking over the world."

"How did you find me?"

"A vampire called Günter gave me your number. He's dead for real because he did. To be cliché about it, I'd like his death to mean something."

"Günter is dead? Did you see?"

"No, but I trust the person who told me."

"How did you know...?"

Harry waved his hand and shook his head. "No. Enough about me, how did *you* know him?"

Anton relaxed back in his chair, staring out the window. "He saved my wife's life before we met. He became her friend and then mine before he went to America." With a sigh, Anton stood. *"Bon appétit,* it is as you Americans say, 'on the house' then drive away and wait at Etzelweg and 9. I will meet you there."

On full alert again Harry barely tasted his meal. He scrutinized the customers again. He tensed at every new arrival, watching for any suspicious movement. They ignored him.

"Trust no one" kept running through his thoughts. Finally, feeling totally exposed he left a third of his meal and a tip and escaped to his car to find Etzelweg and 9. GPS knew where that was.

Harry followed Anton's van through open green fields to a two-story farmhouse nestled in the corner of a large patch of fir and beech trees. Most of the farmhouses were in the open; this one was out of sight of all the others. Harry wondered if that was coincidental or by design.

Dusk lowered as they drove up. Anton motioned for Harry to wait in his car while he opened the door of a well-worn white barn. Cars parked and barn door shut, they walked toward the house. A light came on above a side door, the door opened, and a German shepherd ran out and enthusiastically inspected Harry.

"You are with me," Anton said with a smile. "So he will not eat you."

Harry stood still for the sniff test. "I'm glad I didn't try to come here by myself."

"*Moi aussie*. I would not like to clean up the mess."

A handsome women appeared in the door, her dark hair in a ponytail and her hands in jeans pockets. She watched, amused at the dog's antics. "Thor, *venez!*"

The dog ran up to her, waited for a pat on the head, then sat, keeping an eye on Harry.

"My wife, Maddie. She runs the farm."

"Hello, I'm Fred." He managed not to wince at her strong grip.

In the modern kitchen inside, Maddie and Anton offered Harry a beer, which he took half to be polite and half because he really wanted it, food, which he declined, and a shower, which he wanted to decline because he really wanted to be on his way, but which he seriously needed.

"Thank you, but I only need to know where to find the person who knows how to find Meir. Then I will leave you alone."

"No," Anton said.

Instantly on alert, hand ready to draw his weapon, Harry asked, "No?"

Maddie read his sudden tensing. "Fred, please, calm yourself. You are tired, yes? A long day?"

"I believe he flew from America this morning," Anton said. He turned back to Harry. "We have to call first. We must be sure where he is. It is nighttime. You need to rest."

"You will stay with us tonight," Maddie said. "I see how tired you are. While you shower, I will call. Come, I show you to your bed."

Harry had only had two sips of the beer and already could barely keep his eyes open. Justine might be in trouble, waiting for him to help, but he wasn't far enough gone to realize that driving at night in an unfamiliar country to an unknown place was not a good idea. He almost fell asleep in the shower, but made it through.

In the kitchen they had set three places at the small round table.

"Anton said you ate at the restaurant. This is my *Ragoût de poulet*, chicken stew, you must have some."

"Thank you." Though he didn't think he was hungry the stew smelled and tasted delicious. "Did you call?"

"Yes. The man you want is Peter. He lives in Davos which is one hundred and twenty kilometers south of here." Maddie passed him a paper and an envelope. "Here is his address and phone number and a letter from me. I did not speak to him. I left a message that a friend would come to see him. No names."

"I will call him again tomorrow," Anton said.

Harry stared blearily at the paper. He could barely keep his eyes open. The address could have been on the moon. He didn't like that Peter did not answer the phone—his paranoia again, well founded or not as it might be.

"Thank you. I'll leave first thing tomorrow."

"Lucky for you we are early awake. A good breakfast for you then I will show you to highway 3."

"Go to bed, Fred," Maddie said. "You are sleeping already. *Bon nuit.*"

Harry trudged up the stairs and fell asleep ten seconds after lying down on an incredibly comfortable bed.

# Chapter 28

Two vamps came for Teresa. While Juno's block of her powers was effective, they didn't quite trust it. They always had two vampires deliver her because she couldn't overcome them physically, but if she should somehow regain her powers they might be able to overpower her before she destroyed the laboratory complex.

Teresa was ready. When the two vamps, a male and a female, came for her, she summoned a tiny bit of the magic she'd accumulated and forced the male vamp to not tighten one hand restraint.

This was the second time she'd done that. The first time, she'd managed to have the sloppy guard tighten the restraint around her hand and not her wrist. While Gerry and the guard had all their attention on the pregnant women, she slipped her hand out of the restraint and released her other arm. They caught her with one leg still restrained. She'd fought and screamed, but ultimately was no match for the vampires.

Gerry, though a vamp himself, kept his distance from Teresa and usually had one or two guards with him as they painfully sucked the magic from her. He remembered what happened in the Louisiana bayou. He came within seconds of capturing Teresa. She had punched him in the face, giving Justine enough time to take her away. Humiliated, he took pleasure in all of Teresa's suffering.

The vamps wheeled her into the extraction room and left her. One of Gerry's assistants, a young Hedge witch called Tita, entered and hooked Teresa up to the monitoring equipment. Tita, Teresa knew from direct observation, had a major, if unwise, crush on the vamp guard, Hans. Hans, whether on his own impulse or with a boost of cute Tita's magical influence, returned the crush. With the extraction procedure set up and started, the two lovers retreated to share their attraction in a more physical way than exchanging long sappy looks.

As soon as they were gone, Teresa freed her arm and the rest of her restraints. "Just relax, *chicas*. I'll be back in a few *minutos*."

The corridor leading to the extraction room had a door at each end.

To the left were the double doors they brought her through from the cells. To the right was a single door. Barefoot, Teresa padded to the single door, finding it locked, of course.

Months ago Teresa had begun training with Grace, once an escaped slave, now an incredibly powerful vampire witch. Teresa, a powerful witch in her own right, had only recently discovered her powers. Called to help Justine and Simone track down a girl sold by the Sinakov vampire Family, Grace had hastily installed much of her basic magical knowledge into Teresa. Teresa had no idea what spells or powers were in her head, until she needed them. It had turned out, with a little coaching from Harry, that one of the powers enabled her to unlock locks—including this one. Teresa only had to touch the handle and she heard the lock click.

She stared down at her hands in wonder for a moment, then shrugged and slowly opened the door.

It led to a corridor more finished than the ones Teresa had passed through. One side was smooth bare stone, the other manmade material with four doors, all of which had small windows. She heard voices in the far distance. The closest room, seen through the window, looked like a chemistry laboratory. The second appeared to be the same, the third looked more like a medical or biology lab. Through a small window in the fourth door, she saw a modest office, with file cabinets, a desk, and a large white board scribbled with, her nurse's eye recognized, genetic calculations.

Voices from a cross corridor interrupted her indecision about whether to use a bit more of her power to open the door. Totally exposed, she had no choice. The door opened at her touch and she slipped inside. With the voices coming closer she searched for a place to hide. Under the desk was too exposed. Two tall file cabinets in a corner, one against each wall, left a six inch gap between their front edges and a space behind the gap.

Teresa was no size zero slip of a girl. She was a tall, big-boned woman and even after weeks of short rations she could not squeeze between the cabinets. A key in the lock spurred her to action. Whether by magic or adrenaline, she lifted herself up until her legs could get through the gap, then dropped into the tight space against the wall, sitting with her legs pulled against her chest.

The door opened. Two mortal men wearing white lab coats entered.

*"Que cherchez-vous?"*

Teresa had picked up a little French from hanging around with

Simone. She knew *cherchez* meant look for.

"*Le dossier du garçon.*"

"*Le petit garçon, Nix?*"

Teresa tensed at Nix's name.

"*Oui.*"

"*Pourquoi?*"

"*Il est fini.*"

"*Ah, La mort?*"

*Mort?* Death? Teresa's fists pressed against her knees. Her breathing froze.

"*Quand?*

"*Demain.*"

*Demain. Hier, aujourd'hui, demain*—yesterday, today, tomorrow. Tomorrow they were going to kill Paul Nix.

# Chapter 29

Hedy stepped out of the gondola as if nothing untoward had happened. She walked through the building to the restaurant, hoping no one asked any questions about why she was the only passenger.

In the restaurant several men and a woman were finishing their breakfast. She asked where she could find Peter Raza. They told her he was working at the top of the Gügglbahn lift.

She forced thoughts of assassins, vampires, and world domination out of her head as she strode down the path to the Chalet Guggl, another mountaintop restaurant. She focused on the surrounding vista of mountains, some already snowcapped, the clear blue sky, the warmth of the sun on her back. She was just another tourist out for an early morning stroll.

Her reverie ended soon enough. She found Peter replacing planks in the large outside deck. She watched him for a minute, silently apologizing in advance for what she was going to ask him.

"Hello, Peter."

He looked up. A solidly built man about five-ten, his dark brown hair peppered with touches of gray and just long enough to be shaggy, he cocked his head, attempting to place her.

Hedy moved closer. "It's Hedy Duchene."

Peter's face lit up and his thin lips spread into a broad smile. "Hedy. This is a surprise. What are you doing up here?" He stood and moved closer. "Is your mother all right?"

"She is fine, Peter. But I need your help."

He studied Hedy's grim expression. "What can I help you with?"

"We need to find Konrad Meir."

"No."

"Let me explain."

Ten minutes later he still said, "No," but with less conviction.

"Peter, people have died because of this. They've tried to kill me and the vamps I'm with. Two people died in the gondola, following me, looking for you. You're the key here. You know where Konrad is. If Rubicon's people find you, you *will* lead them to him. He'll be dead, you'll be dead. Come with me, we have a chance. I know it's a cliché, but I believe if Rubicon succeeds it's the end of the world as mortals know it."

"Konrad swore he would never go back there."

"Let us convince him. You and he will be found eventually."

"Peter Raza?" a voice asked from behind them.

<h1 style="text-align:center">Chapter 30</h1>

At seven a.m. Harry, a bit bleary eyed, sat down in front of a breakfast of eggs, sausage, potatoes and toast. He grinned as he sipped the superb coffee.

"Did you sleep well?" Maddie asked.

"Yes, I did. Thank you."

Thor entered the kitchen door ahead of Anton. The big dog sniffed Harry and Harry scratched his ears in return.

Laughing, Anton pushed the dog away. "Thor. *Arrêtez, arrêtez.*" While Thor checked out his bowl for any breakfast morsels he might have missed, Anton said, "When you finish the breakfast we will go, yes?"

"I can go now. I should go now."

"No, my friend, you must eat. You do not want to hurt Maddie's feelings, do you?"

Maddie made a smiling-hurt-feelings face. Harry ate.

Ten minutes later Anton and Harry left the house by the kitchen door. Maddie held a barking Thor back.

"Thank you, Maddie, for everything."

"*Je vous en prie,* Fred Mann. *Bon chance.*"

Headed for the barn and their vehicles, Harry and Anton stopped when a man appeared from around the far side of the barn.

"*Qui êtes vous?*" Anton asked.

"Are you Fred Mann?" the man asked. He was dressed like a stereotyped movie bad guy—dark turtleneck, black pants, knee length coat, black watch cap. "Or Harry Frazier." He spoke with an English accent.

"Who are you?"

"My name doesn't matter, Harry." Hard eyes on him, the assassin drew a large handgun from his shoulder holster.

Harry, one step behind Anton, was already drawing his weapon. He pushed Anton aside and fired simultaneously with the assassin.

The assassin, not expecting another weapon, jerked sideways. Harry's shot creased his arm as the assassin's shot hit Anton just above the hip. The assassin was quick to fire again, creasing Harry's leg just above the ankle, causing Harry to stumble to his hands and knees.

The assassin quickly took advantage of Harry's vulnerability. Gun raised, he took two steps forward. Harry was a dead man—or he would have been if Thor hadn't ripped full speed from the house. The assassin whipped his weapon around, fired at Thor, then turned back to Harry

Thor, hit in a front leg, stumbled, rolled, gained his feet and launched himself at the stranger. His jaws clamped on the assassin's arm just behind the gun. Thor's momentum yanked the man to his knees.

Harry, on his feet, strode up and put two bullets into the guy's head.

Maddie had followed Thor with a shotgun to her shoulder. She didn't give the dead man a second glance as she ran to Anton.

Harry kicked the assassin's gun away and patted Thor's head. "Good dog, Thor. You can let go now."

Limping along with Harry, Thor followed as Harry and Maddie carried Anton into the house and laid him on the long rustic dining table. Maddie dug a sizeable first aid kit from a closet as Harry wrapped a clean dishtowel around Thor's leg.

"What do you want to do?" Harry asked. "Call 911 or whoever you call?"

Maddie began to strip Anton's shirt off as he hissed in pain. "No. I call another, more private doctor. Hold this."

Harry pressed a towel over the entrance wound while she called someone, and using a weird type of German, a form of the famous Schweizerdeutsch, persuaded them to come right now.

She took over the towel.

Harry said, "I assume you would prefer the body disappeared."

"Yes. We prefer there not to be any questions. You also, I think."

"He must have a car somewhere up the road. I'll find it. Put the body in and drive it into the woods."

"Harry, we have hogs behind the barn." She looked sideways at Harry, waiting to see if he got the drift.

"Hogs? Man, that's nasty. Really?"

"The body must never be found. I believe you call it plausible deniability in America."

"You guys aren't just simple farmers or restaurant owners, are you?"

Maddie flashed a grin and shrugged. "One hundred meters up the road is a turn off. He is probably parked there. Follow to the end and then push the car down the bank. Let me see your leg first."

"It's okay."

"No. Sit."

Harry sat and allowed Maddie to clean and bandage his leg.

"How did this guy find me? He knew my name and why I was here."

"Rubicon has resources. Money, power, people and vampires. Not many can resist all of that."

Harry searched the assassin's body, not surprised to find no ID. He stuck the gun in his belt and threw the body over his shoulder. The idea of throwing it to the hogs made him cringe. But Maddie was right, the body needed to disappear completely. Somebody would come looking for him. Vamps would easily smell a grave as well as find him in the car. Still, Harry had to turn off the cop in himself to strip the body and place it the hog pen. He did not stay around to see what happened next.

He found the car, an inconspicuous Volvo, parked where Maddie said, the keys under the passenger seat. Wearing gloves, he drove it about three hundred meters down the narrow track until it ended at a steep bank covered with undergrowth with a small stream at the bottom. Harry pushed the Volvo over the edge and the car sank out of sight into the brush.

By the time Harry returned, a van with *Vétérinaire* on the side had parked next to the house.

Maddie came to meet him. She handed him a bag filled with his clothes and some food. "Better nobody else sees you. The name and address of the man you want is in here."

"I'm sorry for all this. Will he be okay?"

"Yes. Our veterinarian helps all animals. You should go. *Bon chance,* Harry."

"Thank you. You too."

Due to construction delays, regular traffic and getting lost a time or two, it was mid-afternoon before Harry drove up to a small, well kept two-story chalet style house at the end of Edenstrasse at the north-west edge of Davos. The other houses in the area, all separated by grass already browning up for the winter, were larger.

Harry parked across the street, facing down towards town. He surveyed the area for anything suspicious—surveillance vans or loi-terers with dark glasses and trench coats. He had no idea what might be suspicious in that neat and tidy neighborhood. He saw no vehicle parked at the house, which was not a good sign.

He knocked, waited, knocked again. No answer.

*Well, shit.* Drawn curtains blocked the one lower window. There were no fences in the neighborhood, only grass separating big and small houses. Harry walked around the side of the house, finding a small stone patio with a picnic table and a few lounge chairs.

"Hallo?" a woman's voice called out.

Harry jumped at the unexpected call. He looked around until he spied a middle-aged woman in a yellow housedress and an apron, her blonde hair tied up in a messy bun. She leaned on the rail of a lower balcony with a cigarette in her hand.

Harry gave a half wave and walked toward her. "Hello. Do you speak English?"

"Yes, a little."

"I am looking for Peter Raza. He is not home?"

"Are you a friend?"

"No. Some friends in Freienbach told me to see him. Will he return soon?"

The woman took a deep drag and let it out slowly while she considered him. "No. Maybe two three days. He is up the Jacobshorn."

"Up the… Jakob… ?"

The woman laughed. A pleasant laugh, Harry thought. "Jakobshorn, is a ski mountain. He work there, fix for the winter."

"Is it possible to call him?" he asked, hand to ear.

"No. He and many other men turn off cell phone. They no want to speak to wives and girlfriends or business." She had a very sexy chuckle. "I think little work and much beer." Harry had to smile and nod. He could relate. "If you have to see him, go up mountain. Take gondola in morning."

"Not today?"

"I think gondola finished today."

"Okay, ah, *Dankeschön*, ma,am. *Dankeschön*."

"*Bitte schön*, sir."

Harry felt her eyes on the back of his neck as he walked to his car and drove off in search of a hotel.

# Chapter 31

Arm in arm Justine and Simone wandered the city, window shopping, with the occasional stop for a glass of wine. Justine sent some gifts back to Bailey and Susan.

They spoke little, and never about Rubicon or what might happen the next day with Hedy and Peter Raza, or Teresa, or Harry and his secret mission.

When they'd first walked out Justine thought she felt Harry's presence. The feeling was faint, slowly fading, but there.

"I feel Harry," she said.

Simone focused her senses, then gave Justine's arm a squeeze. "I feel him, too—from you. You miss him and worry about him."

"I know I shouldn't. He has managed to take care of himself and us before. But…."

"But you love him."

"Yes. I have to call Claire. She seems to know… a lot."

"I know you do. Be careful what you say."

They found an area with little pedestrian traffic. Justine turned her phone on and tapped.

A sleepy voice said, "Hello."

"Hi, it's us. I need to know about a certain guy."

"You okay?"

"All good. Waiting. Tomorrow could be a good day. Have you heard from him?"

"It's confidential."

"Don't care."

"He's fine. Had a little trouble earlier, got a scratch or two, but he's fine."

"Do you still think someone is listening?"

"Still a possibility, yes."

"You can't tell me anymore about…?"

"I don't know anything more. Sorry."

"This waiting is a bitch."

"Tell me about it. Communicate if you have to, otherwise, carry on."

"Right. Bye."

"He is all right," Simone said as Justine turned off her cell phone and stuffed it in her pocket.

"A little trouble? A scratch or two? Fuck."

"Come, wine is necessary, I think."

After a glass they strolled more, with another glass here and another glass there. It was late and not a weekend, there were no events or international meetings—the big one would be in January. They met few pedestrians. Even so, in the back of their minds, they were on continual alert, searching for vampires. Surprisingly, they detected none...until they were having a last glass in a working class bar.

Justine had had enough small talk. "What do you think they're doing to Teresa? How are they getting the magic out of her? Taking blood, some kind of helmet, sticking wires up her butt, maybe cutting...?"

Simone bumped her with her shoulder. "I am worried for her, also. Do not make yourself crazy about something you cannot know. We are doing...." Simone sat up, alert.

Justine stared at her, then felt it too. Vampires.

"Where?" Justine asked, surreptitiously scanning the bar.

"There," Simone said with her vampire *sotto voce*, pointing with her eyes.

Two men stood at the door, taking in the last call crowd. One was six feet tall and slender, wearing a casual suit jacket and a dark shirt, very stylish. The other was shorter and muscular, wearing a hip length leather jacket.

"Time to go," Simone said. "Slow, to the toilets."

Past the toilets and an office and storeroom, they banged out into a narrow alley—right into the arms of two waiting vamps.

Simone exited first. A vamp grabbed her from behind, lifting her off her feet.

Justine, focused on Simone, didn't see the other vamp until he grabbed her from behind as well. Seeing an opportunity, instead of trying to break loose Justine raised both legs and kicked Simone's captor in the back, forcing him toward a brick wall.

Simone, also being quick to seize an opportunity, threw her weight sideways, spinning her vamp around so he slammed his back against the wall. She threw her head back, smashing his nose. Shaking loose, she hit the ground and ran behind Justine's vamp. She punched his face, slammed her elbow down on his elbow, breaking his arm and Justine loose, and then kicked his feet out from under him.

They turned to run out of the alley, but the two vamps from inside blocked their exit with guns aimed at their heads. Together the women spun around, only to find another vamp holding a gun on them. They hesitated for a moment, long enough for the jacket wearing vamps to grab their collars and press guns to their heads.

Vampires can recover from most injuries, but a bullet in the brain is like decapitation from the inside. There was no true coming back from that—it did happen once but that didn't end well.

*"Qu'est-ce que vous voulez?"* Simone asked.

"What do *I* want?" Leather Jacket said in her ear. "*I* want to go home to my girlfriend and watch television. Instead I'm out here tracking you down for The Girl."

"What does she want with us?" Justine asked, all innocent.

"She wants to talk with you. Or kill you herself. Or both."

"Where is she?"

"You'll find out. Come, or I shoot you."

Still gripping their jacket collars and holding guns to their heads, the two vamps pushed their captives toward a van at the back end of the alley. The others followed, holding up their injured partner.

"Nils, get the restraints," Leather Jacket ordered the other vamp with a gun.

Justine, with eyebrows up and eyeballs glancing at Simone's left hip, caught her partner's attention.

Simone nodded.

Nils brought two pairs of over-sized handcuffs from the van, holding them out like a precious offering.

Simone nodded. *"Maintenant, Chère."*

Justine fake dodged left, then spun right , dropped her head out of the line of fire, reached out and snatched the gun from Simone's belt hidden under her jacket, and shot Leather Jacket in the leg.

Taken totally by surprise, he fired, barely missing Simone as she, too, spun away.

Leaving her jacket dangling in his grip, Justine kept spinning out of her captor's grasp, came up behind her vamp and shot him in the head.

"Halt!" Nils shouted as he fired at Justine. Justine felt the bullet ruffle her hair.

Simone smashed her elbow into Leather jacket's ribs. When he bent over, she yanked his gun from him and shot him in the head.

Together, they used their now fully dead captors as shields, rushing into hand-to-hand proximity with the two that first grabbed them. Only one vamp had a firearm. They slammed the dead vamps' bodies into him. Before he could reach past the shields and shoot either woman, Simone drew her machete and stabbed him in the neck. Unlike mortals with such a wound, he could still function. He swung his arm around to shoot, but Justine smacked the weapon out of his hand.

Justine and Simone quickly cut the two vamps down.

Justine shoved her blade into its sheath. "We have to get out of here."

"Too many questions if we leave them, *chère.*"

"Okay, throw them in the van, take it, leave it, run."

*"Rapidement!"*

At full vamp speed they threw the bodies in the van. Simone, usually a more sedate driver, raced away as sirens drew nearer. After five minutes they parked at the edge of the Vaillant Arena. Then they ran, carefully, back to their hotel.

They knew the back entrance had no security camera. Thanks to Simone's skill with locks—learned from a locksmith friend thirty years earlier—they slipped in unnoticed. The stairway and the main elevator had cameras, the service elevator did not. On their floor, they'd already slightly adjusted the security camera's angle so as not to cover their room door.

Safely inside, Simone sat on the bed and watched Justine pace. "How the hell did they find us? They knew exactly where we were. Who told them? We didn't notice any other vampires. Who here would know us?" She pulled out her cell. "Should we report to someone, Claire?"

Simone nodded to the phone in Justine's hand, eyebrows raised.

"Oh shit. Shit, shit, shit. The call. The bastards were listening. My fucking fault." She dropped on the bed, away from Simone. Head in hands, she moaned, "My fault. If the world goes to shit it will be my fault. Fucking immortality won't be long enough to forgive myself."

Simone put her arm around her friend's shoulders. *"Ma amie, if* the call brought them to us, it is *our* fault, not only yours."

"I wish I could cry and slap myself a few times and get that over with. But those damn tears just won't come, will they?"

*"Non chère,* they will not." Simone gently slapped her face. "That will have to do."

"You are so mean to me." Justine laid her head on Simone's shoulder. "So what do we do?"

*"Rien.* Nothing."

"Nothing? There must be something we…." Justine sat up straight, running fingers through her hair. "Wait. I turned my phone off after the call. It's been a couple of hours since then. Those guys knew exactly where we were."

"Ah, *merde*."

Justine jerked as if shocked. "The tracker implants. Somehow they figured out how to connect with them. I forgot all about those damn things."

"*Moi aussi*. We must remove them."

"Right. You do me, I'll do you." Justine shed her coat and drew off her long-sleeve T-shirt.

Simone opened the razor sharp two inch blade of a small penknife. She felt along the back of her partner's left shoulder for the slight bump of the tracker. "Ready?"

"No. I need a mirror so I can glamour myself not to hurt."

"*Bon*." Simone sliced through the thin layer of skin to the tracker. Ignoring Justine's, "Ow. Damn it!" she pried out the inch long device, about the thickness of a pencil.

Band-Aid on her small wound, Justine returned the favor. "Your skin is so smooth," she said as she ran her hands over Simone's shoulders. "We could make a lot of money if we could make some skin cream out of you. Vampire Skin Lotion—Be Immortal. Make a fortune."

Simone chuckled. "I'll give you a fortune if you don't grind me up and bottle me. Ay. Careful, that skin is still mine, *chère*."

"I'll take it. But first…." She snapped each tracker in half and used an ashtray to crush the pieces. "Now, we must proceed as planned. Looking forward, not backward."

"We must stay without motion," Simone said. "If we lie quiet we are harder to sense."

"Seriously?"

"They will be searching for us. I believe we are safe here. They cannot sense us here."

"Even if they walk past our door?"

Simone shrugged and wiggled her fingers. *Maybe*.

"Great. I'm taking a shower first. If you want to wash my back, I won't object."

# Chapter 32

Harry missed the first gondola. He caught the second, which he shared with several hikers and workers. He hadn't slept well. His thoughts kept jumping from what had happened in the last few days, what he was doing holed up in an anonymous hotel as Fred Mann, and all the million things that could go wrong in the next few days. Then there were those sirens that sped by just as he dozed off.

He did manage to take in the spectacular view as the Jakobshornbahn Gondola rose up the mountain toward the first landing.

Looking down after transferring to the second gondola, he thought he saw a body lying among the trees. The cop in him wanted to call it in, but the civilian in him knew the last thing he needed to do was get involved as Fred Mann. It could have been an optical illusion, anyway.

He got odd looks when he asked a group sitting with their coffee where he could find Peter Raza. Maddie had shown him a photo of Peter, and Harry easily recognized him talking to a woman. He didn't like to be rude, but the fate of the world might depend on how fast he could find Konrad Meir.

"Peter Raza?"

Wary, Peter said, "Yes."

"My name is Fred Mann. May I speak with you, alone?"

"What is it about?"

"Günter sent me."

"From California?"

"Yes." Harry considered lying about Günter. But that might piss the guy off and make him uncooperative, as well as making it awkward later. "I am sorry. Günter is dead." He glanced at the woman, "Fully dead."

Peter slumped, "Ah, *tot*. He was a good man, but I am not surprised. How?"

"I don't know. I learned of it as I was leaving. I don't know who, exactly, killed him, but it happened after he told me that you would know how to contact a certain person."

Peter glanced at Hedy then said to Harry, "Konrad?"

Harry couldn't keep his eyebrows from rising.

"The look on your face tells me yes."

"Konrad Meir?" Harry said.

Hedy stepped up. "You're Harry."

Harry tensed. "No, I'm Fred Mann."

"That's probably not what Justine calls you."

"You know… her?"

"I do, and Simone. They are waiting for me to convince Peter to take us to Konrad Meir, who, by the way, is my stepfather."

A thrill ran up Harry's spine. He opened his mouth to speak, but wasn't sure what to say. *Justine, so close.* "Ah, okay. That's why I'm here, too. We need your help, Peter. Konrad Meir is the only one who knows about the back door into Rubicon's secret lab, or whatever it is. We believe Teresa is the key. If we can rescue her we can stop him."

Peter held up his hand. "I understand. I admit I was skeptical, but two of you now. I'll take you to Konrad, but I know he does not want anything to do with that back door."

Harry and Hedy exchanged *Yes!* glances.

Harry tried to contain his excitement. Justine was there, waiting for him. "Is it possible to leave here now? I'm sure we can make up any pay you miss."

Peter laughed. "For most of us this is a volunteer thing. Our pay is food, beer, and a cot that only sleeps one. You could buy me lunch and a beer."

Harry smiled and nodded. "That's something like what your neighbor said, 'They go up there to eat, drink beer and talk dirty.'"

"That's about it. Let's go."

On the gondola ride down the mountain, Harry asked Hedy how she met Justine, and how they all got there.

"I'll let Justine tell you, if she can keep her hands off you. She misses you madly."

"Me too." He looked out the window. "I thought I saw a body in those trees on the way up." When Hedy didn't answer he glanced at her. He knew guilt when he saw it. "You know anything about that?"

Hedy turned her back on the window. "It's not something you need to worry about."

"Yeah, I get it, out of my jurisdiction."

Hedy studied the trees where two bodies lay. She shrugged one shoulder then the other, deciding. "Well, maybe it is something to worry about."

"Okay… what happened?"

"Well, there were these two assassins…."

When she finished Harry looked at Hedy in a whole different way than when he first met her. He should have known. Any mortal that traveled with Justine and Simone had to be able to take care of herself. But two pro assassins out the door—badass. "Yes, I'd say that was something to worry about."

As they transferred to the lower gondola Harry noticed Hedy's nervous scrutiny of the area. "Expecting…?"

"Lately, anything."

"That why you're carrying?"

"Yep. You?"

"Yep."

"Good."

As the gondola approached the lower station Peter stood casually next to them, hands in pockets, away from the tourists and other workers. Quietly, he said, "You two look nervous. Expecting trouble?"

Hedy opened her mouth to say one thing, then said, "From now on, always." She handed him a business card for the hotel. "If anything happens and we get separated, room 301."

He studied the card. "What have you gotten me into, Hedy?"

"Saving the world, Peter. Saving the world."

They left the bottom station with the five others who rode down with them. Though it was a short walk to Hedy's hotel they decided to take Harry's car.

Harry stopped, swore to himself, and said, "Wait. Those police are looking at my car."

"It's a short walk," Hedy said. "Come on."

One of the cops waved at them. Peter waved back. "I know that officer. Is that a rented auto?"

"Yes."

"What name?"

"Fred Mann."

"You have ID for Harry?"

"Yes."

Peter walked forward to meet the officer.

"Hallo, Peter."

*"Guten Tag, Louis. Wie gehts?"*

They spoke in German while Hedy loosely translated for Harry. "Blah, blah, been awhile, what's with the car? Stolen? Looking for the driver, seen anyone around? No. Friends of yours? Known her for years. The guy? Her friend. What's his name? Harry."

Louis studied Harry. Eyebrows raised, Harry studied back. Louis stepped around Peter and approached Harry.

*"Louis, was machst du?"* Peter asked.

Louis ignored him and asked Harry, *"Sprechen Sie Deutsch?"*

"I think you asked me if I spoke German. No."

"Is that your auto?"

As a cop, Harry was all about truth. Lying didn't come easy, but he was way out of his jurisdiction at that moment. "No."

"How did you arrive here? Your papers, please."

Harry hoped he remembered which pocket had Fred Mann's papers and which had Harry Frazier's. "Train."

"Louis, why are you doing this?" Peter said.

"We are looking for a dangerous man. Full name?"

"Harry Stephan Frazier."

Louis frowned at the passport as he paged through it, then snapped the passport closed. He tapped the little book as his frown deepened.

Harry was cool on the outside, but inside… *What the fuck is this guy doing?*

A grin broke Louis' frown as he turned to his partner. *"Hey Gerhard, Harry ist ein Polizist."*

In English, Gerhard shouted, *"Ja?* Maybe he can help us find this guy?"

Harry forced a smile. "No, no. I'm just here for a vacation. No police work."

To Hedy, Louis said, *"Dieser Typ ist okay, Ma'am?"*

Hedy affectionately squeezed Harry's arm. *"Ja, er ist ganz okay."*

Gerhard called, *"Louis, Kommen Sie. Forensics sind hier."*

Louis handed Harry his passport. "Peter, good to see you," he said as he walked away.

With Hedy still holding his arm, and still holding his breath, Harry turned away and started walking. "There are cameras all over. Eventually they'll see me with the car."

"Then we had better hurry," Peter said.

# Chapter 33

Justine stopped pacing and lay down next to Simone. "Where is she? She should be back by now."

Simone held her hand. "She has proved resourceful. She will return, though I share your anxiety."

"You do? I've come to like Hedy. Where the hell is she, where the hell is Harry, every vampire in the city is looking for us, and who knows what the hell's happening to Teresa, and we're basically stuck in this hotel for the next seven or eight hours. Those anxieties?"

"Oui, *chère*, those ones."

"Well, I'm glad we're on the same page."

Five minutes later a knock on the door had them on their feet, senses on full alert.

Justine mouthed, *No vamp.*

Simone answered. *The Girl?*

Weapons in hand, Justine peeked through the peephole and saw Hedy with others outside the peephole's range. Hedy broke into a grin. She stepped aside and pulled someone else into view. *Harry!*

Still alert, Justine unlocked the door. She glanced at Hedy and the other man, then grabbed Harry and pulled him into a hug that stopped his breathing until Hedy tapped her shoulder and said, "Easy girl, don't kill him."

Relief flowed through Justine. She hadn't fully realized just how much she had worried about him and missed him. Her happy face vanished when he winced as she held his arm. "You're hurt."

"Nothing a little magic can't cure. We need to get inside."

Once inside the room, Justine, Harry, then Hedy, shared quick summaries of how they all got there.

After Justine spoke, Harry commented, "They deserve that for hitting on my girlfriend." Before Hedy spoke Harry said, "I see why you have Hedy with you."

"Harry, you don't have to say anything," Hedy said, shoulders hunched high.

Grinning, he said, "Sure I do. You're a total badass. Your badassery is right up there with these two."

"And what, *chère* Hedy, did you do to impress Harry who has his own share of badassery?"

"Well, there were these two assassins…."

"Hedy, I knew we had you with us for a reason," Justine said. "But…?" She nodded to Simone.

Simone summed it up. "The police will soon be searching for Harry and also Peter. Rubicon is already searching for Harry and Fred Mann. Because Hedy survived an attack by two assassins, they will also be looking for her. The Girl is here and searching for us with four of her minions. Did I miss anything?"

"That's plenty," Justine said. "But this has all been for nothing if Mr. Raza won't lead us to Konrad Meir."

All eyes turned to Peter who had leaned against the wall, arms crossed, listening to their stories. He asked Harry, "Is Anton going to be okay?"

"As far as I know. A doctor was working on him assisted by Maddie's magic fingers."

"Good. I will take you to Konrad, but I'm telling you he will not talk about that project and will not go there."

Justine, sitting on the end of the bed rubbing shoulders with Harry as they held hands, said, "Regardless, the bottom line is that we need to get out of town now."

"Okay, but it's high noon out there. What about these two?" Harry asked.

Hedy stood and stretched. "Not to worry, we have that covered."

Fifteen minutes later Hedy braked a van to a halt by a side entrance. Thirty seconds later she took off with Justine and Simone safely in the back with Harry. Peter rode shotgun. "So, where to?"

"East out of town. It's not far, maybe thirty kilometers."

"This what you guys have been traveling in?" Harry asked as he settled into a new, low set, folding beach chair next to Justine.

"I just bought it yesterday. We knew we would need some day-or-night transportation. Got a good deal."

Harry spoke softly to Justine. "I hope this good deal doesn't become a bad one as soon as we leave town."

"I heard that," Hedy said over her shoulder. "I know my cars."

Harry laughed. "Another badassery category for Hedy."

Hedy raised two fingers for victory.

Once on the open road, Justine asked Peter, "How do you know this Konrad Meir?"

Peter stared out the window. "My grandfather worked with him in the mountain. Helped him escape. They caught my grandfather and killed him, but he died free. I was told his last words were, *"Je suis libre."*

"I am free," Simone said. "A good way to die."

"Yes, yes. When Konrad escaped himself my father and I helped him. We became close."

"So where does this back door lead to?"

"I don't know. He would never say anything except it was the back door to hell."

Hedy added, "Brandt had similar thoughts about the place."

"Great," Justine muttered.

About twenty kilometers farther on, Peter had Hedy turn left onto a narrow paved road that turned to gravel a short kilometer after the turn. Fields, done with crops until spring, turned to thick trees on the flanks of the steep narrow valley.

Peter had Hedy turn west onto a barely noticeable track that led across a field to the beginning of the foothills, then jogged left around a spur of trees to reveal a steep roofed log cabin. The sun had traveled far enough west that the cabin, built in the edge of the trees, hid in shadow.

Hedy parked in front of the cabin and cut the engine. She said to Peter, "You're up."

"No, we are up. He's your stepfather."

"I know, but…."

"No buts. He is less likely to kill me for bringing strangers to his house with you there."

Hedy started to speak then thought better of it.

Peter huffed out a deep breath. "Get out, but you three wait here."

All of them exited the van. Peter and Hedy walked up to the cabin's solid wood front door. Peter knocked. "Konrad, it's Peter and Hedy." He knocked again. "He's not here."

"Peter, I know you don't want to do this, but you know how important this is."

"He's hiding in the trees," Simone said. Hedy and Peter gave her a quizzical look. "That's what I would do."

"Then let's go find him," Hedy said.

Justine could hear everything they said. She walked after them as they moved around the corner of the cabin toward the trees.

Peter said, "No, wait. You will spook him."

"If he's waiting in the trees he already knows we're here," Justine said.

Peter shrugged. "Stay back and don't try to force him."

Hedy spoke loudly into the trees. "Papa, it's me, Hedy. Please, I must talk with you. We need your help."

"Konrad, I'm sorry to bring these people here, but you are the only one who can help them."

Konrad stepped out from behind a tree. A burly man with unkempt graying hair that hung to his wide shoulders under a black toque, he looked like an old farmer or woodsman in his heavy boots, trousers and coat. He didn't move, didn't speak, just stood still, hands jammed into coat pockets.

"Papa, please, you can trust them. Rubicon is trying to kill them."

There was a long silence. Then Konrad spoke. *"Warum?"*

Simone stepped up to the edge of the trees. "Walter, Rubicon has taken a friend of ours. She is a witch. He is using her magic to breed vampires who can walk in the sun. I'm sure you will have no problem imagining what he plans to do with them."

"He wants to take over the world."

"Yes. We want our friend back, and to stop him."

Konrad stared at Simone as he slowly approached her, his face alive with mixed emotions. Less than a meter and more than a century separated them. The others did not exist.

"Simone?"

"Walter."

"Nobody has called me that for a hundred years."

"You like Konrad better?"

His voice caught when he said, "No."

"You went to Switzerland without me."

"I'm sorry. I thought you were dead. I searched."

Simone broke into a wry smile. "The Resistance was good at keeping secrets."

*"Ja."*

They were silent, though there was so much to say.

Konrad reached out to touch her cheek, hesitated. "Simone, I...."

"I know."

He touched her cheek, gently caressing her flawless skin. "Simone, I am so sorry."

He pulled his hand away. Simone stopped him, held his hand to her cheek. "Walter, don't. It was a long time ago. You did what you felt you had to. I did not like it, but I understood."

Simone felt the heat rise behind her eyes. She knew he felt it, too. A bittersweet smile, a kiss to his hand, and she let go.

"You have a family now. You should be proud of Hedy. She would have been great in the Resistance."

"I'm not much of a father. I left them."

"To keep them safe."

He looked at Hedy, standing apart and watching. "She is hurt."

"Saving us, helping to find you."

"Is Rubicon really doing what you say?"

"Yes. We need your help. Show us where this back door is. That's all you need to do. Please."

Konrad studied each of their faces, judging their seriousness. "You will never find it on your own."

Hedy stepped up. "Papa, please."

Konrad stepped back and glared at Justine and Harry. "I don't trust them."

Hedy waved a finger at the others. "Rubicon's people have tried to kill them several times. They have tried to kidnap and kill me several times. Simone and Justine have saved my life more than once. I trust them. You should too."

Peter pointed at Harry. "That's Harry. He is a policeman from America. He was sent by the Vampire Family Council to find you. A very good friend vouches for him. He would not have been sent by them if it wasn't important." He moved closer. "Konrad, I know you don't want anything to do with Rubicon, but if what they say is true, and I believe it is, you have to help."

Justine walked up to Konrad. "My name is Justine. When one of Rubicon's assassins tried to kill me he killed Brandt instead. I believe he was a friend. We cannot stop Rubicon without your help. As soon as possible you can return here. If—"

Konrad held up a thick hand. He looked at Hedy. "Brandt is full dead?"

"I'm sorry, Papa, yes."

"He always wanted to die. He finally got his wish."

"I know. If it matters, the assassin is also full dead."

"You?"

"Justine and Simone. Papa, please help us. This is important to *everybody*. Just show us the way and we will go from there."

Konrad's clenched fists and tight lips signaled his reluctance. He turned his gaze to Peter.

"I only learned of this a few hours ago," Peter said. "Having listened to their stories, I have no doubt of their sincerity. I've seen their wounds. Hedy is convinced, so I am also."

Konrad's deep set eyes studied each of them in turn. Justine felt his gaze in her head searching for the truth. She felt his hate and anger, and his reluctance to release his feelings. She recognized those feelings because she had felt them when her daughter was murdered. Maybe not the reluctance. She had begged Simone to change her so she could serve blood justice to her killer.

Hedy went up to Konrad. Hands on his chest, she said, "Please, Papa."

He touched her cheek, father to daughter, then stalked to his front door. "Come in." He walked inside, leaving the door slightly ajar behind him.

✵ ✵ ✵

At a long plank table flanked by benches in front of a rough stone fireplace, they discussed a plan.

"To get to the entrance is a one kilometer hike. The passage is two hundred and eighty meters until the laboratory."

Simone asked, "If we're going through this back door, there must be a front entrance. Where is it?"

Konrad chuckled for the first time. He went to a shelf and took down a book. He opened it to a page and with one finger slid it over to Simone. "Here."

"Schloss für die Jahre," she read. "Castle for the Years. I have not heard of it."

"Few have," Konrad said.

Hedy took the book, which was in German, and quickly scanned the short description. "It is just across the border in Austria. Basically it's a thick, round tower built about eight hundred years ago into a mountainside a kilometer up a valley. It is privately owned. The only interesting thing about it is a very complete museum of medieval weapons and artifacts. It is open to the public three days a week."

"So Rubicon's secret laboratory is in this castle?" Justine asked.

"Behind it," Konrad said, tapping hard on the photograph. "In the mountain."

"*Merde*," Simone whispered. "This back door goes through the mountain?"

Justine rubbed her eyes then ran her fingers through her hair. "So, what's the plan?"

An hour later they had a plan of sorts.  As they sat sipping wine or beer, Hedy moved next to her stepfather. "Papa, Brandt said you saved his life in that tunnel. What happened?"

"I said I would take you to the entrance, you want me to talk about it, too?"

"*Bitte, Papa,* we need to know about it."

The old vampire stared into the dying fire.

"Rubicon built that castle to protect his stolen wealth. He knew of the cavern and caves. Over the centuries he expanded the system. Around nineteen hundred he determined that one of the caves ended only two hundred meters from the other side of the mountain.

"Using mostly slave labor it progressed slowly. We met during the war. He hired me to supervise the finish of the passage." He held a gnarled hand over his mouth as if to keep the words in. "When the passage was finished he sent vampires to kill everyone who worked on the project, including me.

"Brandt was my friend, a foreman. When I realized what they were doing I hid him in a fissure. Two of the killers discovered him. I killed them, hid their bodies in the fissure and escaped. But Brandt had been wounded, he was dying." His fists and jaw clenched as he relived the past. "The only way to save him was to change him. So I did. I knew soon enough he did not like it. I am glad he finally got his wish to die."

# Chapter 34

They let Peter out of the van a few blocks from his car in the Jakobshorn parking lot.

"Thank you, Peter," Hedy told him. "Without you…."

"Good luck to you. I hope to see you all again. Konrad, I am sorry I brought this trouble to you, but I think it is important."

"Do not be sorry, my boy. Perhaps I have been hiding too long. If I don't survive, you know the cabin is yours and Hedy's."

"I'll arm wrestle Hedy for it when you get back."

✴ ✴ ✴

With little nighttime traffic and Justine driving, they made good time towards the Austrian border.

Hedy occupied the passenger seat, Konrad and Simone sat together in the back seat next to Harry, who sat behind Justine.

Konrad stared at the dark passing landscape for a time. "I'm sorry," Konrad said. "I was blind to what was going on in Germany before the Great War. Germany had been good to my family."

"Walter, I understand. I was blind, also. All I saw was you. I was not happy you left, but I was proud of you doing it."

"Not only me, thousands of Jews enlisted. Most were sent to the front lines. Seventy thousand died. Because my name was Rinman, not Meir, I became a Captain."

His head bowed as he remembered. "I led a squad to take out a Russian gun emplacement, but it was a trap. We were hit hard. Then, when the Russians thought we were all dead and they left, a band of scavenging vamps attacked us. Those of us left fought back. I killed a male. When I was wounded badly, dying, a female vamp said, 'You killed my man, so you will take his place.' She bit my neck and I blacked out.

"I stayed with them for three months. Anna taught me how to be a vampire. I came to like her. She was intelligent, smart, and kind, to me.

152

There was no shortage of blood."

He glanced at Simone who watched him, silently neutral.

"Another woman, Gretchen, the kind of vampire that gives people nightmares, lost her husband in a raid. Instead of changing a new victim she wanted me. Anna fought for me." He shook his head at the absurdity. "Imagine two women fighting over me."

Simone laid a hand gently on his arm. "I can." Konrad laid his hand on hers.

"I killed that woman and left."

"*Je suis désolé*. You loved this woman, Anna?"

He turned to her, raised a shoulder and managed a wan smile. "Not like I loved you."

"Yet, you left me to fight for your country as Walter Rinman."

He chuffed, sitting back. "I had no idea what was important back then. The first weeks I was filled with national fervor, then I missed you terribly. My greatest regret."

"I should have fought harder for you. One of many regrets. But, you… we cannot go back to that time. You should return to your wife. She misses you."

"No, we cannot return to that time, except through our memories. Yes, I would like to return."

Simone sat back and studied the ceiling. "*Je sais.*"

✳ ✳ ✳

After a bit more than an hour on the road, two large sedans caught up to them.

"Two sets of lights coming fast," Justine said.

Tension filled the van.

Hedy jolted awake. "Coming for us?"

"Don't know. Probably."

"How would they know?"

Justine had a good idea how, but wasn't going to say anything to Hedy. "Let's see what happens in the next minute or two."

All were alert, weapons out, watching and waiting.

The vehicles slowed and hung back of the van.

Harry said, "If you see a bazooka or a big ass machine gun appear, say something."

A minute later the lead car pulled out and paced alongside the van.

Justine kept one eye on the road and one on the big Mercedes sedan.

She saw the right window drop down and a shotgun poke out. Without hesitation, she swung the biggest handgun they had, a .45 semi-auto, toward the sedan and put a couple of shots into the open window. They heard a cry of pain and the shotgun vanished.

The sedan sped up, cut into the right lane, and the brake lights flashed. Justine kept her foot on the accelerator, smacked the sedan's right rear bumper and with a quick jerk of the wheel spun the sedan around. She kept contact as the vehicles screeched to a stop.

Both of the spun sedan's passenger doors flung open. Two male vamps burst out. At full speed one ran around the front of the van and one around the back.

Simone threw open the van's sliding door. Her first quick shot grazed the vamp in front. He stumbled for half a second, long enough for her to run to him and use her blade to take his head.

The vamp behind the van opened fire as he came around toward Justine. She flung her door open in his face as he reached it and shot him as he fell.

Harry threw open one side of the back doors and fired into the second sedan stopped behind them.

All four doors of the rear sedan sprang open and four vamps jumped out, one of them The Girl. Harry recognized her immediately. He tried to aim at her, but gunfire from the others drove him back behind the van's back doors. One of the vamps, in full vampire face, jerked open the back door and reached through so fast Harry had no time to react. He dragged Harry out and threw him on the hood of the sedan. The vamp was overwhelmed with blood hunger and this mortal was food. Mouth wide open, he knocked the gun away and pushed Harry's head aside.

Helplessness paralyzed Harry. The sound of gunshots and screams fell away. This was how he would die. This close to Justine. He couldn't even shout out. He fought desperately to break free. *Justine! Justine!* he cried out in his head as that horror of a mouth lowered to his neck. He flinched at the first prick of fangs. *Justine!*

Like magic, the jaws vanished. Too fast for Harry to follow, they reared back then slammed into the van's bumper. Konrad drew his own blade and jammed it into vamp's neck, ripping it halfway though. Another slice and the body fell away. Konrad held the head, regarded it with disgust and flung it away.

The vamp behind the one who attacked Harry had run past him after Justine. In full vamp mode he seemed to forget the purpose of the gun in his hand. He grabbed her and tried to smack her head with the gun. He had no idea of her martial arts training. She easily blocked his strike and punched his chest, forcing him back. They charged each other, wrestling, punching, kicking too fast for a mortal to follow. Justine managed a side kick that knocked him back to the sedan. Konrad stepped out and drove his blade into the vamp's head.

Instantly, the fourth vamp ran between the vehicles, stepped on Harry, and collided with Konrad. They tumbled onto the road, the vamp on top. The vamp wrenched the blade away from Konrad and raised it to finish him. Justine grabbed the blade just as Harry shot the vamp in the head.

Simone saw The Girl coming at her. Finally, Simone had a chance to take her out. Blades out, they clashed at the side of the road beside the guardrail. Their blades clanged and clicked like an old fashioned movie sword fight.

It had been at least a hundred and fifty years since Simone's last real sword fight, yet she remembered the moves—feints, blocks and thrusts. Simone easily held her own. The Girl didn't have Simone's experience, but her diminutive size and quickness and her unwillingness to play by any rules made her a problematic opponent. She proved this by suddenly rolling under Simone's strike and grabbing her legs, pulling her down like a linebacker.

The Girl had planned her move. As Simone fell, The Girl twisted her legs so she fell on her stomach. Up in an instant, she kicked Simone's ribs, twice. The crack of broken ribs rang loud in the nighttime silence. The Girl couldn't resist. "Finally, Simone, the death you deserve." She kicked again and was about to say more when Hedy launched herself out of the van side door, crashing into The Girl and dragging her over the guardrail and down a dark embankment.

"Hedy!" Justine shouted. With her vampire vision she saw the two roll down a few meters before separating. Hedy scrambled to the left. The Girl stood up and began climbing up the bank until Justine shot at her. She stepped back, even in the dark her hatred obvious on her little girl face. Harry shot at her, then Justine shot again. One of them hit her. They kept shooting.

The Girl ran into the night.

Simone, holding her ribs, helped Hedy over the rail. *"Merci encore une fois."*

"You're welcome. You're hurt." She helped Simone sit in the side door opening. To Justine, who stood arm in arm with Harry, "Is she gone?"

"For the moment. We need to go."

"There's a break in the rail up ahead."

"Right. Are all the vamps dead?"

"I'll check," Hedy offered.

A gunshot a minute later broke the silence. "Wounded at the beginning. Leg caught when we rammed them."

Five minutes later, cars sent down the embankment and vamp bodies hidden in the underbrush, they continued their journey.

Curled up in the passenger seat, Hedy asked, "How did they know?"

"Only one way," Justine said.

"I know, Peter. Shit."

# Chapter 35

"I'll arm wrestle Hedy for it when you get back."

Peter watched the van leave the COOP Supermarket Davos and turn east on Talststrasse. He didn't know exactly where they were going. Simone had suggested he stay outside while they discussed their plan. From other meetings with Konrad and what he did hear, he had an idea of their general destination.

He was not a fighter, vampires scared him. He had done his part, good luck to them.

He strolled the opposite way down Talststrasse toward the car park. As he reached his car, a Volvo sedan and a black Mercedes SUV pulled up and stopped beside him.

"*Sie Peter Raza?*" a man asked from the front seat.

"*Ja.*"

Without another word, the rear door opened and an incredibly strong man came out and punched Peter in the face, then forced him into the back seat. A second man pressed a knife to his ribs and told him to keep quiet or....

They drove to a large chalet at the edge of Davos, a compound isolated by trees and a high wall with a gate and a guard. They took him through the lower level into a bleak white room with a wooden table and two chairs. They told him to sit, then left him.

Peter had no doubt his kidnapping had to do with Konrad and Hedy and the others. He had little time to contemplate his predicament and silently thank Simone for preventing him from hearing their plan. What he didn't know he couldn't tell.

The door opened and a girl walked in and sat opposite him. Casually, she set a large kitchen knife on the table's corner. Sixteen maybe, thin, could be pretty if she let her chaos of black hair grow out. Her eyes though... he'd heard of eyes hard and dark as diamond, but he'd never really seen such a thing, until now. This must be The Girl he'd heard mentioned with capital letters. He'd been nervous and worried before; now he was scared.

"You are Peter Raza, yes?"

"Yes."

"You know things that I want to know. You will tell me, quickly."

"Things about what?"

"Konrad Meir, Justine Kroft and Simone Gireaux."

"Okay."

"Where are they?"

"I don't know?"

"Don't lie to me. I'll know. Where are they going, right now?"

Her eyes never wavered from his. Not blinking, not narrowing or widening, just boring a hole in his brain. She wasn't glamouring him. He'd been glamoured before and he knew what it felt like. "I… I don't know."

"This morning, you met Hedy and Harry up on the mountain, then you met Justine and Simone. Are you saying you have no idea of their plans?"

"Yes. No. They are going someplace. I don't know where."

Her eyes flicked to the knife then returned to his. "Are you sure?"

"Ye… yes." Anger flared for a moment as his voice broke. He wanted to be brave, but he wanted to live. He forced his fingers to stop tapping his leg.

"Where do you think they're going?"

"I don't know. Not close."

"Who is with them?"

"Nobody. Just them."

"You are lying." She reached for the knife and slid it closer. "Who?"

Shit. Peter had the feeling if he told her it would be bad for them. He didn't want to betray Hedy or Konrad, but the knife and her unblinking eyes terrified him. She probably knew or had a good idea who was with them already. Did she know about this back door? If he told her it was Konrad she'd know they were going for the back door. If she knew about it. It seemed like it was a big secret. If she found them and killed them then maybe it would be the end of the world and it would be his fault. "Nobody."

"I told you do not lie to me."

In an instant she was around the table and next to him. Peter found himself slammed back onto the table with her eyes drilling deep, and he fell and fell and fell into his own head. Glamour. Blackness. And questions questions questions.

Then light.

"I told you not to lie."

His head was being held sideways on the table. He saw the knife still in its place. That wasn't what pierced his neck, but it was the last thing he ever saw.

# Chapter 36

They crossed the border into Austria with no problems and continued on the zigzag road to Nauders, a picturesque village in a narrow valley. In the darkness, only the vampires could see the well-groomed fields and evergreen woodland that surrounded the town.

They dropped Hedy and Harry at the Hotel Tia Monte. According to the plan, they would be visiting the Schloss für die Jahre, to check out the weapons museum and be on hand to help, if possible. Konrad had told them the location of a door to the laboratory area. It was a very play-it-by-ear plan.

The pleasant young woman behind the desk took their passports, Harry handing over his Fred Mann papers. While he signed in, Hedy moved close to him and unobtrusively but firmly dug her elbow into his ribs.

Harry turned his head to speak, but stopped when he caught her steady gaze. Having gotten his attention, Hedy indicated the desk clerk with her chin and eyes. He was so tired, it took him a few seconds to get it. When he looked back at the desk clerk his cop instincts kicked in. Something wasn't right.

The woman held the two passports down on the counter with two fingers each. Eyes wide with alarm, she looked back and forth between them and the papers. In halting German she said, "I... I will be right back."

"Is there a problem?" Hedy asked.

"*Nein. Nein, kein problem. Ein oder zwei Betten?*

"*Ja*, two beds."

Harry turned to a window where he could see Simone, arms crossed, leaning against the van, watching. Harry gave her a subtle *come-here* gesture.

He met her at the lobby door. *Sotto voce*, he said, "She recognized our names. She was told to be looking for us. Probably all the other hotels, too." He glanced at the desk clerk, who was picking up a telephone. "She can't report us if she doesn't remember us," Harry suggested.

"*Oui*, I agree."

Quickly, Simone strode around the front desk right up to the clerk. Not giving her time to react, Simone grasped her face, looked deep into her eyes. A few seconds later they both disappeared into the back office.

Harry reached over and took back their passports.

"She knew our names, didn't she?" Hedy said.

"Yes. Rubicon, or The Girl, probably called all the hotels. So much for surprise."

"Maybe they don't know we know about the back door."

"Maybe. Looks like no comfy bed to sleep in tonight."

Simone joined them, alone. "She won't remember anything when she wakes up."

Harry asked, "What about security cameras?"

"Erased."

Harry gave her a raised eyebrow look.

"What?" Simone patted his cheek. "*Cher*, I have been around long enough to learn a few things."

Back in the van, Harry said, "Change of plans I think."

✵ ✵ ✵

"So where is this castle?" Justine wanted to know.

"About two kilometers west." Konrad said.

"What does it look like?" Harry asked as he stared west at a half moon in a partly cloudy sky.

"Not much of a castle, more a fortress," Konrad said as if tired of repeating the words. "Round, thick stone structure thirty-two meters in diameter. Is built into the mountain thirty-five meters high at highest point. It cannot be seen from the road."

"No fairytales then."

Konrad's lips twisted tight. "Nightmares."

Justine, behind the wheel, asked, "So where do we go?"

"Opposite way," Konrad said.

They left Nauders heading east, then turned south for two kilometers, passing through what seemed like two mountain ranges.

"Slow down. There. Left."

Justine turned onto a dirt track between fences.

"Lights out."

With her fine night sight, Justine had no trouble following the track between two small fields. A small farmhouse sat off to the left. The track led through a copse of trees and brush at the entrance to a narrow, steep sided fissure in the steep mountain.

"Push through bushes, ten meters up there should be a space to right."

Slowly, Justine drove through a thin wall of brush.

"Back in," Konrad directed.

Parked, they all got out and stretched.

"Nice job," Harry commented. "Just right for a fast getaway."

Justine punched, gently for her, Harry's arm. "For you mortals, anyway."

Harry held her face and kissed her. "Glad I can trust you for help."

"Uh huh." Hedy stood next to Simone. "We can leave you two in the van for, say, fifteen minutes, then you can catch up."

Simone bumped Hedy's shoulder. "Five minutes I think is enough."

"Hey, come on," Harry said.

Konrad said, "Enough. We go now, or never. No lights here."

Five minutes later, packed up with every weapon they had and ready for a hike, they followed Konrad into the fissure, about three meters wide at that point.

They walked beside a streambed of rounded stones, dry except for a trickle of water. "This can be a meter deep in the spring."

They crossed the streambed. There was no trail as such, just a scattering of irregular basketball to baseball-sized stones, talus from the high walls. The mortals followed close behind the vamps until Konrad said it was all right to use a flashlight. Hedy followed Simone with a light. She held it down, sometimes holding it back to illuminate a bigger rock for Harry who followed Justine.

The fissure narrowed, then widened to five meters. A rising narrow shelf littered with stones came into view. The half moon cast a ghostly glow all the way down a steep, rocky slope to the streambed now fifteen meters below.

Hedy, paying more attention to keeping the light on a particularly large rock for Harry than on where she was stepping, slipped on some loose rubble and her foot slid over the edge. With a short yelp she fell over the rim of the shelf.

Justine, two meters behind thinking about the moon and how she and Teresa used to sit on the beach and watch it and talk of the future, missed Hedy's outstretched hand.

Simone, lost in the memory of a time three centuries ago when she and her lover made a similar trek through a similar passage that they hoped would lead to safety, also missed Hedy's hand just behind her.

Konrad, absorbed by his memory of the horrors of creating the passage he was headed to and with the possibility of twisting Rubicon's head from his body, was oblivious to what happened ten meters behind him. Hedy's yelp was lost among the screams in his head.

Harry, paying attention to the light, seeing Hedy's foot slip and knowing she would go over, dashed past Justine and reached for Hedy's outstretched hand. He grasped it, but her momentum dragged him over with her. Together they slid several meters down through the jagged talus before Harry grabbed onto an embedded boulder.

"Hang on, Harry, I'm coming," Justine called.

Justine's vamp speed was no help, as the surface was too unstable. She slipped and fell right on her ass. Concealing a laugh, Simone pulled her up.

Konrad pulled a coil of rope from his backpack and handed one end to Justine. Holding it, she inched down the slope and grabbed Harry's outstretched hand. Gently the vamps pulled the mortals back up to their slender ledge.

Hedy sat against the rock wall while Simone tended to her cut and bruised leg and hand. *"Je m'excuse, chère. I was not paying attention."*

"Neither was I." With a mischievous grin Hedy glanced up at Harry. "Next time I'll fall slower so you all can catch up."

Harry guffawed. "Okay, Hedy. One for the mortals."

The vamps looked at each other with sheepish grins.

"Smartass," Justine said as she held out a hand to help Hedy up. "Can you walk?"

"Think so. Don't think anything is broken. Hurts. Anybody have any Tylenol?"

*"J'ai quelque chose de mieux. Look at me."* While Justine held the flashlight, Simone knelt beside Hedy and looked down at her.

Two minutes later Hedy shrugged on her backpack and said, "Let's go."

Fifteen minutes later moonlight revealed the end of the fissure. The two sides came together in a blunt point. There seemed nowhere to go but hundreds of meters straight up.

Konrad stopped short of the end and waited for the others to catch up.

"I hope we don't have to climb that," Harry muttered.

Justine gently squeezed his arm in sympathy.

Konrad pointed ahead. "The entrance is there. But you should know about this." He moved past them to the cliff wall. He stepped sideways, and seemed to disappear.

"What the hell?"

"Did he just walk into the mountain?"

Simone moved to the spot, looked around, and vanished.

"Okay, is this a vampire thing?"

Simone and Konrad reappeared.

"There is a fissure here. Very hard to find, even in light. A place to hide if you have need."

With Hedy's flashlight that she'd managed to keep hold of, they inspected the crack. It was about two meters deep and barely wide enough to fit an adult's shoulders.

"Come," Konrad said and walked on. Less than a minute later he stopped again. "Here." Looking forward they saw blank stone. "Behind you." There was a wider, obvious crack, going back into the mountain.

"That's the back door?" Justine asked.

"Yes. Many men died to make it."

"And died trying to hide it," Hedy added.

"So how long is this tunnel?" Harry asked. "Is it guarded, monitored?"

Konrad crossed arms over his chest, staring at the entrance with tightly twisted lips that expressed his fear, loathing and disgust for the passage. "The manmade section is two hundred and eleven meters. It was a narrow crack ten, twenty centimeters wide at the end of one of many offshoot passages. To the main cavern, about three hundred meters. From there, I do not know. It has been almost a hundred years. I'm sure it has much changed."

"Cameras?"

"Then, no. Now…?"

Justine checked her gun, stuck it in her belt and drew her blade. "Let's go and find out."

Neither vampire nor mortal said a word as they checked weapons and prepared for a fight that they might not survive.

Hedy, especially, searched her soul, wondering why the hell she was there with people she barely knew trying to rescue a witch she did not know, and attempting to stop a mad vampire from taking over the world with modified vampires, an idea she did not quite buy. But she'd burned her bridges. *Fuck it, let's see how it plays out.*

Justine stood by the entrance, shoulder to shoulder with Harry. Simone stood next to him. "Finding Teresa is my, our, priority. Destroying Rubicon's plans are secondary."

"What about surviving this craziness?" Hedy wanted to know.

Justine's smile crinkled her eyes as she shrugged. "Well, that, too."

Konrad stood by the entrance staring down at nothing.

Simone said, "Konrad, Walter, you do not have to go in. You brought us here, that is all we asked."

He squared his shoulders. "It is easy to get lost. I will show you the way." He flashed them a grin. "Maybe I will get a chance to kill Rubicon."

He turned and disappeared into the cave.

# Chapter 37

Teresa lay on her bunk, fuming with rage, frustration and her desire to just punch somebody in the face without being able to. She could feel the magic burning inside her. There was no time left to build up her magic power any further. She had to act now.

But she had to wait for Condi who was in the extraction room getting the magic sucked out of her.

They didn't have a specific plan, but now she knew the location of Doctor Reich's office and how to get out of the restricted area. The first thing was to find Juno and disable his magic suppression spell. Teresa wasn't sure how to do that. Would knocking him out end the spell? Would he have to be killed? Would that end it? Could she kill him if it came to that? *Yes.*

Grace, a vampire witch considered the most powerful witch in the world, told Teresa in the short time she trained with her that Teresa might be powerful enough to frighten *her.* Maybe now was the time to discover if that was so. If she survived.

Teresa paced the cell ceaselessly. The vamp guard by the far door watched her. He made her reconsider her very vague plan. Scorched earth was her usual feeling. Wipe them out. Kill them all. But that guard, who looked about twenty and could be best described as a fresh faced farm boy, who always seemed to be bored to tears, had never said or done anything against the captives. He'd helped occasionally, brought them extra food or water. Condi smoked; he'd given her cigarettes, lit them when she was out of matches. He'd never said a word to them.

The door to the laboratory section banged open. Two mortal attendants pushed Condi past. She held out a hand. Teresa reached out to touch it.

"Get away from the bars, witch bitch," a young shaven-head attendant said as he slapped her hand away.

Teresa's resolve not to tear down the mountain vanished. She grabbed his arm and yanked him hard against the bars, his head hitting them forcefully enough to make the metal hum. She had to do *something* with her seething emotions.

The attendant grunted his surprise when she grabbed his head with both hands and slammed it again against the bars.

She didn't really know what she was doing then. With her hands on both sides of his head Teresa let her burning anger out. She thought of fire.

His whispered cry of pain rose quickly to a full scream, muffled by the bars against his face, as smoke rose from his hair followed by a short burst of flame. His fear filled eyes bulged out, leaking smoke. She let go. The body crumpled, scorched face sliding down the bars, until it keeled over and lay still.

*"Que diable?"* his partner cried out. He ran around the stretcher and stared at the body. In French he asked, "How the fuck…? You're not supposed to be able to do that!" He looked at Teresa's face. His eyes grew wide and he stepped back. "You can't do that."

He turned to run. Condi grabbed his arm. He yanked free, and ran into the young guard who punched him unconscious with one blow. Still without speaking a word, the guard unlocked Teresa's cell, then dragged the unconscious attendant into an empty cell.

"I guess *la revolución comienza ahora*," Teresa muttered.

Not quite prepared, Teresa quickly helped Condi off the gurney. "Are you ready for this? No turning back now."

Condi revived more quickly than Teresa from the sessions. "Do not worry, Madame Sorceress. I have been waiting long. We must get the boy."

"Right." She took the keys from the attendant's body and handed them to Condi. "Get him. I'll put this guy to bed."

Teresa dragged the dead body into her cell and threw him onto the bed, then covered him with a blanket leaving the unbloodied part of his head exposed.

Condi, whose slender frame was stronger than one would expect, easily carried Paul Nix. "We have to find a place to hide him."

"Wait."

Teresa went to the door of the next cell. The young vamp guard had laid the unconscious attendant on the bunk. Blood stained the silent guard's mouth as it returned to normal after feeding on the attendant.

"Where is Juno?"

The guard turned his head, displaying his wide open mouth. Behind the bloody fangs she saw only a stump of a tongue. No wonder he didn't speak. Instead, he pointed up.

"How do I get up?"

He pointed at the door she went through earlier, then left, then left, then up.

"*Gracias, chico. Buena suerte.*"

"Come on." Teresa grabbed a pillow from her bunk, then led Condi through the doors and down to Dr. Reich's office. She threw the pillow into her hiding place behind the file cabinets. "Put Paul in there."

With hands under his arms Condi lifted the boy up.

"Wait. Hold him in your arms."

Condi cradled the limp, barely conscious boy.

"I don't know if I can do anything, but Grace put a lot of things in my head. Maybe I can bring up something to help."

Teresa stood by him, eyes closed. *How can I give this boy strength?"*

She saw hand movements. Saw a hand on a chest, a hand on a back. Heavy lidded eyes opening.

Teresa opened her eyes. She swayed and had to step back to keep her balance. The power she felt before wasn't there. A thrill of fear gripped her stomach. How could she hope to escape now?

A small hand touched her arm. "Thank you," Paul Nix's feeble voice said.

Teresa focused on the boy. Condi still held him, but his eyes were open with a hint of hope. He managed a smile. She raised her gaze to meet Condi's wide smile. "How...? Did I...?"

Condi nodded. "You did, my friend. You moved your hands then a hand up and down and I felt the energy go into him."

"*Maldición. Gracias Grace.*"

"You must wait for us," Condi told Paul. "Do not let them see you." She lowered him into the corner space behind the file cabinets. Teresa found water and power bars in the small refrigerator, and carefully dropped them in along with the pillow.

As the two witches left, Paul said in a voice that brought tears to their eyes, "You won't forget me, will you?"

"We be back, honey."

At the door Teresa had to breathe deep. "I think I used up my witchy magic." She took another deep breath. "How will we fight Juno?"

Condi gripped her arms. "We find him and punch his face and kick his ass and tell him stop."

"*Sí Sí. Vamonos.*"

"Wait." Condi took a white lab coat from a rack and put it on. "I am doctor, you my no magic patient."

The corridor ended at a natural cavern, judging by the rough hewn ceiling and walls, roughly thirty meters in diameter. Four other passages branched off the space.

They stepped out of the passage then ducked back as a woman exited one corridor and entered another. They hesitated as a scream echoed across the space from one of the openings. Two white-coated attendants ran across the cavern into a corridor. Approaching footsteps from behind spurred them on. Following the guard's directions, they took the corridor to the left.

In the corridor, steps carved out of the rock led up to a circular hall with rough-cut windows. At the top of the steps, Condi quietly asked, "Where to?"

Teresa backed against the outside wall. Her body vibrated as she forced herself to breathe deep and slow.

Condi shook as if hit by a blast of freezing wind. She gripped Teresa's arm. "Do you feel it?"

Teresa sucked in a deep breath. *"Sí. Él está aquí.* I feel his power."

"Do he feel us?"

A wave of fear washed over Teresa. "We have to hurry. Do not hesitate. We must attack him. Do what we must before he can stop us."

They ran around the hallway until they found, more by internal feel than sight, the source of the power they felt: an ancient, but solid wooden door. They exchanged a quick look, then Teresa pushed the door open.

# Chapter 38

Konrad led them through the tight, smooth-walled passage. He went slowly, stopping every five meters or so to scan for cameras or sensors. Peering around a curve where the walls transitioned from artificially cut to natural stone, and the original cave ceiling rose into darkness, Konrad stopped and turned off his flashlight.

To Justine, behind him, he said, "Two cameras, one forward one back possibly four meters up. They may be infrared. I am an old vampire who cannot jump so well. You must move as fast as you can and jump to push them up."

"I'm no spring chicken, but I can do that."

She carefully peeked around the corner to locate the cameras. A very faint light from ahead illuminated the devices for her enhanced vision like a searchlight. "I'll be right back," she told Harry, then planted a quick kiss on him as if she was leaving for six months.

If he could have seen her in the dark, she would have vanished, appeared under each camera, leaped to shove it upwards to scan the ceiling, then reappeared two seconds later.

"Told you," she said to Harry. To Konrad she said, "It gets light ahead. Where to?"

"From here, is new to me. We move ahead. Look, ask, fight."

Konrad continued around the curve. Just before the passage ended, a man wearing a blue guard's jacket turned into the passage. He saw them. He stopped, drew his gun, and fixed eyes on Konrad.

Konrad stared at him. "Gasqu?"

The young guard opened his mouth, but no words came out. He glanced behind him then approached Konrad.

Grinning, Konrad stepped forward and gripped the smaller man by the shoulders. "Gasqu, you survived."

Gasqu also grinned and gripped Konrad's arms.

"Do you know this man, this vampire?" Simone asked.

"His name is Gasqu. He worked with me."

"Why are you here?" Simone asked Gasqu.

The vamp winced, tapped his mouth with a finger and waved the finger across his mouth.

Konrad's grin vanished. He held Gasqu's chin and looked into his mouth. "What have they done to you? *Bastardes!*

"He worked in the tunnel. He brought food and water to the mortals. He brought bandages and other supplies to treat injured workers because if they couldn't work they be killed. Several times I've seen him work for a man so they could rest. A good man."

"You said they killed all the mortals at the end."

"*Ja, ja, die Reinigung.* The Cleansing. A terrible evil thing. When three vamps came to kill us all I saw one attack him. I killed that vamp and carried Gasqu into a little used chamber. He was dying. I did the only thing I could do for him."

"You changed him, like Brandt."

"Yes. I had to leave him and try to save others. That is when I helped Brandt. But they sent more to kill us and they drove us out." Konrad faced Gasqu. "I am sorry. I wanted to come back for you, but it was impossible. I thought you were dead. I am so sorry I left you."

Gasqu gave a wan smile and touched his hand, palm down, to his cheek—I know. He started to use sign language but stopped when it became obvious Konrad didn't understand. He pointed to the group and threw up his hands in the universal gesture of *Why? How?*

Hedy stepped forward, her hands signing quickly. Gasqu brightened as he signed back. The others watched for several minutes as they communicated.

"I had a deaf friend as a kid. She taught me. Okay, quickly. A mortal man found him. Gasqu tried to talk to him. The guy thought he talked too much so he cut out his tongue then stabbed him." Gasqu pulled down his collar to reveal an inch long scar. "He survived and escaped and survived. They're paying real good money to work here, even if they're basically prisoners."

"What about the guy who cut you?" Harry asked.

Gasqu smiled and drew his finger across his neck.

"As a cop I should arrest you, but, it's not my jurisdiction, so…" He gave the young vampire a thumbs up.

Finally Hedy said, "Teresa, another witch, and a boy have escaped their cells. They have gone after Juno the head sorcerer who has put a blanket spell over this place that suppresses all magic."

Justine said, "If Teresa can use her magic she could take over this place."

"If she has learned her lessons. Or remembers them," Simone added.

"There is that. How do we find her?"

Gasqu signed. Hedy said, "He'll take us there." More signing. "He helped her escape. There will be an alarm anytime."

"Then let's go." Blade gripped tight, Justine bounced on her feet, jaw set.

Simone rested a hand on her shoulder. Communicating silently, she projected *calm, calm.*

They followed Gasqu down the natural cave tunnel and up stairs cut into the stone. As they reached the top of the stairs, they all felt the frisson of potent magic. At the same time a cry echoed through the cavern and passageways.

Frozen by the rising power of magic, the sudden rise of tension and the approaching drum of running footsteps they turned to Gasqu. He drew his gun and raised his hand, but the attention of the others had shifted from him to the two women running toward them.

# Chapter 39

Teresa stumbled when she barged through the heavy wooden door. Magic hit her and enveloped her. Condi, too, gasped as they broke through a barrier from nothing to everything. Unfettered magic filled the room. In an instant full power infused both of them.

Hundred-year-old cabinets crammed with books and bottles lined the circular room's walls. In the center, suspended by no apparent physical support, floated a four foot diameter globe. On it a map of the world dimmed, or blurred, or changed color as it slowly spun. Above it a huge brass funnel penetrated the wood beam ceiling.

On the far side of the room Juno leaned over a desk. No taller than five foot eight, he was slender with a completely shaved head except for a dark van Dyke beard like a comic book sorcerer. He jerked around.

Driven by the sudden surge of power she wasn't prepared to handle, Teresa ran to Juno and smashed into him. They tumbled across the floor.

Juno gained his feet first. "Of course, Teresa. Reich has more experiments for you. He will be disappointed." He raised his arm to strike her down with magic.

A large, slightly misshapen dog growled and leapt at him, knocking him to the ground.

"Fuck you, Juno." Teresa used her fist instead of magic. Before he could retaliate she put all her strength into a punch that laid him out cold. Fascinated and a bit grossed out, she watched Condi transform back to her human form.

Breathing hard, they held still for a few seconds before they heard a cry of alarm and then the ear-piercing squeal of a real alarm.

Condi said, "They be coming here. Even with power we maybe be trapped. We must get Paul and depart."

Teresa sneered at the unconscious sorcerer. "I wanted to kill him."

"Then do it or not. We must go."

"Halt!" Two blue jacketed vamp guards filled the door, sidearms up.

Teresa kicked Juno then spun and let loose a fireball that drove the vamps backwards, landing with a dull smack against the corridor wall.

Without a word the women ran out of the magic-laden room, heading for the stairs.

A group of people at the top of the stairs, not guards, froze. Some of them seemed familiar. Stunned, not able to breathe, Teresa halted two meters away. They were not real. Some mind trick of Juno's. Hallucinations. She raised a hand to blast them away.

"Tee?"

"Teresa?"

"Ah, *Dios*. Justine? Simone?"

Forgetting the danger, Teresa and Justine came together in a joyful hug that almost cracked a few ribs.

"I knew you would come for me."

"What else do I have to do?"

"*C'est un plaisir* to see *la sorcière* again." Simone allowed Teresa to sweep her up in a happy hug.

"I knew you would escape if you could," Justine said.

"Not yet, new friends," Condi said. "Teresa, they come."

Three guards rushed up the steps.

Teresa stepped away and sent a fireball toward them. But the flame came out tiny and tame. One of the guards swatted it away like a snowball.

She looked at Condi. Simultaneously they realized what happened. "The globe holds the magic."

"It has to be destroyed."

"I will do it." Condi turned away, then turned back. "The other women. Yes?"

"Yes. *¡Vamos!* With magic we can help them."

Condi raced back to the magic room.

Teresa said, "Antonia and the other women, we have to help them."

"Where are they?" Harry asked.

"I..." Teresa noticed Gasqu. He smiled and nodded. "He'll show us."

The guards, moving more slowly in case Teresa's fizzled fireball was just a warm-up, mounted the steps while shouting in German. One didn't have to speak German to know what they wanted. Instead they got Justine and Simone. Their heads rolled except for the fourth, who ran across the open space into a bullet in the head from Harry.

"Nice to see you again, Harry," Teresa said.

"Always good to have a cop around you, Teresa."

Gasqu led them down another passage to a heavy locked door. Justine opened it with one well-placed Kung Fu kick. Through the door they found three rooms with six cots each. Two of the rooms held six women, one three. Their ages ran from teenage to midlife, various ethnicities, all in different stages of pregnancy.

The reactions on both sides were variations of "Holy shit." Many of the women cried out and cowered in their beds at the intrusion.

More guards came. Justine and Simone, attempting not to kill them, ruthlessly immobilized them. One, who refused to accept the inevitable, lost his head.

Hedy took over. In several languages she said, "Do not be frightened. We are here to get you out. Get up and come with us, now."

Konrad and Harry helped her get the women out of their beds and to the door. Most were weak, their cheeks hollow, their ragged hair cropped short.

Teresa paced by the doors, occasionally encouraging a woman she recognized. "Do you know Antonia? Where she is?" she asked in English and Spanish. No one did.

"Where is Rubicon?" Simone asked the conscious guards. None knew where he might be. "Konrad, where would Rubicon be? Is there an office?"

"I do not know. None of this was here before. I believe he planned an office up where we were."

Teresa shook clenched fists at the universe. She pounded her fists on the bare wall with each question. "Where is she? Where is Condi? Where is the magic?"

"Tee, easy. We'll find her and take her home."

Teresa's face froze as she stared at Justine as if she was a total stranger. Then something else drew her frustrated glare.

"Gerry!"

Gerry, in his white lab coat, carrying his clipboard, looked up and stopped in his tracks. "You. You are the alarm? How did you…?"

Though he was a vamp, many times stronger and faster than Teresa, he backed up when she rushed him. He had to look up as she pushed him against the stone wall.

"Where is Antonia?"

"I don't have to tell you." Hands on his clipboard as if loath to actually touch her, he forced her back.

"Where is she!"

"What does it matter, Witch. You will be dead soon."

Simone and Justine picked him up and slammed him against the wall. His eyes bulged as he searched for his dropped clipboard as if searching for a shield in the middle of a sword fight.

"It matters to us, Gerry," Justine informed him.

"*Où est* Antonia?" Simone asked, her insistence backed up by her blade against his crotch.

Cringing from the blade, it took a few tries for him to blurt, "Sheisdeadandyourmagiccanotchangethat."

Teresa could still manage a small fireball. She rushed to him and held it close under his chin. "She can't be dead. Are you lying? Who killed her? You?"

Like a dying fish, his mouth worked, emitting an "I, I, I" sound.

Teresa's anger made the ball flare up. "You killed Antonia."

"*Nein. Nein. Sie hat sich umgebracht.*"

Teresa looked wildly at everybody. "What the hell does that mean?"

"Suicide," Konrad whispered.

Simone whispered in Gerry's ear, "*Hat sie sich wirklich umgebracht? Do not lie.*"

Gerry tried to avoid her hard gaze. "*Nein.*"

"Is she really dead?"

"*Ja.* She fell."

"Where?"

"The cemetery."

"Did you see the body?"

"*Nein*, too deep, too dark."

She looked to Gasqu who had been listening closely. His eyes widened and his lips twisted. He nodded once, clearly not pleased.

"Take us there," she told Gerry, who was also not pleased.

"Simone, what the hell?" Justine demanded.

"He says Antonia died by falling into the cemetery, but he never saw the body."

"You mean she is…?"

"I do not know how much I trust this one. I told him to take us to this cemetery. Konrad, do you know this place?"

"I do not."

Simone glanced at Gasqu. He stood back, his expression unnaturally neutral, except the eyes. He knew something. "Gasqu, do you know this place?"

Keeping his eyes fixed on hers, he nodded once.

*Mon Dieu.* Simone thought she knew what secret Gasqu held. "Will you take us to Antonia?"

Lips a tight line, he nodded.

Hedy had been following the exchange. Simone asked, "Hedy, will you ask him about this cemetery?"

Hedy and Gasqu had a quick sign language conversation. She said, "He will take you where you need to go."

Before they followed Gasqu, Konrad said, "You do what you must. Hedy and I will take the women out the front."

"Is daylight, *maintenant, n'est-ce pas*?"

"*Ja*, but I believe there are two buses that bring tourists. We will use them."

"Where will you take them?"

"The hotel. They already know where we are."

Hedy nodded to Simone, gripped Teresa's arm, said "Good luck," and with Konrad herded the ladies across the cavern and into a passage.

"*Viens*." Simone gripped Gerry's arm.

"Justine, will you go and find Condi? Where you saw us. I should have magic now. She has been a friend."

Justine, who'd been concentrating on not slapping Gerry's smug face a hundred times, gave Simone a shrug and a quizzical grin. To Teresa she said, "As you wish almighty Sorceress, and best friend."

Harry, who'd been standing back trying to follow everything, said to Justine, "I thought I was your best friend."

She took his arm and led him out the door. "You're my best something else."

# Chapter 40

Justine and Harry moved quickly to the cavern. They waited as a woman and a man in lab coats made a crouching run across the space as if they were under fire. Justine headed to the steps, but had to duck into another passage as two well-armed guards ran up the steps.

"Mortals," Justine whispered.

Weapons out, they started to mount the stairs, then ducked back. Juno quick-stepped down the stairs, muttering and tossing a small fireball hand to hand.

Finally, Justine and Harry made their way to the top of the stairs. Two guards were either inspecting the two that Teresa had thrown against the wall, or going through their pockets, checking wallets.

"*Niemand wird diese assholes verpassen,*" one said, chuckling as he stuffed some bills into his own pocket.

"Nice guys," Justine whispered. She ran to them, grabbed an ear of each and slammed their heads together. She handcuffed them, then stared hard into their eyes. They fell asleep. "You guys will be out for a while."

✳ ✳ ✳

Wary, Harry entered the magic room. Inside, he watched Condi drag a table from its place against the wall to just below the ball and funnel.

"What are you doing?"

"I break the ball and let the magic out."

"Will Teresa get her magic back?"

"Yes. We all get magic back. She is powerful, yes?"

"Yes. Very. But untrained."

"Enough to beat Juno?

"Yes."

Condi stepped on a folding chair then onto the table. She reached down for the chair, but it slipped out of her grip and slid noisily to the floor.

Harry picked up the chair and handed it to her. Teresa was worried. You didn't come back."

Chair in hand, Condi nodded at a small, mangled animal cage. "Juno wake too fast. He see me, make a joke. He know what I do so he make me a rabbit, put me in cage." Her body squirmed at the memory. "He said Dr. Reich done with me so I would stay in the cage until someone came to eat me. He say, too, he take Teresa magic. It make him the most powerful sorcerer."

"Not as long as Justine is around. Teresa is her best friend." He looked around the room. "Where is she, anyway?"

Harry headed for the door as Condi swung the folding chair at the globe. As if in self-defense, the globe pulsed a shockwave throughout the room that knocked them both to the floor.

Piled up against the wall, Harry shook his head then waited a minute for the dizziness to fade. "What the fuck happened? Condi, are you okay?"

"I think maybe so."

Harry, a bit unsteady, made it to the other side of the room and helped Condi stand. He pointed to the folding chair, now a tangled mess of steel tubes. "You hit it with the chair."

She nodded, flexing her fingers.

"Can't you do a spell or something?"

"I am not that kind of sorceress." He gave her an inquiring look. "I am what you call a shapeshifter. I become any animal."

He glanced at the mangled cage. "Like a rabbit?"

"Yes."

"No rabbit did that."

Condi pressed her fingers to her forehead. "He forget that in here I have all my ability. After he leave I became a tortoise. There was not enough room for that, so...."

"I don't know about rabbits or tortoises, but we could use a rhinoceros about now."

"I do not think that will help."

"Well, how about something little?" Harry drew his gun and shot the globe.

✳ ✳ ✳

"Justine," a familiar deep, scratchy voice said. "Feed on them if you like."

She spun around, instantly on full alert.

He stood a little back from the stairs. She knew it was him. The first time she'd seen him she'd thought a thousand year old vampire would somehow look like a thousand year old vampire—not like a stoutly built forty-year-old real estate salesman who'd made good. He was maybe six feet tall, with a square face surrounded by fashionably long, dirty-blond hair, a broad nose, and full lips that naturally settled into a frown when he was listening. Good-looking, but no model for a supernatural romance cover. A man you wouldn't look at twice on the street.

"I wondered where you were hiding." Justine wrinkled her nose at his moldy ancient dirt scent. He might not look like much, but he was not to be dismissed.

"You came for Teresa. Your loyalty is to be commended. But I am not finished with her, yet."

"Yes, you are."

Almost as fast as magic, even to her vampire eyes, Rubicon appeared beside her, grabbed her arm and dragged her past the stairs and through a short roofless passage into another circular area in the center of the round main tower—his office. He planted her in a desk chair. He strutted away, spun and favored her with a twisted, arrogant grin. He tapped his leg with her blade.

Justine allowed herself a slight touch of fear.

"Where is your Girl?"

"On her way. She wanted me to save you for her."

"Does she want me to beat her again?"

"You are quite resourceful. Come, work with me and you may survive to see the dark again."

"All we want are Teresa and Antonia. Then we will leave and you can return to your world domination plans."

"Vampires have been despised and hunted for a thousand years."

"Deservedly so."

"But we are stronger in every way. Sunlight has been our nemesis. Kept us in the dark." Rubicon paced the room, excited, hands waving, eyes wide. "Soon, my Sunwalkers will change that and mortals will be the hunted. They will serve us and we will own the Earth, and beyond. Space is too big for mortals. Soon we will own the universe."

"You will still need the mortals."

"For food and breeding."

"And you think you will rule it all?"

"Yes, yes! I have had a thousand years to think of this. Now is the Vampires' time."

"I'm a vampire, so it's my time, too."

Two fast steps and he grabbed her by the neck and held her two feet off the floor. "No! You have ruined too much for me. You killed that Sinakov."

"He was crazy."

He dropped her. "True. I would have had The Girl finish him."

"He was her master."

He spun and pointed a thick finger in her face. "But *I* was *his* master," He grabbed her neck again and pulled her close, their eyes inches apart. "As... I... am... yours...."

His eyes held hers, penetrating deep into her body, brain and soul. *He's glamouring me.* She tried to avert her gaze, but couldn't. She squirmed in his grip. It seemed like he was a snake in her body, slithering about, exploring.

Using all her will power, Justine managed a slow blink. Free for two seconds, she raised her arms and tried to break his steely grip. She reached for his eyes. He held her at arms length. His grin never faltered. She felt the tip of her blade against her body.

*Helpless.* That realization sent a thrill of despair through her body, ending in a burst of panic and surrender. Helpless. She'd always hated that feeling and made sure she'd never feel it again.

Her Kung Fu instructor once told her there was always something you can do if you feel helpless. "You are never helpless," he said. Those four words had served her well since then. This time they banished any thoughts of surrender. Able to look away from those terrible eyes for a moment, she looked down. Ah, the old classic.

In the half second between her decision to do it and doing it, Rubicon realized that like all men he had at least one vulnerability and began to close up.

A quarter second ahead, Justine grasped the arm that held her, then kicked Rubicon in the balls.

He partially blocked her kick, though it managed to distract him enough so she could twist away. A side kick knocked him on his ass. But he rose up and charged.

They fought then—full force, full speed. Justine ignored some cuts. Rubicon took some hard hits and his left arm didn't work quite right. The office fared much worse.

The fight lasted barely thirty seconds. A gunshot echoed through the connecting passage. A second later a pulse that made the air shiver passed through the room, knocking them both down.

Rubicon recovered first. He didn't pause to figure out what the pulse was; maybe he knew. He didn't hesitate to pick up Justine's blade and go after Justine. Standing over her, he raised the blade to take her head.

Justine saw the blade and knew she couldn't stop it. A millisecond of anger. Two of regret. Three of NO, she had moves.

Then it didn't matter.

Rubicon flew off her and slammed into the stone wall. She thought she heard his spine snap as his body hit the corner of a window.

"Never thought you would be *una damisela en apuros.*"

"That better not mean what I think it means." She took Teresa's hand. Justine tilted her head toward the twitching vampire. "I assume that means you have your magic back."

"Harry shot the magic ball."

"Ah… okay."

"Can I get you out of here now?"

"One more thing." Justine picked up her blade and turned to where Rubicon lay. He wasn't there. "Where is he?" She spun around, searched the floor, checked the still intact window. "Damn it, where…?"

"No, Teresa, you may not get her out now." The voice came from across the room by the entrance. Rubicon stood up, working his back and shoulders as he rose. Laughing, he said, "Unlike mortals Vampires heal quicker as they grow older."

Teresa and Justine, stared, stunned, frozen except for Teresa's lips and fingers.

"Something you two will not have to worry about."

Justine tensed and stepped forward, ready to defend Teresa and herself. Teresa grabbed her arm and pulled her back.

Blade raised, Rubicon rushed them. But he never reached his prey. Instead, he slammed into an invisible force field Teresa had formed over her and Justine. He bounced off and backpedaled until he backed into a desk.

"Clever, Teresa. However, you have a problem, do you not?"

Teresa whispered in Justine's ear. "I cannot keep the shield and move us at the same time. There will be a few seconds between."

Justine whispered, "Do it now. Right now."

Trusting her friend, Teresa made a chopping motion.

Justine felt a slight change in air pressure.

Rubicon threw a knife with a six inch blade at Teresa as he rushed them again.

Justine bumped Teresa sideways, taking the knife blade in her shoulder. With her machete she parried Rubicon's underhand strike. Continuing her circular motion she swung down, aiming for Rubicon's thick neck. A few inches from contact Rubicon slapped the blade aside, receiving a long, deep slice down his arm instead of a severed head.

Justine thought she had time for another strike. Before she could swing,  she and Teresa vanished.

# Chapter 41

Konrad, gun in easy reach, helped a very pregnant woman across the cavern. Hedy brought up the rear, gun out, fully alert. They had abandoned stealth mode at the cavern entrance.

A vamp who had watched too many bad movies advertized himself by yelling, "Halt! Halt!" before rushing at Hedy.

She wasn't having any of it. She shot him in the head from two meters away. He tumbled past her, skidding to a sprawling stop on the stone floor polished smooth from centuries of vampire, mortal and at one point animal feet.

Several women screamed, holding each other, wide-eyed with fear. One strode over and with a hateful sneer, muttered, *"Ya kalab,"* and spit on the dead-forever vamp.

Hedy figured that was Arabic for something not good. A quick scan revealed a few faces peering out from the passages, but no imminent threats. Konrad studied her from a passage entrance. He might have nodded, he might have tilted his head a centimeter and shrugged, he might have shown her a half smile. Either way she took it as *well done.* She looked back to Simone who nodded *good job.*

Calmly, Hedy got the women settled down and herded them toward the exit.

Cool on the outside, her insides quivered. She knew that if the vamp hadn't yelled before he rushed, she could not have stopped him and she'd be done. Surreptitious deep breaths helped her regain her equilibrium before she exited the cavern.

A short passage led to a wooden door held together by thick, black iron bands attached to massive iron hinges. Konrad waited, his hand on a heavy latch.

In several different languages he explained to the women they were entering a public space, the lobby for the museum. They were to wait by the main entrance while he prepared a bus for them. He apologized that he did not have warmer clothes for them. A few women translated for others.

Konrad lifted the latch and peered into the lobby. *"D'accord mesdames, suivez-moi."* He swung the five centimeter thick door open and led them through.

Bunched together, moving with quick little steps like a raft of baby ducks, they followed him into the U-shaped lobby, ten meters wide by thirty long with modern double doors to the outside.

Part of the original eight hundred year old stone construction, a small alcove served as souvenir shop and ticket booth. Two women and an older man huddled behind the counter staring dumbfounded at the procession of white-gowned pregnant women.

The man picked up his cell phone.

*"Nein!"* Konrad pointed a finger at him. *"Nein!"*

The man put the phone down.

*"Mesdames, attendez ici."* Konrad stalked around the women. He handed Hedy his gun. "Shoot anybody you don't know."

"You might need that weapon."

"You might need it more."

"Papa, let me go. It's freaking daylight. That's not good for your complexion."

"I have thick skin. Beside, is cloudy."

From the door Hedy watched him descend the ancient, well-worn steps—four flights with landings, leading to a narrow parking lot. At the bottom a stone path led to a five meter diameter stone pad surrounded by a heavy stone wall a meter and a half high with one narrow gap serving as entrance and exit. The view from the wall looked out over the broad valley below.

Konrad didn't bother with greetings for the bus driver who was checking the tires of the tourist bus. Konrad held his long-haired, long-bearded head and hard glamoured him.

Hedy swore out loud, *"Oh Scheiße,"* when the early sun broke through the clouds.

Konrad felt it, too. He squinted at the sudden light and instinctively hunched his shoulders against the coming heat. He knew he had about ten minutes before sunlight, the vampires' natural enemy, brought on the first debilitating pain. Fifteen minutes and he might survive the burns. Twenty minutes brought smoke and a painful final death.

"Be ready," Konrad said to the driver, then raced up the steps to join Hedy.

"Papa, I can take them. You don't have to go out there."

"I helped make this place what it is. People were tortured here, experimented on. I heard about them, and to my shame I did nothing. I cannot let these women stay to be experiments. I did nothing before, now I can. *Verstehst du?*"

"I understand. Go. I'll bring up the rear."

Konrad held open the door for the women. It was a chilly morning and they wore only hospital gowns. "*Je suis désolé, Mesdames.* It is cold, but the bus will be warm."

Chattering in several languages, complaining, crying, helping, they shuffled through the entrance and started down the steps. Hedy followed, gun out and alert.

"Halt!"

Hedy spun to see two guards bang out of the door—a mortal and a vampire. The vamp, in his forties with a bit of a belly, stopped and looked up at the patchy blue sky. The mortal, six feet tall and well built, weapon up, ran right out toward her. "Stop, you must not take those women."

Hedy hesitated. He was a mortal; if she shot him there'd be no waking up a vamp.

He fired at her. The bullet grazed her arm.

She shot him. A few of the women yelped as he skidded to a stop.

A second later, a shout from the door demanded her attention. The vamp guard held up his blade and rushed at Hedy.

When Hedy saw the first guard, a mortal, die she had a flash of regret. He was a mortal trying to kill her and return the women to their experimental captivity. Nevertheless, she didn't really want to kill him. The second she heard the vampire's shout, she knew she was going to die. She accepted it, as long as the women were safe. That desire must have enhanced her reflexes. She shot the vamp in the forehead.

Not quite fully dead, he continued running, knocking her aside as he tumbled past her and down the steps.

Hedy barely glanced back. Ready to defend the women's freedom she strode to the middle of the terrace and stood like an avenging angel, daring anyone, alive or dead, to confront her.

The women bunched up, cringing away from the twitching vamp. Two of them broke ranks and approached the vamp.

"*Cochon!*" One spat at him and followed up with a kick.

"*Connard!*" The second spat and kicked. "*C'est bien, tu es mort pour toujours.*"

Arm in arm they joined the others who murmured agreement.

Hedy turned to watch them. A slight scuffing sound warned her too late. The Girl slammed into her.

# Chapter 42

Gasqu led Teresa, Justine, Simone and a very reluctant Gerry down a darker passage with several offshoot fissures. He stopped at one barely wide enough to walk through. They all faced away from the distinctive odor of decay and death.

Gasqu held his hands, palms down, in front of him and rolled them down as if ready to dig.

Simone said, "That is the cemetery, *oui?*"

Justine patted Gerry's back. "Is that where you belong, Gerry? The cemetery?"

Gerry tried to back away, but Justine stood immovable behind him. "*Nein!* She run in and fall down by herself. Not me."

Simone asked Gasqu, "Where is Antonia?"

Gasqu grinned and pointed to a wider fissure two meters behind them. He slipped past them, giving Gerry a "fuck you" grin, and led the others a few meters into the fissure before turning into a three by four meter cubicle. The room had a basic table and chairs and a makeshift kitchen. A small rough-cut doorway opened to one side. It smelled of food and people.

Gasqu turned to Simone, held up four fingers and tapped his chin, pointed at her then pointed into the room.

"Speak?" she asked.

Gasqu nodded.

*"Hallo, est quelqu'un ici?"*

A young woman's face peeked out the door. "Gasqu? Who are...? *"Mamá, ¿qué haces aquí?"* Antonia asked with surprise and skepticism.

"I have come to rescue you, of course."

Antonia rushed into her mother's arms.

Teresa hugged her daughter tight. She had dreamed that her daughter's body might have the coolness of a vampire, but it was warm, alive and Teresa's chest expanded with relief. Tears wet her cheeks. A deep breath helped her keep herself together.

"How did you get here? When? How did you get in?"

"They did not tell you?"

"What?"

"I have been held here for weeks. They have been taking my power to create spawn like they did to you to make their sun walking vamps."

"Oh my God, Mama." Hand over her mouth, Antonia jerked her head around, scanning the others. Could she trust them?

Teresa said, "You can trust them, except for Gerry there."

"Gerry?" Antonia strode to Gerry, who cringed at the hate on her face, and slapped him.

The others started at the unexpected violence.

"Henri!" Antonia yelled.

"I know he deserves that and more," Teresa said, "but...?"

"Antonia?"

Everybody turned to look at the young, handsome man with light brown skin standing in the open doorway to another part of the living quarters.

"Gerry," Antonia spat out, nodding at the vamp holding his clipboard like a shield.

Henri's face twisted with disgust. Without a word he drew a long blade from the sheath on his belt, rushed at Gerry and stabbed him low, then yanked the blade up, eviscerating him.

Gerry screamed.

Holding his blade horizontally, Henri pressed it to Gerry's neck.

*"Attendez!"* Instinctively, Simone and Teresa moved to pull Henri back.

*"Violeur!"* Stepping back, Henri spit on the sobbing Gerry who had dropped to his knees, holding in his guts.

Antonia told them, "He raped several of the women. One became our friend. She killed herself."

Still holding his blade, Henri broke free and with one anger fueled strike removed Gerry's head. He kicked the corpse to the floor and stood over it, his body quivering. If Henri had been a mortal he'd have been breathing deeply while composing himself, but as a vamp he vibrated, shoulders hunched, head bowed until Antonia hugged him, speaking low in his ear.

"Antonia," Teresa said. *"¿Qué demonios?"*

"Henri was a medic in Vietnam. He took care of some of the women here when they were first pregnant and after the babies were born. Henri cared about the women Gerry raped."

※ ※ ※

Henri's platoon heard the shooting and smelled the smoke before they saw the village. On full alert they rounded the corner of a narrow dirt road. Three huts were burning as the Viet Cong fired into each hut then set them on fire.

The platoon went in hard after the ten enemy soldiers. The enemy fought back, setting fires as they retreated. Two of the platoon were wounded, one killed. Henri ran into the burning village to tend his wounded men and the villagers. From his vantage point he noticed a hut slightly away from the rest. He saw a Viet Cong soldier enter the hut shooting, but not came out.

When the shooting stopped and he'd done what he could for the injured he approached the separate hut on full alert.

"No! No! You no go in," a man shouted. "No go. *Rất nguy hiểm cho con người.*"

The platoon's translator approached the shouting man. "What's he saying?" Henri asked.

Looking slightly bewildered, the translator said, "He says that hut is not safe for humans."

"What? Why?"

The two men talked quickly. Henri heard a child cry. He entered the hut.

Inside the dark hut he found the soldier on the dirt floor covered with blood, his neck a bloody mess. On a bare mattress laid over straw was girl nine or ten years old. She, too, was covered with blood from a bullet wound in her right side. Beside her a woman around fifty held a bloody rag against the wound.

With surprisingly little accent she said, "Please. You must help her. She too young to change."

Henri thought that was an odd thing to say, but he sedated her and set to work. Fifteen minutes later the translator said from the door. "Fortin, we pull out in ten minutes. All okay?"

"Yeah. Ten minutes."

The translator left and within minutes the shooting started up again.

An enemy soldier appeared in the doorway as Henri clipped the last stitch. He laughed and shot Henri.

In an instant the woman grabbed the shooter by his shirt and threw him to the ground. With blurred vision Henri saw the woman rip the soldier's neck open and with a weirdly distorted jaw capture the spurting blood. The last thing he saw was the old woman's face looking down on him.

"You good man," she said. "No need to die."

He stayed with the woman for several months, learning how to be a vampire and helping the locals, especially the children and mothers. Eventually he moved on, traveling to other villages helping children and mothers, hiding from the Viet Cong and his own people. In Ho Chi Mihn City he was recruited to return to Switzerland where he was born and monitor at-risk pregnant women.

✷ ✷ ✷

Teresa nodded, trading a quick glance with Simone who shrugged back. "So who is this Henri to you?"

Antonia's face took on that raised eyebrow *oh-now-we're-getting-to-that-question* look. She took Henri's arm and faced her mother. "He is my boyfriend. His name is Henri Fortin." Teresa glanced again at Simone. Henri had been the name of Simone's long lost brother, also a vampire. Justine had ended him for good reason. Simone was okay with it, but still, he had been her brother.

Simone acknowledged the reason for Teresa's look with a raised eyebrow and the slightest of shrugs. Both of them looked to Antonia for more.

"Mama, after my son was born I was very afraid and confused, but I felt good, physically. But soon, I didn't. I guess I have some magic in me. It was used up and I could barely move. Henri helped me and we fell in love."

The older women looked at Henri.

"*C'est vrai,*" Henri said. The way he looked at Antonia confirmed it. "She is a very strong woman, kind, and beautiful. How could I not *tomber amoureux d'elle?*"

Teresa opened her mouth, but no words came out. Simone lightly gripped her arm for support.

Before Teresa could find her words a young voice said, "Mama?"

All eyes turned to a beautiful boy, apparently about five or six years old, who was studying the headless body, then the new people.

"Oh." Antonia winced, then squared her shoulders. "Mama, this is Carlos, your grandson."

Shocked into silence again, Teresa looked from the boy to Antonia to Henri.

Simone broke the awkward silence. "Is he one of Rubicon's new vampires?"

Antonia stood behind Carlos, protective hands on his shoulders. "Yes."

"Does Rubicon know he is here with you?"

Antonia's eyes connected with Henri as she shook her head and held Carlos a little tighter. "No. I'm supposed to be dead."

Teresa regained her voice. "You mean… a vamp dead or really dead?"

Henri put a protective arm around Antonia's shoulders.

"Real dead, mama."

Simone said with eyebrows raised in question and a quizzical tone, "Yet you are not really dead."

*"No, muchas gracias Henri."*

✳ ✳ ✳

A week after her baby was born Antonia lay on her bed barely able to move. After the birth she had been tired, but exhilarated. They kept her alone in a small, but well-equipped room where her and the baby's vitals were checked often. But her strength waned and soon she was unable to stand without help.

She knew that a mortal and vampire had never conceived a baby before, so he was special, but she had no idea of Rubicon's ultimate goal. Though he was conceived by rape, and the father was dead for real, he was her baby. Every time they took the baby away to be tested she worried they wouldn't return him.

She had heard Dr. Reich talking to Rubicon. "I think for now is best to keep the mother with the baby. If all goes well for one month, then…."

"Yes, yes. If she has no more magic then we do not need her. I have heard news. New magic will arrive soon."

"Good. I will be ready."

Antonia understood what they meant, but as they continued to draw blood she was soon powerless to do anything but tell Henri who was kind to her. The touch of his hand on her face, or the whisper of his lips were enough to energize her for a short period before fatigue held her down.

A few days later a nurse known for her unforgiving attitude toward the women came to take Antonia's baby. "Give the baby American whore," she said with a thick Eastern European accent. "You finished now. No good mother."

"No!" Antonia cried out, when the nurse attempted to tear the baby out of her arms. Without thinking she thrust her hand out, palm toward the woman and ordered, "Go away!"

Feet off the ground, the nurse flew backwards, stopped by a stone wall. Without a sound she slid to the rough floor, leaving a thin trail of blood on the wall.

"Antonia," Henri said, rushing to her bedside. "How did you do that?"

"I… I don't know. She wanted to take my baby away and I was scared and mad and…."

"Little bitch," Gerry said from the door, radio already at hand. "You murder her. Finally, you die." His lips twisted into a malicious grin. "We take you baby first."

"It was an accident," Henri said.

"No, murder. I see. Guards come, you die," he said with satisfaction.

Henri stood by the bed so tense he vibrated. He looked at Antonia and the baby she held so tight. Their eyes met. "I love you." Antonia nodded.

Henri strode around the bed to Gerry. "You will still lie?"

Gerry grinned.

"Look, the guards."

Gerry turned his head.

Henri punched his face with all his vampire strength.

Still clutching his clipboard, Gerry crumpled like a half-full sack of potatoes.

"Come," Henri said. "He was right, you must die now." He took the baby and put out a hand to Antonia. "Come."

"I can't. I'm too weak."

"You can. You did that to her. You can walk. You must."

And she could. Slow at first then faster as the guard's shouts reverberated through caves. "Where… are we… going?" she asked, her breath labored.

They ducked into a narrow opening whose walls came together a few feet above their heads.

Twenty meters in Henri stopped and gripped Antonia by the shoulders. "Ahead is a deep crevasse. It is where they dispose of the bodies.

You have to scream as if you fell in. Now, Antonia now."

Antonia looked toward the end. She tried to jerk away and run. "Bodies? In there?"

"Antonia, scream now." He shook her. "Scream! Scream!"

She sucked in a deep breath and screamed a scream full of terror, until Henri clamped a hand across her mouth.

"Good. Come." He dragged her back to the entrance and farther down to an old wooden door in the rock. He yanked it open. "Go in as far back as you can go. Wait. I will come for you when I can. I love you. Go in now." He handed her a flashlight and closed the door. Then he ran back into the narrow passage to the crevasse edge.

The smell was foul, full of rot and decay and death. Even consciously damping his enhanced sense of smell did not lessen the odor. A minute later two guards sidled down to him.

"Where is she?" one said, holding his nose.

Henri pointed down. "I was chasing her. She ran right over."

In the dim depth were bones and several newer bodies in white medical gowns. "The baby, too?"

"Yes. A pity."

"Huh. Maybe."

"Let us leave here, *avant de vomir.*"

"Henri saved me and Carlos. We have been hiding here in his rooms ever since, hoping to escape."

"*Gracias,* Henri."

"Escape to where?" Simone wanted to know.

Before she could answer a shock wave passed over them all, rattling dishes and knocking over bottles.

Henri, Antonia and Carlos fell to their knees. Simone steadied herself against the table, while Teresa held on to her. Gasqu rolled with it.

"*Ca c'était quoi?*"

"*Magia,*" Teresa said, laughing with short, quick breaths. "Magic. Condi did it."

Both witches froze, feeling something the others could not.

Teresa announced, "Justine needs help. Simone, I'll get her. We need to go. We all need to *vamonos.*" She stepped apart from them, closed her eyes, moved her hands, and vanished.

# Chapter 43

The big globe cracked outward from the bullet hole, slowly at first, then faster until fine cracks covered the whole ball. The sphere seemed to shrink as if taking a breath.

Condi, knowing what might happen, yanked Harry down to hide under the table.

"What are you do…?"

The globe exploded with a great whoosh and the pattering of thousands of tiny particles hitting the walls, ceiling and floor. A pulse of power, warm and chill simultaneously, flowed around and through them, jiggling their insides before flowing out thorough the walls.

For a moment sparks swirled around Harry's palms. He felt a warmth grow inside him. He thought of a fireball he'd seen Teresa make, and one appeared in his hand. He jerked his hand back, thinking he'd be burned, but it stayed with him, cool on his palm.

The fire had his full attention. He couldn't believe he had magic. Condi moved. He caught her watching him with a wry little smile.

"You feel the power," she said.

Harry nodded.

"I am sorry, it will not last."

Even as she spoke the fireball dimmed and puffed out. The magical warmth within him that made his heart race and fingers tingle leeched away, leaving him with a sense of loss. "Is that how you feel all the time?"

"Sometime, when all is well, but usually, no."

"I suppose I'll miss that feeling the rest of my life."

"Maybe. You are with the vampire, yes? Teresa's friend?"

Harry nodded with a smile.

Condi touched his arm. "I think you will make your own magic. We must go."

Wary, they exited the "Magic Room" and made their way to the stairs.

Condi held Harry back. "Harry, there was another with us. A boy,

Pauly. He is very weak. They were going to kill him. We have to get him away."

"Why kill him? Never mind. Where is he?"

Condi pointed down the steps. She led him to Reich's office without interference and slipped inside.

Harry looked into the space and saw Pauly hunched in the corner, legs drawn up and head bowed on his knees.

"Pauly, it is Condi. We have come for you."

The boy slowly raised his head, his drawn, pale face trying for a smile.

The door banged open. Dr. Reich, 50, thin, his black hair randomly poking out like a demented scientist from an old horror movie, white lab coat trailing, dashed to his desk. He lifted a dark green messenger bag from a drawer and began to stuff it with papers and files. A single paper escaped, floating toward the edge. Reich grabbed for it and froze. He drew a well-used Luger from a drawer.

*"Was zum Teufel willst du hier?"*

Harry and Condi held still, not understanding German, but with a good idea what Reich said.

"Ach, Condi," he said in broken English while aiming the Luger at her. *"Ja,* I know what you do here, you escape. Is too bad, *ja?* I was not finished with you. But with this chaos brought by intruders…." He swung his aim between them, "I think you must be eliminated." Harry stepped sideways to shield Condi. "And you, also, intruder."

"Why?" Harry asked. He felt something happening behind his back. Condi touched him just below his neck, then he felt the touch run down his spine and taper off. "Your experiments are finished here. What good will killing us do?"

"Ha. Dead people do not speak."

Harry felt something brush his ankle. He glanced down and jumped back against a file cabinet. A long, thick, black snake slithered between his legs and darted under the desk.

As he jumped Harry swung his right arm back as if to steady himself. As he reached behind his back, he lifted his pistol from his belt. Before he could decide to shoot Reich, the scientist let out a screech. Startled, Harry reflexively pulled the trigger. He yelped as his own bullet grazed his hip.

Panicked, trying to lift both feet off the floor at the same time while shooting at the floor two, three, four times, Reich shrieked, "Hexenschlampe! Hexenschlampe! Hexenschlampe!"

Harry took the opportunity to shoot at the dancing doctor, but the big snake striking at the scientist from under the desk distracted him, so he only hit Reich's upper arm.

Dr. Reich had had enough. He thrust a last handful of files into his bag and ran limping out the door.

Harry sagged against the file cabinet while watching with great fascination and a bit of ewww-I-don't-want-to-see-this as the snake coiled up and grew, not always clearly, into Condi.

Back in her human form, Condi shook herself then leaned against the other file cabinet, breathing heavily.

"That was creepy, scary and fascinating at the same time," Harry said. He noticed blood on her leg. "Did he hit you?"

"Just my tail. Be right." She took deep breaths. "To change so fast is very hard."

"And weird. Did you bite him?"

"Yes. Very satisfying."

"He gonna die?"

"Maybe. As Black Mamba I have poison, but it not strong as real one. He be sick some."

A weak voice said, "Condi?"

"Aye, Pauly, I am here. Come." Condi attempted to reach into the corner space. They held hands, but Condi couldn't pull him out.

"Let me." Harry gently pulled Condi aside.

"You are hurt."

"We could go away until I am healed up. Come back next week."

"You very funny for white policeman."

"Not all white cops are mean, nasty, racist, trigger-happy, potbellied men."

Harry winced as he stretched his wounds, but had the emaciated boy out in seconds. Gaunt, pale, barely able to stand, the sight of the boy shocked Harry. Condi knelt and held Pauly reassuring him, and Harry wanted to do that, too.

"Christ, what'd they do to the kid?"

"They try to take his magic."

In a squeaky British voice, Pauly said, "They did not get my power, Condi, like you said."

"I know, honey, but they want to kill you, so we rescue you."

Swaying on his feet, Pauly said, "Thank you and Teresa. Is she okay?"

"I hope so."

# Chapter 44

Teresa and Justine appeared in the same spot Teresa had vanished from. Startled, Henri and Simone had weapons out before they recognized them.

"Mama!" Antonia nearly knocked her over. They hugged tight until Antonia said, "Auntie Justine!"

While they hugged, Justine surveyed the group.

Simone stood a bit apart, hand on the hilt of her blade, watching them all. Justine caught her eye. Their quirked smiles and barely-there nods said all they needed.

Justine had expected to feel the coolness of her honorary niece's body right away. Already amazed to find her alive, to find her still mortal and warm was an astonishment. For a moment Justine felt a warm happy constriction in her chest.

Even more of a surprise was Henri—Black, handsome, a curved scar on one cheek, twenty-something when changed. The way he looked at Antonia and the way she looked back at him told her all she needed to know about him.

"Mama, I am still secret?" the young boy asked.

Topping off the surprises was Carlos, a good looking kid who looked about five with café-o-lait skin, a hairless head and big dark eyes.

Antonia let go of Justine and stood beside the boy, hand on his shoulder. "Aunt Justine, this is Carlos, my son."

That, Justine did not see coming at all. "From Rubicon's yacht?"

"Yes."

"That was not so long ago."

"I know. They grow fast."

"They being… ?"

Simone never took her eyes off Carlos. *Vampires du soleil.* Sun vamps."

"I see. I have questions."

Henri moved beside Antonia. "And this is my boyfriend, Henri."

"Hi, Henri. Now I have more questions."

"Later," Simone said. "We have to get these people out of here."

"Right. I haven't a clue where we are," Justine said. "Can someone get us back to the back door?"

Teresa said, "Antonia, are you coming with us?"

"*Por supuesto*, Mama. We were planning to escape ourselves. Henri has a farmhouse we can go to."

Henri said in halting English with a thick German accent. "I say maybe not go, ah, *jetzt*. I must...."

"Henri, *parlez-vous français?*"

"*Oui. Oui.*"

Simone said. "*Dîtes-moi.*"

They spoke quickly for a minute. Simone ended with, "*Non nécessaire, les femmes ont disparu.*"

Henri's eyes grew wide. "*C'est vrai?*" He glanced at each of them in turn, ending with Antonia.

"He wanted to check on the other women. I told him it was not necessary because they have gone."

"Do we know what's happened with Hedy and Konrad?" Justine asked.

"No," Simone admitted. "I will look for them. You take everyone else out the back exit. Gasqu can guide you." She held Teresa's arms. "I am glad you are not dead, Teresa. I missed you."

Teresa, a head taller than Simone, smiled down with affection at the vampire who had, surprisingly, become a good friend. "Me too."

Justine caught Simone's arm as she made her way to the door. "Where's The Girl?"

Simone's lips twisted in a tight grimace. "*En effet.* I will *fait attention.*" Simone squeezed her partner's arm. "You too, *chère.*"

# Chapter 45

Hedy hit the stone floor rolling. She knew instantly who had hit her: The Girl, small but powerful. Hedy knew the diminutive vampire would win any one-on-one fight, unless Hedy had an advantage, like a gun. Unfortunately the collision had knocked the gun out of her hand and sent it spinning to the top of the steps. She rolled to her feet and faced The Girl from two meters away.

"I wondered when you would get here," Hedy said with false bravado.

"You wish to give me your blood?" The Girl took one step closer.

Hedy had a three inch pocket knife in her pocket. Not much, but maybe she could do a little damage. The gun would be more helpful if she could get to where it had landed, inches from the first step down.

"We already killed Rubicon. You're next."

Hedy took one step back, then a few nervous steps right, then three left, slowly making her way toward the gun.

The Girl's mouth twisted in a combined smirk and sneer. "He is not dead. He is my master, I would know." She managed a small grin of anticipation. She knew what Hedy was planning and wanted to wait until the last moment to dash Hedy's hope of surviving.

"Maybe he's dead. Maybe he isn't. But his fantasy of mutant vampires taking over the world is."

"Maybe it is, maybe it isn't. I don't care. I would rather serve him myself. Just me. No other."

Only five feet away from the weapon, Hedy could dive for it, grab it and shoot The Girl while she was distracted by her fantasy of servitude. Hedy lunged for the weapon as a scream from the bus distracted The Girl for a second.

Hedy snatched the gun. She swung it up and pulled the trigger, but The Girl rushed her just in time to slap the gun away, the bullet missing her by inches.

In a fit of pique she grasped Hedy's arm and yanked her up, then threw her twenty feet to land in a heap in the middle of the stone entrance area. Like a cat playing with a mouse, she picked Hedy up by a leg and dropped her, rolled her over with a kick, swung her around and sent her sliding across the paving.

"Enough," The Girl finally said. She straddled Hedy and held her head tightly to the left. Her jaw unhinged, revealing two fangs.

Hedy watched The Girl lower her head toward her neck. She attempted one last push—after all The Girl barely weighed a hundred pounds. As a nurse she had had to wrestle three or four hundred pound patients.

But The Girl held firm. Hedy kept fighting, to no avail. Those fangs inexorably descended until with an inhuman grunt they slashed her neck.

*What a shitty way to die,* Hedy thought.

Then, with an angry growl, the fangs lifted away along with the weight. She opened her eyes in time to watch Konrad lift The Girl over his head and throw her fifty feet over the low stone wall.

He knelt and studied Hedy's neck. In English, he said, "I think you be okay. I think is not serious."

Hedy gave him an are-you-serious-it's-not-serious? look.

Shrug. "Maybe little serious." He placed her hand over the wound. "Come. We have to go." He scooped her up in his arms and raced down the steps to the bus. As she entered the bus she looked back. On the wall encircling the lower level, The Girl lay splayed out on her back, her body bent over both sides of the wall in a very unhuman way. Dark liquid dripped from her head. She was bathed in full sunlight.

Feeling no pity for The Girl, Hedy sat in the first seat and closed her eyes as the bus started to move. Using the bus's first aid kit, Konrad cleaned and bandaged her neck. "Look bad, but not bad as it look."

She glanced at the bloody gauze in his hand. "*Danke,* Konrad. If you need to feed I have more."

Before he could answer, a strangled cry came from the back of the bus.

Hedy closed her eyes and let her head fall back. "I know that scream." She stood up too quickly. Konrad steadied her as she took a deep breath. "I'm beginning to hurt, but baby calls."

An extremely pregnant young woman slumped on the bench seat at the back of the bus, helped by two others. Strands of raven hair stuck to her sweat soaked brow.

Wincing, Hedy knelt before the woman. In a calming nurse's voice, she said, "I'm a nurse. I haven't birthed many babies, but I have an idea how it works."

She lifted the woman's shift to inspect the situation while another woman translated her words into Italian.

Over her shoulder she shouted to Konrad, who stood two feet behind her, "Papa, are there any gloves in the first aid kit?"

Konrad seemed to vanish, appear at the front of the bus and reappear behind Hedy in less than five seconds. He dropped the latex gloves into her lap.

"About time. You getting slow in your old age? This kid is coming out right now."

Gloves on, world dominating vampires, her latest aches and pains and friends she had no idea what happened to forgotten, Hedy focused on the dark-haired baby emerging from its laboring mother.

"Push."

Screaming, the woman pushed and a minute later Hedy held a wailing baby girl. Hedy did a quick examination, which indicated the girl was healthy. Too healthy. She had a strong, but slow heartbeat. Her eyes were dark and deep and tracked Hedy's every movement. Her grip was purposeful and strong. There were long pauses between breaths though the baby did not seem to be in any distress.

Hedy sat back on her heels. "Well, shit." The baby she held in her arms was one of Rubicon's experimental babies. A freaking Sunvamp.

She considered throwing the newborn girl out the window. Vampires were bad enough, but a Sunvamp meant to turn the world into a vampire buffet with mortals the main course? Then she looked at the woman, sweaty and exhausted, probably raped or forcibly inseminated, gazing at her baby like any new mother.

"*Sta bene?*"

Hedy needed no translation. "Yes, she is healthy. Different, but healthy." She wrapped the baby in a towel and some cloth torn from the women's shifts then handed her to the new mother.

"*Grazie. Grazie.*" The mother and a few others cooed over the newborn as if she wasn't…whatever she was.

Konrad stood close behind Hedy. She leaned back against his legs and breathed out a long sigh. "You did good Hedy." He gently swept her hair back.

Hedy liked the way it felt. For a brief moment she forgot he was her stepfather and wondered what it would feel like if he touched other places. It had been a long time since anybody had touched her. Christ, what would her mother think about that?

Back to reality with a quick painful shake of her head, she said, "Do you think the others are alive, or safe? Did they really find Teresa's daughter? They should know about this infant girl."

Watching the new mother and baby, Konrad said, "They are maybe at the hotel, waiting for us."

Hedy didn't believe that for a second. Before she could come up with some slightly more positive scenario her head spun and her eyes shut and she fell back against her stepfather's legs.

# Chapter 46

Big blade in hand, all senses on high alert, Simone stalked through the maze of the secret laboratory. As she passed a lab area she heard heavy breathing. Inside two mortal men, both on the far side of middle age, stared at her from a far corner. She stared back, wondering if she should kill them just for participating in Rubicon's monstrous experiment.

The younger of the two thought it was safe to vent at her.

"You. You damn vampire bitch are the one who ruined our mission to create a new life form. We were almost there. Three births, each lasting longer than the one before. Now you've ruined it, and our chance for a million Euro bonus. Juno should do his magic thing and burn you. Burn half these useless vamps, for all I care." He grabbed a big knife. "If you didn't have that blade I'd cut your pretty head off."

He let his anger overrule any common sense he might have had and charged Simone. He might have had a chance, because Simone was so shocked that he attacked, she hesitated. Even so it was all over in seconds. She easily blocked his strike, took the knife and sent him rolling five meters down the hall. Making sure he saw her blade come down, she smacked his head with the flat.

To the older man, who seemed amused by this, she said, "Take your friend *et partez*. The experiment *est fini*."

"*Il n'est pas mon ami.*"

Simone cocked her head, raised an eyebrow, smacked the guy's head again, and strode out, wondering for the thousandth time about the stupidity and callousness of people, both mortal and vampire.

As she crossed the cavern, a mortal guard appeared at a tunnel entrance. He started to approach Simone, but stopped when he met her steady warning glare. She did not stop or slow down, just kept her eyes on him. He had the good sense not to move.

Simone strode through the empty entrance hall and banged out of the exit. Standing in the middle of the entrance yard, she cast her senses out. No motion, no voices. Blood scent. She studied the blood. Hedy. *Merde.*

She heard sounds of a vehicle leaving. From the top of the stairs she saw a small van moving fast down the dirt road. Moving to her right she scanned for a bus that would hold a load of scared and abused women. She saw no other vehicles. She could only hope Konrad and Hedy and the women made it out. Obviously, they had not gotten away unscathed.

She walked around the perimeter scanning the stone steps for… something. Nothing. Her skin began to heat in the thin sunlight so she returned to the cool museum interior.

Inside, she heard a familiar voice from long ago echo around the entrance hall. "For a mortal you have caused me too much trouble, Harry. I do not need more trouble, only more blood."

# Chapter 47

Harry, Condi and Pauly had barely made it out of the corridor on their way to the back door passage when a figure at the bottom of the steps stopped them.

Rubicon said, "Condi, Dr. Reich will be disappointed if you leave us. He is not quite done with you."

The three attempted to run around Rubicon, but he was far too quick. He grabbed Harry by the scruff of his neck and held him a foot off the ground with no visible effort. For the moment, he ignored Pauly.

Condi stiffened, face set.

"Condi, don't try to change into a lion or a snake or a bug." He slapped her with a thick hand, driving her to the floor. "I said Reich was not done with you. You stay." He picked up Pauly by one wrist and dangled him at arm's length, inspecting him like a little half-dead animal. "You we are done with, Pauly. You had promise, but you failed, so…." He flicked Pauly away like a scrap of litter.

The boy slid against a stone wall and lay still.

"Pauly!" Condi started to stand. Rubicon pinned her to the floor with a foot on her leg.

"Son of a bitch." Harry managed to draw out his gun.

"Oh, Harry," the vampire said as if disappointed with a child. He snatched the gun from Harry's hand and held it to his head. Then he grinned and tossed the gun away. "You sunk my favorite yacht. That deserves more than a quick bullet in the head, don't you think?"

Harry breathed with difficulty, but managed to croak out, "Yes. I deserve a medal."

"Ha. You always were a cheeky one. I wonder if you will be so cheeky with no blood."

"Your Girl tried for my blood. She didn't like it."

"I do not think so. That Girl likes all blood."

"Where is she?" Harry carried a small folding knife. He reached it, but it took two hands to open. He would have to open it right in front of the old vamp. "I think we killed her earlier."

"She is here, sucking the blood from your mortal friends while your vampire friends watch."

"You wish. I bet…." Harry started, his eyes grew wide as he managed a glimpse to his left behind the old vamp. "Oh shit!"

Rubicon glanced behind his shoulder, his eyes off of Harry's hands for two seconds. A thousand years old and he still fell for that old trick. Pocket knife open, Harry realized the arm that held him a foot away from the vamp's body was the only bit of Rubicon available to stab. And he'd better do it, right now.

Holding the knife in his fist, thumb along the blade, Harry swung the knife up. He had a flash of satisfaction when the blade jammed into Rubicon's arm.

Rubicon cried out, more from surprise than pain. He threw Harry down, grabbed his arm, snatched the knife out and slashed Harry's chest, his strength enough to cut through jacket and shirt and deep into flesh.

With one quick snap he broke Harry's arm and threw him to the stone floor. "For a mortal you have caused me too much trouble, Harry. I do not need more trouble, only more blood."

Rubicon pulled Harry up by his unbroken arm and bent his head sideways, exposing his neck.

That's as far as he got.

Simone slammed into him, knocking him down. Harry slid across the floor, ending in an unmoving lump.

Blade at the ready, eyes on Rubicon who knelt calmly watching, Simone squatted by Harry.

"Harry, you alive?"

"More or less." He roused himself. "Hurts."

Simone lifted him to his feet and steadied him. She turned him so she could see Rubicon behind Harry. Rubicon did not seem inclined to move.

"Look at me, Harry." Quickly, staring deep into his eyes, she did a quick pain glamour. Behind her, a tiny scrape on stone warned her. She spun 180 degrees to put her back to Harry and block Rubicon's blade from taking off his head. "Run, Harry. You know where to go."

Rubicon backed off. "Simone Gireaux, why am I not surprised you are here? You are friends with the witch are you not?"

"Harry, *vite.*"

"No Simone," Rubicon said, his blazing eyes on Harry. "He cannot go. He owes me his head."

Condi ran to Harry and quickly led him away.

"No. He is mine." Rubicon went after Harry.

Simone forced him to fight her.

Though larger, stronger and more experienced, Rubicon needed all of it to hold off Simone. She was a survivor. From day one of being accidentally changed she had had to survive on her own. She'd dealt with vampires of all types, using her relatively small stature, quickness and brains to survive them all.

She darted in, feinted, ducked and dodged, drawing Rubicon's attention away from Harry, Condi and Pauly. Barely dodging a strike that left a six inch slash across her ribs, she lost sight of them. They were there, then five seconds later, they were gone.

She had to assume they'd escaped down the passage.

# Chapter 48

Gasqu led Teresa, Antonia and the rest down the passages toward the cavern.

"Justine," Teresa whispered in Justine's ear, forgetting that most everyone was a vamp and could easily hear her words. "Simone is fighting ahead. Might need your help."

"Yeah, I get that. Take everyone down that passage. Keep going, it comes out in a ravine, at the bottom is a van. Wait there. Gasqu can show you. Go. Go."

Without waiting to see if they obeyed her, Justine ran to join Simone. Simone and Rubicon fought in the center of the cavern. Simone had cuts on her ribs and leg. She'd never admit it, but she needed help.

Cavern in sight, Justine rushed in. She had a gun and her blade. She raised the gun with the intention of shooting Rubicon in the head immediately.

Rubicon hadn't survived as long as he had by luck alone. With his experience he could anticipate an opponent's actions. "Justine, I knew you would turn up." In the second before she could aim at him he rushed her and smacked the weapon from her hand. "You were trying to cheat. Now we are on even ground."

He swung at her. Justine, after years as a high end real estate broker, could anticipate, too. Dropping down, she swung and managed a slice to his leg. Even on a mortal, the cut would have been minor.

But Rubicon was not accustomed to wounds. He hesitated, and slowly backed up as she pressed her attack and as Simone joined her.

# Chapter 49

Gasqu led Teresa, Antonia, Henri and Carlos along the edge of the open space and down the back door passage. Just out of sight of the cavern Teresa looked back, thinking she should help her two friends. Instead she saw a wave of magic, a visible shimmer, move down the passage. It bumped into Teresa, knocking her back, and stopped.

Teresa placed a cautious hand on the barrier, expecting to be stopped. Her hand passed through.

From beyond the barrier, Antonia came over and did the same. "What is this?" She stepped through it with no problem.

"Try your magic," her mother said.

Antonia concentrated, moving her hands. "Nothing."

"It's a magic shield, like what we've been living under."

Antonia stepped back and repeated the hand movements. A small fireball appeared. She let it fade away. "You want to help Justine, don't you?"

"I won't be any help without magic."

Gasqu tapped her nervously and motioned her to follow them down the passage.

Teresa looked at Henri standing next to Antonia, holding Carlos' hand. She looked back through the shimmer toward Justine and Simone. *Dios. Dios.* They would have to take care of themselves this time. To her new family she said, "Okay, *vamos.*" With a last backward glance, she followed Gasqu.

Farther on, the passage widened into a small chamber about three meters by thirty meters. On the left the walls slanted down to a low, narrow horizontal opening. At the far end the chamber narrowed vertically so that only one person at a time could get through.

Just before he entered, Gasqu froze, looking back with his head cocked. Henri followed suit. Their eyes met. Gasqu pointed at the side opening. Henri nodded and ran to it.

"Quick. Quick. In here. Rubicon comes. *Schnell! Schnell!*"

Gasqu crawled in first, then Antonia. "Eww, bones," she said.

"They won't hurt you," Teresa said. "Move in."

Carlos, Teresa and Henri followed. Though it was a tight fit, they pressed back out of sight.

This was another time when the spells that the witch Grace put in Teresa's head in case of an emergency came in handy. Teresa didn't know she could put up an invisibility screen, but she felt she needed to, so she did it.

Seconds later Rubicon, still moving fast despite his injury, limped into the chamber. Teresa sucked in a quick breath at the sight of him. Instead of his usual smartly styled attire, his trousers and shirt had several black blood stains from cuts, including one just above his ankle.

He'd heal, Teresa knew, but the wounds were slowing him down. She assumed and hoped that Justine and Simone were pursuing him, but she saw no fear on his face when he glanced over his shoulder—more like surprise. She doubted he had ever run from a fight. Being bested by two women, plus the loss of his world domination project, would be quite a shock for him.

Just before exiting the chamber, he looked all around the space, eyes locking on hers as if to say I-know-you-are-in-there, then he vanished, and Teresa released the breath she'd been holding.

Seconds later Justine and Simone ran in, both looking the worse for wear. Wary, they scanned the chamber as they moved through, spending several seconds on the hiding place.

"Teresa has been here," Justine said.

"*Oui,* I feel her, too."

"That means she's safe, doesn't it?"

Simone squeezed her shoulder. "*Oui, j'espère.*"

"I hope so, too."

Teresa waited a minute after they left before letting the invisibility screen fade. "How much farther?" Teresa asked Gasqu. The tongueless vampire held up his hand, thumb and index finger an inch apart. "*Bueno,* one inch to go, *vamos.*"

Also watchful, Gasqu led them on. In some of the narrow spots Teresa had to suck it in to get through.

Antonia squeezed her hand, "Mama, did they feed you too much while you were here?"

"I've known stray dogs who ate better. But thanks for asking."

"*De nada.*" Antonia hugged her mother tight.

Teresa's tears ran freely. No matter what she'd told herself or Justine, she had not totally believed she'd ever see her daughter again. To hold her once more dispelled those doubts, allowing, for the moment, joy and perhaps even lasting happiness.

Henri and Carlos gave the two their moment as they watched with small smiles on their vampire faces.

"Antonia, we must go."

Teresa held her hand on her daughter's cheek.

Antonia pressed her hand to her mother's. "*Tan cálida*, mama. So long since I felt a warm body."

At the end of the passage Gasqu cautiously looked outside. On full alert he studied the overcast sky, noting a few patches of blue. He scanned for Rubicon, detecting traces of him and the two women vampires, but sensed no vamps or mortals in the near vicinity. The rest stepped out into the shadowed ravine. Free, they all breathed deeply, whether they needed to breathe or not.

"There is a van down there," Teresa said. "We should go now."

A dismally familiar voice said, "You cannot go quite yet, Teresa. I will not allow it."

# Chapter 50

Harry was too out of it to direct Condi to the correct passage. Instead, they ran down the next tunnel they came to. A few meters in, the passage made a right turn and narrowed to one meter wide, until it widened into a chamber about ten meters by four. A natural cavity, the chamber had rough walls and deep cracks in the ceiling. A well used wooden table and chairs occupied the center. It seemed to be a break room of sorts with a shelf holding water, soda and beer.

Desperately needing some calm and quiet, they rested arms and heads on the table. Condi brought over a beer for Harry and a Pepsi for Pauly, taking only water for herself. "This is not the way out, is it?" she said.

Harry shook his bowed head.

"A break room," she said. "Hope no one comes in. Maybe they all dead."

Pauly sat quietly, sipping his soda. In a meek am-I-allowed-to-speak voice, he asked, "Do you know the right one?"

Harry nodded, waving his good arm behind himself. "Yes. Next one back." Wincing, he slumped in his chair. "In a minute."

Condi said, "I saw you and Simone. Did she glamour your pain?"

He nodded.

"But it hurts now, yes?"

Harry nodded again, grimacing.

Ignoring her own pain, Condi knelt beside Harry. "I cannot glamour you, and I am not a real witch like Teresa, but I have learned one or two things. May I touch you?"

Voice strained, he said, "Please do. Don't do anything to make Justine jealous."

"I will not."

Gently, she slid her hands over his leg while murmuring incomprehensible words. Immediately, Harry breathed more easily as the pain faded. His racing heart slowed. Still murmuring, Condi slid her hands over his arm. Harry sighed and melted into his chair.

"The pain will return," she said. "We should go now."

Harry sucked in two deep resigned breaths and nodded. With Condi's help, he stood up and tentatively put weight on his leg. He wasn't going to run, or even walk, a marathon, but he could move. "Okay, let's go."

*"Wer zur Hölle bist du?"*

Harry's head snapped up. "Well, shit," he muttered.

Two guards stood by the exit. The guards' eyes marked one of them as mortal, one a vamp. The mortal, a slim guy under thirty, stood tall, but carried an extra ten pounds under his belt. A holster with what looked like a .45 semi-automatic hung from the belt. The vamp looked over thirty with broad shoulders and a mean face. He carried an extra twenty pounds all over as well as a large machete blade.

*"Wer bist du?"*

Harry didn't speak German, but it wasn't hard to figure out what the vamp asked. "I do not speak German."

*"Ha, English. No English."*

*"Parlez-vous français?"* Condi asked.

*"Français?"* The mortal spit on the floor. *"Non putain française."*

The guards had a quick conversation in German, then the mortal drew his gun.

Condi said quietly to Harry, "I heard the word 'Blut.' I think that means blood."

"I don't like the way he's looking at me."

"Maybe he gay?"

"Maybe he hungry."

The vamp grinned, though it looked more like a snarl. "English blood, *ist gut.*"

"I'm American, actually."

*"Ah, Amerikaner. Ist besser."* He hefted his blade and moved toward Harry, who limped backward.

Mortal waved his weapon at Condi. *"Die Frau? Das Kind?"*

Vamp made a throw away motion with his blade.

Mortal grinned. *"Französische Hündin."* His grin turned into a sneer. He raised his gun. No screwing around, he was going to shoot her.

Vamp had Harry backed to the wall. His jaw opened to full vampire mode. His blade hovered inches from Harry's gut.

Condi could transform into any animal, but not instantaneously. She breathed in deep and went for the change, knowing a bullet would kill her at any time during transition.

Mortal's arm suddenly dropped as if kicked—or as if an invisible, eighty-five pound kid had jumped on it.

In the few seconds of resulting distraction, Condi changed her target creature from mouse to chimpanzee, a large and fast chimpanzee. Mortal recovered first. He managed to fire at Condi, leaving a bloody furrow along her right cheek, before she snatched the gun from his hand and pitched it across the chamber.

Harry, riveted by Condi's transformation despite Vamp being on the point of skewering him and sucking him dry, caught the gun. With barely enough room strength to raise the gun, Harry shot him in the ear.

Mortal, a bit slow on the uptake, just had time to look into Condi's chimpanzee eyes before she twisted his head around way further than it should go.

Several minutes later, Harry, Condi, and Pauly sat together at the end of the long table, checking to make sure everyone was okay as they let themselves calm down.

Condi put an arm around Pauly's shoulders. "Thank you, Pauly. You save our asses."

Harry ruffled Pauly's hair. "That was very brave, Pauly. Thank you for saving me and the chimp."

Pauly giggled and managed a rare smile. "I didn't think I could do that anymore." The smile disappeared. "I thought they sucked it all out of me. I'm glad they didn't."

"You can make yourself invisible?" Harry asked.

Shyly, Pauly shrugged. "Yes."

"A good skill to have. No wonder they wanted you."

Condi squeezed Pauly and kissed his head. "I too am glad they did not." They sat quietly for a minute. "So what now?"

"We get the hell out of here."

# Chapter 51



"**Y**ou cannot go quite yet, Teresa. I will not allow it."

Teresa had been gazing down the ravine, joy, hope and freedom swelling in her chest—all of them just down the trail one kilometer. All of them crumbled when she heard that voice behind her. Juno had stepped out of the hidden space Konrad had showed the others.

For a long moment after the unexpected appearance of the smarmy, arrogant sorcerer, Teresa contemplated jumping away. She forgot she had her magic back. All she could see was Juno standing over her, grinning as the tubes stuck to her body sucked the magic power from her. That vision began a heat buildup inside her body. She envisioned herself a giant fireball engulfing the sorcerer, hearing his screams as he burnt to ash.

With the heat came the knowledge that she could jump. Eyes open she saw her new family wide-eyed at the sudden appearance of Juno. If she jumped her family would be left behind. That was not going to happen. They'd all been through too much. She breathed deeply to gather control of her power and turned around.

"Juno. I will leave here. You've had enough of me." She instinctively knew what the hand motions he was performing meant. If he cast another no-magic spell over her none of them was safe. There were subtler weapons in the magic armory, but she didn't know them, so the fireball was her only choice in the one second she had to decide.

Clumsily, she flung a small fireball at Juno. He easily deflected it, but it disrupted his spellcasting. She flung another, bigger one. And another and another.

Juno vanished and materialized behind Teresa, his back to the end wall. "Enough," he called out.

"Not yet." From the small vault of spells Grace had hidden in her mind for just that kind of situation, Teresa sent a massive, invisible ball of power at him.

Taking him by surprise, the ball knocked Juno off his feet and rolled him up against the mountain. Though shaken, he levitated himself to a standing position ready for Teresa's next attack. "Teresa, you will come with me."

Juno intentionally deflected the next power ball so that it swept Antonia, Henri, Carlos and Gasqu off the trail. Caught off guard, they tumbled down the steep rocky ravine face. Antonia reached out with her magic to catch Carlos just before he smacked his head against a sharp rock.

"You will return with me, Teresa, or I will bury your friends."

Gasqu moved to the left to get behind Juno, then began to climb.

Juno made two quick hand movements, then with palm down he pointed one hand at the cliff wall a meter to the right of the vampires. He made a slow slicing movement. In a straight line the stone split apart and fell into the ravine, just missing the vamps.

Henri started climbing up the rock face. Juno punched him with a fireball even his vampire resilience could not fight. Henri hit the bottom hard with the fireball stuck to his chest and didn't move. Antonia jumped down and brushed the fire off him, trying to revive him.

"*Pendejo puta madre*," Antonia shouted, "I will...."

A few meters from the top of the slope, Gasqu rushed Juno. Juno spun at him, and using the same slicing movement that had split the stone, he cut Gasqu in half. Before he fell, Juno sliced backward and removed the young vampire's head.

"*¡No, maldita sea!*" Teresa ran toward Juno, firing multiple fireballs with a huge invisible power ball mixed in. Juno, concentrating but grinning, easily deflected them, many into the ravine.

"I had hoped you would come willingly," Juno said. "But this is tiresome. You will come... now." He held fists in front of his face, closed his eyes to gather his power, then flung both hands at Teresa.

Teresa attempted to push back, to hold her ground, but his power overwhelmed her. She flew backwards, up, then down hard on her back. The power seemed to sit on top of her, holding her down.

Juno stood at her feet, peering down as if she was an annoying bug. "I have use of you yet, but not your friends. Antonia is supposed to be dead anyway." He faced the ravine.

Teresa attempted to move—to kick him, or fireball him, or squash him like a cockroach. Her feet and hands stuck to the rock. "No! I will go! We all will go."

"Too late." He gestured with his hands, pointing them at the rock above the vamps.

A roar broke his concentration. A huge tiger leaped on him, smashing him to the ground. The tiger sank her teeth into his shoulder and with a flick of her massive head flung him against the rock wall. Then she pounced on him, her massive paws holding his hands tight against the rock.

Free to move, Teresa rose and shook herself then walked slowly toward Juno and the tiger. Harry and Pauly stood together by the back door entrance.

"Condi, I hope?"

Harry raised his good shoulder and grinned.

Teresa glanced into the ravine where the others were climbing out.

Juno shouted at Teresa as he struggled to free himself. "You think you can best me, Teresa? I am Juno, one of the most powerful sorcerers in the world. Even with this beast on me—Condi, I assume—I can still overpower you. I can raise you up and let you drop a thousand feet, strangle you with somebody else's hands, squeeze your heart. I will—"

The tiger roared full-throated into his face. The sound echoed through the high cliffs up into the mountains. Juno cringed from the blast, eyes clenched shut, showing no small amount of fear. Finished with her display of power, Condi licked his face with her sandpaper tongue.

Juno spit and could barely speak through his rage. "I'll kill you. I'll kill all of you. Let me up, Condi. I'll let you live. Rubicon will end all of you. He needs me. Not you." The inch or so of his exposed fingertips wiggled in a frenzy as he tried to do magic with them. Deliberately, Condi slid a huge paw to cover the fingers. "Ahhhhh! You won't beat me, Teresa. I am too powerful, and you know nothing, nothing!"

"Oh, I know some things." Teresa had had enough. "Condi, thank you."

The big tiger's head swiveled to look Teresa in the eye.

Condi lowered her face to an inch from Juno's, looked him in the eyes and emitted a deep warning snarl. Then she leaped away.

"You are dead." Juno started to get up. Fingers extended, Teresa held her hand palm down over him, pushing him back down.

"You say you are one of the most powerful sorcerers in the world. Well, I know Grace, *the* most powerful sorceress in the world. I may not know as much as you, but she taught me a few things." Invisible force from her hand still holding him down, she knelt beside him. "One thing she taught me: that an ego driven magician who was willing to help destroy humanity doesn't deserve his power."

Juno started to speak then peered into Teresa's eyes. With his wide eyes and lips tight against his teeth he projected real fear. "What do you mean?"

"I mean, you do not deserve your power."

Teresa held her hand up in a particular position, then tapped each fingertip with the other index finger.

"No. No. You cannot take it away. I will leave you alone. Your family, also."

"You kept us locked up and sucked us dry. Now you will know how that feels."

Juno's "No!" turned into a scream when Teresa jammed her hand into his chest.

Teresa immediately felt his power flow into her. In her mind's eye she saw it rush into her hand and through her arm and spread throughout her body. A liquid, gaseous mix of colors, pure white, darkest black, red, orange, yellow, even a bit of blue. She felt a warm rush. Her heart beat stronger than ever before. She felt potent, invincible.

*This must be what it feels like to take drugs,* she thought. *This is what it feels like to be high. Queen of the World.* Then she looked down at Juno…his back arched, his head thrown back, his mouth a rictus of horror, pain and loss. She could feel the flow ebbing. Though at that moment she truly believed he deserved to lose it all, she couldn't do it.

She withdrew her hand, as the power continued to expand through her. At once she felt exhausted and exhilarated.

Juno's body slowly relaxed, his scream died, and a tear rolled down a cheek.

Antonia helped her mother stand. Teresa looked to each of the others. Some had tiny tight smiles—*It had to be done, but I don't like it.* Teresa agreed.

"What now?" Antonia asked.

"There's a van at the bottom. We go and wait."

# Chapter 52

Rubicon may have been ten centuries old, but he still had moves. Slowly they wore each other down. It took almost fifteen minutes of full on, vamp speed attacking, defending, close quarters kicking, punching, striking, slicing, and blade work. Slowly the cutting and bruising took their toll.

Rubicon, used to defeating his opponents quickly, slowly lost his edge. Maybe he also lost a tiny bit of his confidence, not to mention arrogance.

Justine, too, as the fight went on, grew frustrated at the stalemate. The pain of her several wounds seemed slower than usual to fade, becoming distractions. Simone also seemed to lose focus.

Justine caught her eye. Communicating silently, Justine signaled *attack, full on. Let's end this.*

Rubicon understood their intent and ran.

Taken aback, and suddenly having no target, both women became acutely aware of their many wounds and hesitated to pursue Rubicon.

Justine, back against the wall, blade dangling, said, "What the hell? What do we do now, like I didn't already know?"

"*Courez, Chère, Courez.*" Simone limped over to lean on the wall beside her partner.

"I assume that means run after him. Can you run?"

Head bowed, Simone said with little enthusiasm, "*Certainement.*"

"Bullshit. Let's just walk fast."

Entering the small chamber where Teresa and the others still hid, Justine knew Teresa had been there. They had been friends long before she was a vampire and Teresa discovered she was a powerful witch. She and Simone, who was her maker, had their vampire connection, but she and Teresa had a powerful connection, too. Friendship. Whether by scent or vibe Justine knew her friend had passed there.

"Teresa has been here," Justine said.

"*Oui,* I feel her, too."

"That means she's safe, doesn't it?"

Simone squeezed her shoulder. *"J'espère."*

"I hope so, too."

They did not encounter Rubicon anywhere along the passage nor at the exit. They were cautious as they searched the exit area. They looked up and down for a sign or a trap. They found nothing until Simone concentrated on his scent.

Justine followed her down the trail until Simone stopped, puzzled. Then she looked up. "Did Konrad tell us about a trail up the mountain?"

"No. But Rubicon would know about it. Doesn't look like much of a trail. You ever climb a mountain?"

With a wry smile Simone said, *"Une fois ou deux."*

"I assume that means yes. Lead on." One didn't have to be a mountaineer to follow the trail after the first three or four meters. There was only one way to go, along a ledge, around a corner, through a steep narrow defile—the perfect place for the ambush which they expected—that opened up to a vast open meadow.

The oblong meadow, an uneven mix of grasses, shrubs, patches of low flowering plants and rock, stretched for kilometers left and right until lost from sight. Two kilometers away the meadow ran into high, craggy peaks separated by a steep couloir rising to a narrow gap spotted with snow, between high cliffs. Above them the sky was a pristine blue, but to the right a massive bank of dark clouds roiled toward them.

Simone spied Rubicon halfway up the couloir. "Can you run, *chère?*"

"I would rather take a leisurely stroll, but yeah, I can run."

"A leisurely run, then."

"Not too leisurely." Justine pointed to the approaching clouds. "I'm a Southern California girl. I don't feel like trudging through six feet of snow."

At first glance, the meadow looked smooth, but both women took tumbles among the hummocks, hidden boulders and veiled dips. They were halfway across when a loud cracking sound reverberated among the peaks. They looked up in time to see, high up on the right side, a huge buttress shear off. As it crashed into the couloir it sent snow, dirt, boulders and vegetation outward in a spray that flew hundreds of meters in all directions, including Rubicon's. It looked like he took the full force of the rockfall as he disappeared in the debris spray.

Justine and Simone swore in several languages and ran full speed across the meadow and up the couloir.

A dirty mist hung over a jumbled mess of rocks, snow, and dirt, in some places reducing visibility to only a few meters. Opening up their senses they scanned for signs of Rubicon.

"I'm feeling him all over the place. Maybe that big ass rock, you know, smooshed him," Justine said.

"Possibly," Simone said. "But I do not see any part of him."

They searched the area, Justine checking the spread of the debris, Simone hunting through the gigantic remains of the buttress.

Simone searched the upslope side of the thirty meter fallen rock. She sensed him everywhere, but could not find any pieces of him. She was searching the far end when Rubicon jumped from the rock, landing behind her.

She spun to attack him. He kicked dirt in her face, then struck the blade from her hand.

"Simone, did you think I was dead? Crushed into a thousand pieces?"

He waved his blade in front of her—left, right, left, right, backing her against the huge fallen rock. A lunge sliced her sword arm.

"Almost did get me, I will admit. But I haven't survived this long to be crushed by a big rock."

Suddenly he lunged, piercing her body through. Then he smacked her head with the flat of his blade.

"I might let you live if you call Justine over here. Yes?"

Simone took a few seconds before saying, "I believe in English they would say, 'Fuck you.'"

"Ahh, too bad."

Justine raced around the corner of the rock. "She doesn't have to call me. I'm here."

"I know." He kicked jagged stones at her. When she flinched he struck her head with the flat of his blade, knocking her down. "I am an 'oldie but a goodie' as they say in English." As Justine tried to regain her feet he scooped up a basketball sized rock and launched it at her. Justine went down again. "We have fun now, yes?"

He strode to Simone, flipped her over with his foot and sliced her legs, cutting them to the bone.

Grinning, totally in charge, he said, "Catch me if you can, Justine." Laughing, he ran toward the top.

Justine crawled to Simone.

"*Non, non. Allez*, finish him."

Still feeling a broken rib or two, a few cuts from the earlier fight and limping from a cracked ankle bone, Justine climbed to the top of the couloir. An obviously new cluster of boulders narrowed the pass-through to ten or eleven meters. At a similar distance was a sharp drop off.

Wary—Justine was very tired of being wary—she passed through. She knew Rubicon's arrogance would not allow him to run again. Now he was playing cat and mouse.

On the other side of the pass the rock-strewn ground sloped slightly to the drop-off. He waited there somewhere.

A pebble bounced off her back. She spun about in a crouch. Another pebble landed in front of her. She scanned above her, saw nothing. Another stone fell to the left, then there was a crunch to the right. She blocked Rubicon's lackluster strike. He was playing; she wasn't.

Already in a crouch, she spun, knocking his feet from under him. She continued the spin, came up and struck for his blade arm.

He blocked, rolled away, and came up flinging a stone.

She swatted it away and attacked. For a minute blades flashed, their clang echoing in the mountain air. Justine managed a front kick to Rubicon's chest.

As he stumbled back, he grabbed her leg, sliced it then yanked it. As she fell she kicked up with her other foot, landing a solid shot in his crotch. The distraction allowed her to wrench her leg free.

He recovered quickly and attacked before she could stand up. He kept at her, forcing her to crawl backward, toward the edge.

She used his trick, a handful of rubble in the face. Reaching forward she sliced his leg, a long slice along the bone. With a quick cry of pain he swung down before she could withdraw her blade, aiming to cut off her blade hand. She snatched her hand away before he connected.

Not playing around anymore, he came for her.

She scrambled backward, just able to avoid a killing blow. She'd lost her big blade, but she had a small one, a flip knife with a five inch blade in her back pocket. She looked for an opening before he pushed her off the edge. There—his strike swung too far. She had a half second.

In an instant she threw herself forward while extracting the small knife. Lunging up from her knees she flipped open the blade and sunk it into Rubicon's gut. Her attempt to eviscerate him failed when he back-handed her with his blade hand.

She slid through the loose small stones to end up dazed a half meter from the brink. On hands and knees, she got her first look over the edge. It was not a gentle slope, nor a short fall any mortal could survive. At some point, a giant had cleaved the mountain in two, leaving a flat, thousand foot sheer wall, with a rocky streamed at its foot. Not even a vampire could survive that fall.

Black blood from her face pooled on the stone in front of her.

Rubicon limped toward her, leaving black blood footprints. His free hand dripped blood.

Justine attempted to stand, still not giving up, but too slow. He kicked her in the ribs, lifting her up to fly over the edge. Full sunlight blinded Justine for a moment, but she didn't need to see to do one last thing.

When Rubicon's foot slammed into her ribs, she reached out and grabbed it. In midair, with Rubicon on one leg at the brink, she fell, dragging him over with her. As he fell after her, she thought she saw someone behind him, though it might have been a trick of the sunlight. Certain that he was falling with her she pushed him away, deriving some satisfaction from his scream.

Falling backwards, Justine looked up and saw a figure looking down at her.

Teresa? The figure's arms stretched out as if reaching for her. Justine felt it then, giant invisible hands cradling her, slowing her fall. Then lifting her up. Closer and closer to… Teresa, reaching out, pulling her up. Just before she got to the ledge, Justine glanced down in time to see Rubicon bounce off an outcropping and fall and fall.

Suddenly Teresa's warm outstretched arms gathered Justine in a hug that lasted what seemed a very long time. Justine clung to her oldest friend. She felt the heat behind her eyes from tears that could never be shed. It was okay, though—Teresa's tears left warm tracks down both their cheeks.

Warm relief filled her chest. It was over. All over. Her friend was safe. She was safe. Everybody was safe. Surely they were.

It seemed like hours before they relaxed their hold.

Justine held Teresa's face in her hands. "I knew there was a reason I came to rescue you."

Grinning, Teresa held her friend's face. "I knew you would come." They touched foreheads. "You are warm, *amiga*. The sun is out."

Justine pulled the hood over her head. Smile fading, she asked, "Simone?"

"That way. Healing."

Together they began to move back toward the pass, Justine wincing and limping, and leaving black blood footprints.

"Can you walk?"

"Apparently I can fly, so I should be able to walk."

"Should be, but you're not doing a very good job of it." Teresa wrapped an arm around her friend, carrying her over the rough ground.

Through the narrow pass they spied Simone hobbling uphill. No one spoke until they met together. "I was coming to help you," Simone said before she fell into Teresa's arms. She, too, felt the witch's tears.

"You know, I did not like you at first," Simone said,

"And now?"

"You are okay."

"I'm happy for that."

*"Moi aussie."*

"Okay, unless you want to walk down, I can get you to the van quicker. There are people waiting."

"Harry?"

"Harry."

Without waiting for an answer Teresa gripped each of them by one arm.

"I thought you lost your power," Justine said.

Teresa's smile faded. "I found some more. Ready?"

She closed her eyes, thought of where she wanted to go, and all three vanished.

Harry paced, his mind sorting through all the bad things that could be happening to Justine. She was a vampire, immortal, smart and tough, and she had Simone as a partner, but still. Rubicon was all those things and had centuries of survival experience. Anything could happen. His heart hammered, his brain twisted and turned and he kept his hands in his pockets to keep them from shaking. *Where are they?*

A small whooshing sound and a quick blast of displaced air put him out of his misery. "Justine, I was worried about… you." He went to her, taking in the black blood, the wounds, her limp as she came to him. "With good reason, I see." He glanced at Simone, similarly beaten up and leaning on Henri. "I hope that's not all your blood." He was going to say more, but Justine's kiss shut him up. At that moment he didn't care about anything except that she was there, in his arms where he had feared she never would be again.

Usually she felt cool to his touch, but suddenly she felt warm. He'd been around vampires enough to know that was not good. He pulled back and looked up. They stood in full sunshine with black clouds peeking over the mountain. Giggling like kids caught in the rain they joined the others by the van.

Henri the caregiver had insisted, in a mix of German, French and English, that Simone sit in the van to heal. "Maybe walk now, maybe no walk later." He insisted Justine join her.

Justine looked around. "What happened to the mute kid who helped us?"

The joy of their reunion vanished. Harry said, "Juno." He drew a finger across his throat.

"That sucks. That kid deserved much better than that. And Juno?"

All eyes turned to Teresa. Justine studied her friend, then looked to Simone who nodded confirmation. "You took his power."

Eyes downcast, Teresa said, "He was not doing good with it. And as you said, Gasqu deserved better."

Justine reached out and squeezed her shoulder. "He did."

Breaking a slightly uncomfortable silence Simone asked, "Konrad, Hedy?"

Antonia squeezed her mother's arm. "Harry went out into the open and managed to call her."

"They're fine," Harry said. "At the hotel we tried before. A baby was born on the bus. Maybe another any time."

"Let's go see," Antonia suggested.

Minutes later Harry drove the van into the light surrounded by snowflakes.

# Epilogue

## *One week later*

"That's the last one," Antonia said, watching from the farmhouse porch as an expensive sedan drove down the long driveway.

"She might be back. Her family did not seem happy to be reunited with their ruined daughter." Hedy patted the younger woman's shoulder. "But at least for now it's done. Everybody can go home."

"And where are you going?"

Hedy shrugged and stuffed hands in her jean pockets. "Konrad and I are going see my mother. Don't know how long I'll stay. I don't think a regular day to day job will work for me anymore."

"You're always welcome here."

"Well, I might have to come and check up on your two, maybe three, sunnyvamps."

"You don't think the Vampire Family Council won't be checking them out enough?"

A young woman of about twenty-five, with dusky skin similar to Henri's, short sun-streaked brown hair, not pretty, but quite attractive nevertheless, joined them. "Tell them they can no see kids until they milk cows, collect eggs, and clean stalls before breakfast. They not come around so often."

Hedy offered, "Nikita, put your great-uncle, or whatever Henri is to you, to work. This is his place, too, isn't it? He can work all night, right?"

Nikita chuffed. "Henri is too busy with his new *famille*."

"So, this farm is part his, right? Officially, I mean."

Nikita nodded. "My father left to me two hundred hectares, but I am not farmer. They pay Henri many Euros to come here and take care of women. He gave the money to me so I give him half. I, too, think he make a good night farmer."

Antonia said, "The women with no place to go who are staying here are basically free farmhands."

"Of the three, I think only one seem strong enough to do real work here."

Konrad stepped onto the porch from the shady side and stood behind Hedy, hands on her shoulders. "Ready to go?"

"After the sun sets, Papa." She leaned back against him. "Have to be careful of your complexion, you know."

Justine led Henri out of the kitchen.

Henri took Simone's hand and gave a short bow. "*Dankeschön. Vielen Dank.* And thank you for rescue."

"*Bitte, Henri. Bitte.*"

Justine and Simone stood together, watching the sun set behind a mountain. "What did you offer him?" Justine asked. "Money? I thought the Council was paying for the women staying."

"Advice."

"About?"

Simone bumped shoulders with Justine. "How to live with a mortal."

"He could have asked me."

"You give advice from inside, *chère.* I give from outside. Better."

Justine threw her arm around her vampire partner. "Maybe in ancient times, *chère*, but modern times, me is better."

"I think, *mon amie*, we must agree to disagree on this subject. *Oui?*"

"*Oui.* This place seems to be doing okay. You came from a farm. You still remember it?"

"I was happy there for a while."

Justine tightened her arm around Simone's shoulder, "Weren't we all."

Teresa came out of the barn holding Carlos by the hand. He happily kicked his way through the foot of snow left by the season's first big storm. The setting sun did not seem to brother him at all. When they got to the porch the boy said, *Danke, Großmutter* Teresa," then ran to his mother. Teresa stood shoulder to shoulder with her two vampire friends.

"Harry back yet?"

Justine nodded to an approaching vehicle making its way closer on the snowy muddy road. "Souvenirs for Bailey and Susan. And news?"

"You ready to go home tomorrow?"

"Yes I am, now that I know you're safe."

Teresa rested her arm on Justine's shoulders.

"*Muchas gracias* and *merci* for coming for me."

"*De nada mi amiga.*"

"*De rien mon ami.*"

Harry parked the old Opel sedan and took out three shopping bags.

"Harry," Teresa called with a laugh. "I have a one bag limit. Extra charges may apply."

"One bag, Teresa. One big bag."

"Harry," Simone said. "What did the Council find?"

He set down the bags and shook his head. "Not much. There was four meters of snow at the bottom of that cliff. They found no trace of Rubicon. He could be dust already or frozen under the snow and rock that keeps falling off. Might have to wait until spring."

"There's no way even Rubicon could survive that fall. I saw him bounce off that outcropping then fall into the rocks," Justine insisted. "No fucking way," she added to herself, not quite as confident, her gaze held by Simone's carefully neutral expression.

"And The Girl?" Teresa wanted to know.

"They definitely found blood and traces of dust where Hedy said it would be."

Konrad opened his mouth to say something, but stayed silent.

"Reich?"

"Not a trace. He has a big chalet in Gstaad, a big tourist and ski town, but he hasn't showed up there."

Justine said, "I imagine he has a lot of Rubicon's money. He'll probably set up a lab somewhere and make Sunvamp mice."

"Then I guess we should notify the mouse trap makers to step up their game," Harry said, throwing his arm around Justine's shoulders.

A blood red aura surrounded the sun as it sank behind the distant mountains.

✺ ✺ ✺

About nine the next evening Teresa, Justine, Simone and Harry, arm in arm, appeared in the parking lot of Harry's apartment building. They all took a minute to savor the beach air and listen to the waves.

"Looks like somebody's home," Harry said. "I'll go get a key."

While Harry went for a key to his door, the women stood together, not speaking, not looking at each other.

Simone said, "Teresa, if you have enough magic left after that last jump, I want to go to Grace's place while she teaches you to control your new power. I do not have a home here anymore and these two do not need me as a third wheel hanging around. If you believe you have enough power to take me with you."

"Simone, *mi amiga*, right now I want to throw out fireworks, I want to flip that noisy car, if you wanted I think I could take you to the moon.

It's scaring the hell out of me. I would love it if you came with me."

They both looked at Justine. "You don't need my permission. Teresa, go, before you explode. Simone, take care of our baby." She gave them quick hugs and backed away. With a smile she said, "Go, now, before you do something we can't explain."

Teresa looked up at the apartment building's second floor. She saw Bailey and Susan and Darwin, watching from the landing.

Harry joined Justine. "It's okay. They're working with Darwin. Long story."

Simone shook her head in amazement and gripped Teresa's arm.

Teresa, her body vibrating with the urge to do magic, closed her eyes, made a few hand movements, and they vanished.

Finally, after promising his neighbors and Darwin a full update soon, Harry closed the door to his apartment. Together he and Justine slumped on the couch and put their feet on the coffee table.

Eyes closed, head laid back, Harry said, "It's good to be home."

Justine stared at the ceiling. "Is this my home, too?"

"Yes."

Justine snuggled up to Harry and laid her head on his shoulder. "Then I agree. It is good to be home."

## *The End*

# About the Author

David Burton has been a boat builder, sailor, and custom cabinetmaker and has traveled by thumb, motorcycle, and sailboat. Upon returning from sailing in the South Pacific, he turned to writing. His first published book was a mystery, *Manmade for Murder* (Write Way Publishing, 1997. Paperback, Worldwide Mysteries, 2000). It was a selection of the Detective Book Club. *Hell Cop* (Silver Lake Publishing, 2004), a supernatural adventure story, was his second published novel and won 3rd place at the 1998 Colorado Gold Writers Conference. The ebook version was a finalist for the EPPIE awards.

He has also written screenplays, including an adaptation of his *Hell Cop* and *Fear Killer* novels. The screenplay adaptation of *Hell Cop* won 1st place at the Pikes Peak Writers Conference in 2002. Another screenplay, *Time For Love,* took 1st place at Pikes Peak in 2001. David now lives with his wife in Southern California and is working on more stories and characters that pass thorough his life and brain in both novel and screenplay form.